Growing Pains

by the same author from The Gay Men's Press:

Unnatural Relations
Conduct Unbecoming
Out of Bounds
Full Circle

with other publishers:

Quick Singles
Coppers: An Inside View of the British Police
Fine Glances
One Over Par
Max: The Life and Music of Peter Maxwell Davies
Turf Accounts
Nice Tries

GAY MEN'S PRESS

Growing Pains

by Mike Seabrook

First published 1999 by Millivres Ltd,
part of the Millivres Prowler Group,
3 Broadbent Close, London N6 5GG

A CIP catalogue record for this book is available
from the British Library

ISBN 1 902852 05 2

Distributed in Europe by Central Books,
99 Wallis Rd, London E9 5LN

Distributed in North America by InBook/LPC Group,
1436 West Randolph, Chicago, IL 60607

Distributed in Australia by Bulldog Books,
P O Box 300, Beaconsfield, NSW 2014

Printed and bound in the EU by WSOY, Juva, Finland

As always, I have to thank my wife Perviz for her immense contribution to this book. In particular it is dedicated to her, and to my sister-in-law, Khorshed, for sitting for hours one afternoon in 1983 in the garden of The Feathers at Dersingham, patiently talking me into believing that my ambition to write stories for my living might not be quite as impossible of fulfilment as I then gloomily — and wrongly — assumed.

"How pleasant it is to have money, heigh-ho!
How pleasant it is to have money."

(Arthur Hugh Clough)

1

"Bonjour, vin," said Stephen Hill, raising his glass and squinting at the sunlight fractured in its oily yellow contents. "Bienvenue à mon estomac." There was a chuckle from the handful of early drinkers in the little café-bar. Stephen, a handsome, well-made boy of nineteen, with clear grey eyes and an untidy mop of dusty-blond hair, took a hefty slug of the wine, grunted appreciatively, and resumed shoving dirty glasses into the round mesh cage, ready for the dishwasher. He was lifting his glass for a second mouthful when the door opened and Graham Curtis walked in. Stephen's hand halted half-way to his mouth, which remained open in surprise.

"What's up?" he said, quick concern registering simultaneously in his face and voice.

Curtis, a stocky, athletic-looking man of about thirty, stood on the threshold for a moment while he took off his sunglasses and allowed his eyes to accustom themselves to the inside light. He waved a hand easily towards the half-dozen men at the bar, including Stephen in the wave, and grinned at him, reassuring him that nothing was amiss. Then he ran a hand through his hair and tramped through the room to the bar. As he came closer Stephen, who was intimately familiar with his entire repertoire of facial expressions, saw clearly that he was under the influence of some kind of shock or surprise. But he had enough sense to keep quiet and wait for Graham to volunteer explanations — of why, for example, he was back in Saint-Hippolyte barely an hour after leaving for Strasbourg. Graham looked hard at him, saw the question marks all over his fair, youthful face, and laughed.

"Gimme a beer," he said. "A *sérieux*, not one of those fart-arsing *demis*."

Stephen served him a half-litre of *pression*, watched appreciatively, and yet with a tinge of anxiety, perhaps of insecurity, by Graham as he moved easily behind the bar. He had insisted on taking the job within days of his arrival from The Hague, declaring that he wasn't going to be kept by anyone and was going to earn his keep. Graham hadn't tried to talk him out of it. Indeed, he had thought it was a very good idea, with himself away in Strasbourg all day. Stephen had found the job as barman at a nearby café-bar, got it on sheer strength of personality, having nothing else in the way of qualifications to recommend him for it, and had picked it up in hours. Now, six months later, Graham reflected with a faint twinge of envy for the boy's youth and quickness, he looked as if he had been born with a bar towel in one hand and a corkscrew in the other.

He took a deep pull on the beer, gasped as the cold liquid hit his stomach, wiped his mouth with the back of his hand, then grimaced in disgust at himself and plied his handkerchief. Meanwhile Stephen kept working behind the bar according to his usual routine, serving coffees and beers, filling a *pichet* with Alsatian wine and dextrously twirling glasses along the bar for six Pastis-guzzling old men who had arrived after Graham, flushed and leg-pulling after an early morning *boules* challenge on which some mighty sum had, apparently, changed hands.

The old men crowded noisily off to a side table, chattering like starlings, and Stephen leant easily across the bar as Graham swigged at his beer once more. "Aren't you going to put me out of my misery," he said at last, "and tell me what's brought you back like this?"

Graham grinnned at him. "I was waiting to see if you were in any misery to be put out of," he said softly. He drew from his jacket pocket a fat, strange-sized manila envelope. "Had a letter this morning," he said, passing the envelope over to Stephen. "Didn't have time to open it till I got stuck in traffic in Strasbourg. Soon as I read it I turned straight round and came back again. Mainly," he went on, watching Stephen closely as he slid his long, slim, off-spinner's fingers into the envelope and drew out the contents, "to discuss it with you. See what you thought we ought to do. Go on, read it," he added, jerking his head in the direction of the letter in Stephen's hands as the boy hesitated.

Stephen raised the sheaf of papers and read rapidly down the first sheet. As he read the others at the bar suspended conversations, set down morning papers and drinks and waited to see what news had brought one of their resident *Anglais* back so unexpectedly. They saw a look of stunned surprise dawn on Stephen's face, followed, rapidly in turn, by shock, disbelief, and finally a flush of pleasure, still slightly shocked, that made his eyes sparkle.

"I can hardly believe it," Stephen said quietly after a few moments gazing into space as all the various possibilities struck him. "I mean, I had no idea he had all this... What shall we do, do you think?"

"That's what we've got to talk about," said Graham, draining his beer. "Can you get time off from here, d'you think?"

Stephen shook his head. "Shouldn't think so, for a minute," he said. "I'm on my own in the bar till Nicole comes on duty at three. Does it matter? I mean, we'll have all night, shan't we?"

"That we shall," assented Graham. "I've got to go into work some time, anyway. I'll leave you here, love, all right, and go in? I'll take tomorrow off, and you do the same here. I'll just borrow their phone, if it's all right by you, and let them know I'm on my way." Stephen made way for him to slip past behind the bar, and grinned a minute later as he heard Graham blaming his tardiness on an imaginary malfunction in the car. Five minutes later Graham was gone, speeding back to Strasbourg. Stephen continued serving and washing up the enormous traffic in glasses, his mind far away from his work, daydreaming happily of things to come.

* * *

It had been a different story three months before.

It had been, then, three months since Stephen had descended on Graham, tousled, desperately tired but joyous, straight from the scenes of debauchery marking the end of the cricket tour in The Hague. They had been three months of joy, unmarred by the slightest difference of feeling. They had spent the time getting to know each other, finding out all the small things about each other that lovers spend the first few months of married life discovering. Stephen had taken his job at the auberge, and Graham had continued exploring the potential of his new work at the language school in Strasbourg. And then, one Saturday morning, everything had changed for a while.

They had been sitting about after breakfast, wondering what to do that day, when the telephone had rung. Stephen, who happened to be nearest, picked it up. "Allo. Bonjour." There had been a pause. "Yes. No, he's here. Just a moment, I'll pass you over." Graham looked interrogatively at him as he went to take the proffered phone, but Stephen had pulled a 'don't know' face. "English," he had murmured as Graham took the receiver from him and sat in the armchair beneath the instrument.

"Hallo, Graham Curtis," he said. There was a squawk from the other end. "What?" said Graham suddenly. Stephen looked up at him sharply. Something in his tone had reminded Stephen of when Graham had been a schoolmaster. He had sometimes rapped out a question in just that tart, not-to-be-denied tone, usually directing it at someone wool-gathering, their attention straying out through the form-room window to the cricket field across the quadrangle... quite often me, reflected Stephen, with a warm smile of reminiscence. It had been one such reprimand that had led to all this, he reflected. But he wasted little time on the moment of languorous remembering, because Graham's face and tone of voice were getting more and more grave, and his questions increasingly sharp and monosyllabic. Eventually there was a long squawk of voice from the other end, and Graham was thanking whoever it was, profusely, and promising to be there, wherever 'there' was, within twenty-four hours. Stephen's heart contracted in sudden fear. He had not been out of Graham's arms for twenty-four hours, let alone his company. He wondered, desperately, over the final few pleasantries uttered tersely by Graham, as if he was in a great hurry to put the receiver down and act, what emergency could have arisen.

Graham enlightened him as soon as he put down the receiver. "That was the London Clinic," he said. He was staring blankly into space, and his voice was strangely blurred and muted. Stephen's eyes opened. "Someone ill?" he said softly.

"Yes," said Graham in the same dreamy tone. "Old Reggie. He's been asking for me, they said. He... he's got forty-eight hours to live. If he's lucky..." He sat, still with that glittering, thousand-yard stare in his unfocussed eyes, and suddenly began to shiver. Stephen, becoming seriously worried for his usually masterful friend, went hurriedly over to him, sat beside him on the sofa and put his arms tightly around him, rocking him slightly out of some instinct.

After a few moments of this Graham pulled himself together and turned a pale, shocked face to Stephen. "Thanks, love," he muttered. "I... I'm sorry to crack up like that. It was just... just that coming out of the blue like that... I thought the poor old chap was making a fine recovery, and to hear it baldly, out of a clear sky like that... I'm sorry, Stevie."

"Never mind that," said Stephen. "What do you want to do? You'll go to London, I suppose?"

"Yes, I suppose I must," muttered Graham. "Well, of course you must," said Stephen, surprised that there should be any supposing about it. "Christ!" he exclaimed. "You'll have to look slippy about it, too, if you're gonna get there in time. You go and get a

10

bag packed," he said, taking charge for the moment, while Graham still sat on the edge of the armchair, all the stuffing knocked temporarily out of him. "Come on, love," Stephen said again, urgently this time, shaking Graham gently by the shoulders. Graham roused himself, gazed at Stephen as if he was seeing him for the first time that morning, and then, abruptly, got himself back in hand again. "Sorry, Steve, my love," he said briskly. "Shouldn't have allowed it to wind me like that. I'll go and pack, as you say. Will you be looking up flight times?"

"Already doing it," called Stephen. A minute later he was bounding upstairs. "There's an Air France flight in two hours and five minutes," he said.

"Okay," said Graham over his shoulder, busy packing a small overnight case. "I'll take a cab into Strasbourg. Have to teach you to drive, you know, Stevie."

"I've booked the cab," said Stephen quietly. "He'll be here in five minutes. And I'll start learning to drive when you get back."

Graham closed the case and twisted the catches to lock it, then turned and looked steadily at Stephen for some moments. "You're a good boy," he said, in a low, serious voice that made the small hairs on Stephen's neck stand on end. "You're bloody good for me, you know that, Steve?" said Graham. He stood like that, gazing levelly at Stephen, for a few seconds more. Then the moment was over, and Stephen was hurrying downstairs, asking questions over his shoulder as he went.

"I can't really answer any of them right now, Stevie," said Graham apologetically, peering out of the window to see if the cab had arrived. "I'll have to stay there as long as I'm needed — or wanted. I'll ring you at the auberge to let you know I've got there, and then again this evening here, to tell you where I'm staying and so on. After that, we'll just have to play it by ear, old chap."

And then the taxi had arrived, and apart from a forlorn little wave through the window of the house they were renting, that was the last Stephen had seen of Graham for a week. Stephen spent it fretting, missing his lover more than he had ever seemed to in the bad days when they had still been schoolmaster and sixth-form pupil. And yet those days had been bad enough, he thought to himself when he was feeling particularly lonely and miserable. They'd been bloody near intolerable. But his reason had supplied the answer readily enough: this was the first time they'd been kept apart since they had been in France, where there was no reason why they had to be apart.

When Graham telephoned one evening to tell him that there had been a slight improvement in the old man's condition, and that he might be in London for a week or even two, Stephen had felt a brief spasm of jealousy, which sinuously, like a dragon forming out of a wreath of smoke, turned into a momentary wish — that made itself felt despite his instant revulsion and suppression of it — that the old man ought to have the decency to die and let Graham get back where he was needed. Then he shuddered, and gave himself a ferocious reprimand, full of self-hatred and contempt. The following day he volunteered for overtime at the auberge, and told no one there about the little impromptu calendar he had made, just like the ones he had made towards the end of term as a very small boy at school, on which he could tick off the hours till Graham was restored to him.

And yet when Graham finally did return, grey-faced and bone-weary from an almost unbroken vigil at his old friend's bedside for the final thirty-six hours of his life, things were wrong. Neither of them, afterwards, could say what exactly had gone wrong; only that something had gone sour between them, for almost the first time since they had known each other. Graham was crotchety and irritable, inclined to bite Stephen's head off at the slightest provocation, or at no provocation at all. He also developed a tendency to slope off on exploratory strolls round the little town, drinking quite hard and late into the evening, ending up, often, at the auberge where Stephen worked, half-drunk and in a mood to force an argument or even, once or twice, an open quarrel. They slept apart quite often, for the first time since they were together in France, and Stephen lay sleepless, staring into the darkness of the spare room and wondering what he had done to offend Graham. He would think himself round in circles, endlessly and fruitlessly, trying to work out rationally something that was far beyond, above or beneath reason, and sometimes crying himself to sleep as the dawn light came up, which he hadn't done since he had been a little boy.

The truth of it was that Graham was a man of unusually highly-developed conscience, inclined to tax himself with duties and responsibilities that few would have acknowledged, and to be very hard on himself when he felt that he had been remiss, or insufficiently responsive to his duty. He was, thus, feeling heavily responsible for his dear old friend's death, believing that he ought to have spent more time with him over the last few years, and that if he had done so he might have spotted the signs of encroaching illness before the old man had seen them unaided.

Stephen, who was a thoroughly ordinary, average kind of boy, with all the insouciance and casuistry of youth, coupled with a generous ration of youth's ability to find extenuating circumstances when duty contended with pleasure and pleasure won, saw much more clearly than Graham himself that Graham's quite unnecessarily hard line with himself was uncalled for, unhealthy and foolish. But if he tried to voice any such opinion he was brusquely shut up by Graham, who preferred to wallow, for the while at least, in the soupy waters of self-flagellation and the opposite side of the same penny, self-pity. He insisted on blaming himself for neglecting Reggie Westwood, swore that the old man's death would have been averted had he, Graham, been more willing to go and talk to him. Stephen found such self-absorption irritating, pitiful and incomprehensible at the same time, and rapidly began to let his feelings show.

There was an awful period of three or four days during which Stephen, whose eyes were clearer during that difficult time, really thought they were going to break up over the matter. He cried himself to sleep at night, reflecting on the absurdity of human emotions, that could enable the two of them to overcome almost insurmountable difficulties in order to force a chance of living together and then, a matter of a few weeks later, look as if it was likely to make it impossible for them to do so.

And then, as quickly and with as little apparent reason as it had come, the bad patch was over and life resumed the slighty uneven tenor of its way. They began being nice to each other again, at first uneasily and hesitantly, then with growing and finally soaring confidence that all was well again. They began to use little endearments between themselves, at first slightly self-consciously, as if faintly embarrassed, like newly-acquainted actors in the early rehearsals of a play, but very soon as unconsciously and unaffectedly as before; they resumed sleeping together, and soon after that they restarted sexual relations, which had ceased almost instantly with the beginning of their quarrel. In a fortnight it was as if there had never been any awkward moment, or any disagreement between them. By a common, unspoken but clearly understood instinct, they agreed to keep away from any topic of conversation that might unduly remind them of the rift; and in a few weeks it was forgotten.

One thing Graham had mentioned, which they had both almost forgotten in the ensuing unpleasantness, was that his old friend had told him, in a rare interval of lucidity, that he had left him most of his estate. When the tiff was over and they were back on the old, easy footing once more, they discussed it briefly, but neither of them thought much about it. "Will it be very much?" Stephen had asked.

"No idea," Graham had replied casually. "He's got that whacking great flat in St John's Wood, and he must have a bit of cash to be able to afford the London Clinic just now. But as far as I know he's not a wealthy man. I shouldn't start choosing the yacht yet awhile."

"I'm not," Stephen had said, grinning. "There's only one thing I want out of life at the moment, and Reggie's money couldn't buy that." He stood up and moved his hips lasciviously. Graham had stared at him uncomprehendingly for a moment, then caught on, and they had gone quietly but happily upstairs. The interlude of coldness between them, inexplicable though it had been, had in one sense been valuable, in that it had made them realise just how blissful their relationship had been, by and large, until then; so when normality was resumed they were both duly grateful and appreciative. It was not destined to last; but neither of them could know that, and they took their happiness while it was there to be taken.

* * *

"Come on, then, Graham," urged Stephen that evening at home. "Let's tot it up. Let's see how much you've got. Christ, you're a millionaire, aren't you?"

"Several times over, by the looks of this," said Graham, still unable to absorb the full import of Westwood's solicitors' tortured legal English. Now that they had the black and white of the solicitors' letter before them to testify to their precipitate and utterly unexpected entry into the ranks of the rich, they found it temporarily paralysing. They passed the letter back and forth between them, reading and re-reading the series of clauses and trying to see real, tangible things behind them.

"Hey! You've got a pub!" had been Stephen's first words when he scanned the letter the first time. For no particular reason that he could analyse, the idea of Graham owning a pub on the Sussex coast struck him as absurd, impossible, almost surreal. Sitting on the floor at Graham's feet, he goggled at the paragraph of the letter until it ceased to have any meaning, and the letters swam before him. Then he leaned back against Graham's legs and roared with laughter, which he could not have explained in any way whatsoever. Graham, oddly enough, had been reflecting on old Reggie Westwood owning a pub, and finding it as improbable as Stephen found the idea of Graham owning the same place, and joined him in the laugh. Then they had gone more carefully through the long series of clauses, discovering that in addition to a substantial fortune in various kinds of stocks, bonds, shares and cash, and the pub in Sussex, Graham was now the proprietor of a small chain of fish and chip shops in the north of England, and a director of a travel agent's in Maida Vale, a chain of nine petrol stations and tyre-fitting depots in the Midlands, a company making electric and gas furnaces and crematoria, and nine other companies across the country.

"Well, come on, then," urged Stephen. "What're you going to do with it all?"

Graham laughed. "Not so fast, boy," he said sternly, and the reversion to schoolmaster was so convincing that Stephen stopped his prattling in mid-flow for a moment, until he remembered, and glared accusingly at Graham.

"To tell you the frozen truth," Graham said after some musing, "I haven't got the slightest idea what I'm going to do with it all. I mean, good God, I've never expected to have anything like this much... never dreamed of being as rich as this, in my wildest day-dreams." He relapsed into silence.

"One thing I can tell you I'm not going to do," he said at length. Stephen looked up at him attentively.

"I'm not going to work any longer," said Graham decisively. "That's absolutely flat. I've read about these twats in the papers that win three-quarters of a million on the pools, and say 'I'll be back with my broom on Monday'. Well, I'm not gonna be back with my broom after this. No way."

"Be unfair anyway, wouldn't it?" commented Stephen. "I mean, keeping someone out of a job who actually needed one."

Graham stared at him for a moment, then laughed. "Christ, you're good for me," he said softly. "I can always trust you to see the thing from an unusual angle. You're going to keep me young years beyond my rightful span, d'you know that?"

That was something else that was not destined to be fulfilled, but once again, they could not know it at that moment.

The following morning Graham went in to Strasbourg to discuss the future with his old friend and Cambridge crony who had given him his job when Graham was in some trouble. He took him to the best restaurant in Strasbourg, bought him a gourmet lunch and told him without much detail of his good fortune. His friend was almost more emphatic than Graham himself that he should give up the daily toil; but they agreed that Graham would remain in place for a while, until his friend had succeeded in finding the right applicant to take over from him, to preserve continuity for the students. Graham accepted this compromise gladly, delighted to be able to offer something by way of compensation. He told Stephen of the decision that evening, and Stephen agreed without demur that it was no more than Graham's friend was entitled to. Stephen, for his part, had come to a similar amicable arrangement with the *aubergiste* on his own initiative.

* * *

In all it took them another two months before they were completely free of all encumbrances. Graham flew to London twice more, to discuss details of his inheritance with Reggie's solicitors, some very sharp operators in Chancery Lane. He shed all his directorships, mostly in return for handsome cash settlements, and sold the fish and chip chain for a small fortune to a consortium of the owners of individual shops. He sat and listened to a whole series of lengthy and detailed speeches from the sharp operators on the best ways of avoiding the maximum possible sums in taxes, duties and other imposts on his money, of which he understood one word in ten, and perhaps one sentence in a thousand. When he gathered that the fount of advice on avoidance had finally flowed to its conclusion he thanked his advisors profusely, candidly admitted the extent of his understanding, and asked if he might perhaps entrust the entire management of his unexpected fortune to the sharp operators. That being precisely the result which the sharp operators had been expecting and hoping for, they congratulated him politely on his impeccable business acumen, recommended that he allow the same firm of accountants to remain in charge as had supervised the making of the original fortune for Reggie

Westwood, and, when Graham agreed without demur, congratulated him once again, offered him a glass of very dry and splendid sherry, and bowed him out of the office with great courtesy but not a grain of servility.

At some point in the proceedings, almost as an afterthought, one of the sharp operators asked if he had made a will. When Graham had said he hadn't there were Jeeves-like coughs and it was politely intimated to him that only a breech-born half-wit would be so insensate and incorrigible as to leave the office in possession of such a fortune and intestate. And so it came to pass that, almost without thinking about it, or even really being fully conscious of what he was doing, so fast did the sharp operators lead him through the seemingly impenetrable morass of legalese, formality and red tape associated with becoming suddenly and unexpectedly rich, Graham quickly, efficiently and almost casually made a will, in which he left everything he possessed to Stephen Francis Hill, currently of 4, Rue de la République, Saint-Hippolyte, Haut-Rhin, in the Alsace region of the republic of France.

2

Stephen swallowed the last dissolving morsel of his Café de Paris entrecôte and leaned back in his chair with a deep sigh of repletion. It turned into a burp, quite a loud one, and he pulled a sheepish face as he glanced guiltily round. Then he grinned. Graham smiled affectionately at him across the table.

They had decided to spend a little of Graham's sudden and rather overwhelming wealth on a leisurely tour round Europe, and had come to rest, after a very short first leg, in Geneva, a city Graham loved deeply and Stephen had never seen. They had been on the mini-train and all the numerous different cruises on Lake Leman. "You could play cricket on some of those lawns," Stephen had remarked at one point as they passed a vast pink and cream mansion inhabited by a recently deposed psychopathic third-world despot. Graham had nodded, and both had unconsciously given the majestic sweep of manicured grass a lightning assessment, for dimensions, flatness and obstacles. Then they had realised simultaneously what they were doing; two heads had come up in the same moment, and they had stared sadly at each other for a long moment. There had been a tacit but unbreachable understanding between them ever since Stephen's arrival in Saint-Hippolyte that cricket should not be mentioned. The sense of loss it brought was altogether too painful. "Sorry," Stephen had muttered, and they had turned back to look at the next palace along the lakeside in a glum silence.

They had cheered up very quickly, though, aided by the benign and relaxed atmosphere of the city, and had gone for a drive later, dining sumptuously at a small but magnificent gourmet restaurant in the mountains overlooking the city. The following day they were going to a concert of orchestral music, the first Stephen had attended. "Time you acquired some culture, then, you little prole," Graham had said when Stephen confessed the fact. Meanwhile, they had decided to take the day in between easy, wandering round window-shopping and buying little presents for people, enjoying the sensation of not having to wonder whether they could afford them. Finally Stephen had felt hungry, and Graham had introduced him to the delights of the Café de Paris and its entrecôte steaks.

"This is the life, isn't it?" Stephen said luxuriantly as his *coupe colonel* arrived.

"Hmph!" grunted Graham, eying the huge confection. "We'll be as fat as a pair of prize saddlebacks if we don't start getting a bit of exercise," he went on, glancing round the packed restaurant and surreptitiously undoing the waistband of his trousers. Stephen muttered "Good idea" and followed suit, and both minds turned simultaneously to the one thing they were both missing poignantly.

Graham sat deep in thought for some time, and Stephen, sensitive as always to his beloved friend's humours, devoted himself to polishing off his dessert in a considerate silence.

"You say 'This is the life'," Graham said at last, gazing reflectively into the middle distance, "and very agreeable it is, I grant you. But if you're missing things... well, what I'm really asking, I suppose, is, would you like to go back?" Stephen gazed at him for a moment across the little round table, his coffee cup arrested halfway to his lips. "I... well... I hadn't..." he stammered, before falling silent once more. "I hadn't really thought about that," he eventually said, thinking about it now. "I mean, I've been enjoying it over here. Very much. Especially since — you know, since we could do things in style, sort of." He sat thinking about it some more.

"But in any case," he resumed, "surely we'd be running the

same risks as before if we were to go back now, wouldn't we? I mean, I'm still not twenty-one, so we could still get into trouble with the law, couldn't we?" He sat watching Graham anxiously, the tranquil contentment that had settled over him since they had started their jaunt blown to shreds by Graham's unexpected question.

"Ah," said Graham, looking shrewdly at him. "Now, that's rather where things are a bit different now. Different from how they were before — before our bit of trouble, that is.

"There's one big difference between then and now." He reached into his trouser pocket and pulled out a fat wad of Swiss banknotes. "That's the difference," he said quietly, slipping the money back. "And it makes more difference than anything else in the world could make, believe you me." Stephen looked questions at him.

"You said just now 'This is the life'," Graham said. "Yesterday, you remember, we were both saying how bloody marvellous it was to be able to pop into any old shop, whichever we felt like popping into, and buying exactly what we felt like buying, without having to count the cost? Same thing the day before, when we went to that flash restaurant up in the mountains, remember?" Stephen nodded.

"Well, that's one... one facet of having money. It buys you things. Great. But there's another aspect of it, that's even more important, and even nicer for the lucky person," Graham went on. "It was spelt out to me once by a chap I knew. Only really rich man I ever knew, really — 'cept Reggie, of course, and he didn't count, because I didn't know he was rich. Not really rich. But this other bloke told me why he was glad he'd got money, and hoped the day would never come when he hadn't got it. Can you guess what he said?"

"No," said Stephen simply.

"No, well, there's no reason why you should, of course. Well, what he said was 'I like having this kind of money, not because of what it can buy me — that's very nice, but there's very little it gets me that I couldn't cheerfully do without. What this is, for me' — and he pulled out a wad about five times the size of that lot I just showed you — 'is Fuck-you money.' He explained to me, and I understood. But I understand better now, Stevie. Do you see what he meant?"

Stephen sat there, thinking about it. "Well," he began, "I think

I do, but..."

"What he meant, Steve, was that when you've got this sort of money behind you" — he gestured at his trouser pocket — "real money, there's nothing anybody can do to you that can hurt you. Because you can always go one better. Whatever they do to you, you can always buy something bigger, or better, or you can buy someone to put right whatever they've damaged or fucked up. Money can buy you practically anything, not to mention anybody. So if someone looks as if they want to do you some kind of disfavour, why you haul out your wad, and you say 'Fuck you, pal', and you buy whatever sort of antidote or prophylactic you need to spike their guns. That's what he meant, and I'm beginning to see just how right he was. Do you see what I mean, though? The relevance of what I've been saying to what we were talking about?"

Stephen pondered the matter for some time, sipping his coffee absently. "You mean, I suppose," he said slowly, "that if we were to go back to England, and anybody started getting nasty about you having me with you, you could use your money to get rid of them. I don't mean get rid of them," he added hastily. "I mean, get rid of the threat they posed, or whatever."

"That's it," said Graham calmly.

"But surely, even having a lot of money can't make any difference to the law," objected Stephen. "I mean, you can't bribe judges and things, can you? I know the odd policeman takes bribes, but you could never take the risk of offering one, could you, in case the policeman you picked happened to be an honest one. You'd be even further in the sh..."

"Not the point, Steve," said Graham. "The point about having money is that you never get to the position where you have to start taking risks like offering bribes. The point is that anyone who ever thought there wasn't one law for the rich and another for everybody else was deluding himself. We're the rich now. So we stop at the kind of hotels where the police only go if they're invited, and call people 'sir' if they do. We've now got enough money to take two rooms, even though we only want one. But we've got enough also to pay our hotel staff, who might say something, well enough that they bloody well won't. No chambermaid or room service waiter's going to jeopardise the kind of tips we'll be giving, just to see the law about under-age sex with you enforced."

Stephen grinned at him brightly. "Fuck-you money," he mused. "Mm, yeah. Got a nice ring to it, as well, hasn't it? So you can stick your finger up at anybody who looks like getting in our way and say 'Fuck you, pal', and there's nothing they can do about it?"

"That's it, exactly. So, what with that and the fact that the British legal system is open to all, like the Ritz Hotel — we'll be in the Ritz Hotel, of course — if you want to go back to England, well, we can. It's as simple as that, really."

Once more Stephen sat for a long time in thought. The waitress came, and Graham smiled winningly at her, gestured at the boy and made gear-wheel motions beside his own temple, and ordered further coffees for them. She smiled, charmed, and went off.

"It's very sweet of you to offer," Stephen said very slowly at length. "But it's not the cricket season yet, is it? What is it, the..." He consulted his watch. "Eighteenth of Feb. There's two months to go till the season starts. I'd like to carry on this trip round, if you're willing," he said after more reflection. "Then maybe we could go back and find a club a bit later on, when the season's under way."

"Okay," Graham smiled. "Just as long as you're happy. But don't forget, if you're really missing cricket, we can go to Australia or New Zealand, if you like. It's only a matter of popping across from here to Heathrow, and then jumping on Concorde. Be there in a couple of days, if you like. Personally, I like this central bit of Europe in the cold weather, and I think you'll like Madrid, which is where I had in mind to trot off to next. But don't forget the offer's open, if you fancy seeing a bit of cricket. Come to that, we could just pop down to Oz for a few days, if you like. Watch a few days' cricket, then come back here and carry on touring round." He chuckled with glee at the idea of doing something so outrageously, ostentatiously expensive. "Conspicuous consumption with a vengeance," he laughed.

"No, thanks, love," said Stephen softly, and seriously, in contrast to Graham's hilarity. "I appreciate it, believe me, dear Graham. It's wonderful of you. But, no, I think I'd like to carry on poodling round Europe for a while yet, unless you really want to do something else. And then it'll make it feel all the better when we do go back. And I'd like that to be for the beginning of next season. That's when I'd like to go back, please, Graham."

"Okay," agreed Graham cheerfully. They said no more about it that day, and only ever spoke of cricket once again.

* * *

The next few weeks were a long series of short hops in aeroplanes, when both of them lapped up to the fullest the wondrous luxury of travelling first class, sumptuous hired cars, comfortable hotels. They wandered from city to city in Spain, spending a day or two in Barcelona, in Toledo, in a ferociously cold Madrid, admired the Alhambra and the other Moorish beauties in Granada, and finally fetched up on the south coast. They stayed for a few days in Malaga, where they discovered a restaurant which Stephen, who was learning Spanish fast under Graham's guidance, christened Los Bandidos, run by two magnificently moustachioed and villainous-looking ex-colonials from one of Spain's former possessions on the North African coast.

They took a taxi along the coast to Torremolinos and Fuengirola, and thoroughly enjoyed the encyclopaedic vulgarity of the resorts, with their "British pubs," representative of all that was worst about such places. "Ah," exclaimed Graham reminiscently as they sauntered into Barry's British Bar. "Watney's Red Barrel. How well I remember that. A headache in every pint was their proud guarantee, I think." They sat under a multi-coloured umbrella drinking pints of the despised beer, watching the antics of the small number of holidaymakers taking winter breaks, and Graham reminisced a little sadly about when the resorts had been beautiful fishing villages with a few white cottages and miles of unspoiled, undiscovered golden beaches. "Still," he said, brightening up, "they're still worth seeing, don't you think, Steve? I mean, it'd be awful to be on your deathbed and never have seen where Club 18-30 used to go for their holidays, wouldn't it?"

An hour or so was enough of the delights of Torremolinos, however, so they fled back to Malaga, and thence to a tiny village along the coast, called Salobrena, which Graham swore was the last unspoiled spot on the whole littoral. "I just hope it still hasn't been discovered by the Cook's Tours shower of shit yet," said Graham fervently as they sped along the coast road and Stephen admired the cactuses growing beside it.

It hadn't, and they spent an idyllic week there, climbing the steep hill to the neat, compact village of white Moorish houses nestling on the hilltop, but mostly swimming lazily in the more or less unpolluted sea, and basking on the vast and almost totally empty beach. As the evenings drew on it became totally deserted, and they made love languorously on the sands every night, and then a good deal less languorously in bed later on.

* * *

"Damn," said Graham mildly.

They were temporarily back at Saint-Hippolyte. After their idyll of untramelled joy in Spain they had decided to return home for a few days "to see what the postman's brought" as Graham put it. They had aired the house and collected a small mountain of mail from the post office, and were rather enjoying taking life easy and opening the dozens of letters at their leisure. Stephen looked up from the letter he was reading and glanced over enquiringly when Graham swore.

"Got to go to London," grunted Graham, pulling a face. "Some papers to sign. Something to do with those bloody directorships of Reggie's. What a pain."

"I don't know," said Stephen thoughtfully. "The season's nearly starting, you know. We could stay over there for a bit and have a game or two. Old Bill'd be happy to have us back, you know that. He says so in every letter he writes, and gets the others to say so as well." They both grinned.

"I s'pose we could give the old bugger a ring," conceded Graham, secretly delighted with the idea. "See if he's got room for us. I wouldn't mind a game, I must say. I hated losing the second half of last season." Stephen nodded approvingly. "Better get the flight booked first, though," muttered Graham. He picked up the telephone directory, thumbed through the yellow pages and scribbled a number, and lifted the phone. Two minutes' fluent French later, he replaced it and turned to Stephen, looking faintly annoyed. "Hmph!" he grunted. "We'll have to travel separately, by the looks of it." Stephen raised his eyebrows.

"They say there's only one seat left, out of all the flights in the next three days — one seat." He muttered to himself in annoyance for a moment, then shrugged. "Oh well," he said, "I s'pose I can take it, and you can follow on a day or so later."

Stephen's face fell. "Can't it just wait a few days till there's two seats?" he demanded. Graham shook his head. "I've got to sign these bloody papers right away, according to the solicitor," he said. "Something to do with tax, from what little I can follow of their gobbledegook." He tut-tutted to himself, shaking his head. "Honestly, I don't know why the hell they bother explaining all this in their letters. I understand about one word in ten. It might as well be in Swahili. And I bet it's costing me a small fortune to receive these pieces of code. Anyway," he said briskly, returning to the point, "whatever this jargon means, it's clear enough that I've got to leap aboard the first passing plane and do the necessary. I'll leave you here, and you can take the next flight."

"Why can't we drive it and go over on the hover?" asked Stephen peevishly. He didn't feel like his own company, and he enjoyed long night drives with Graham.

"Take too long, love," said Graham briskly, dismissing Stephen's attempts to talk him out of it in four airy words. "Might as well wait for the next flight with seats available as do that. We wouldn't be in London till..." He closed his eyes and did a rapid mental calculation. "Next Wednesday," he finished. "No, old love, I'm afraid there's no way round it. Besides, what's the panic? You can do without me for a couple of days, can't you? I'll shoot into Strasbourg now, and you can take the next one. There's the number." He gestured to the slip of paper beside the phone book. "Same travel agents we use normally." And he went off upstairs, whistling, quite happy with his brisk and efficient arrangements. He didn't see the glare of annoyance Stephen directed after him. Stephen remembered it, though, afterwards.

Graham packed a few things in a small overnight bag, and a few hours later he was gone in a taxi to Strasbourg, waving cheerfully to Stephen as the car pulled away. Stephen raised a hand glumly, then went back to the pile of mail, a little disgruntled.

Three hours later there was a brief moment of instant sunshine over the English Channel as an airbus exploded in mid-air. All 298 people aboard died in seconds.

*   *   *

Stephen could never clearly remember afterwards the sequence of events; nor could he ever say exactly how he had managed to get through the first few days after he heard the news. Assuredly he could remember individual moments, but they were jumbled and out of sequence, fading into and out of each other with the insane parody of reality of nightmare, like lighted galleries scattered along an endless corridor of unrelieved darkness.

With the insensate, nightmarish randomness of memory at

such moments, he could remember the precise point the Clint Eastwood western that had been showing had reached when the newsflash interrupted it, and his vague irritation at the French insistence of dubbing an utterly un-Clint-Eastwood-like voice over the action, and the distraction it never failed to bring with it. He could remember the sudden clenching feeling of faintness as the sense of the announcement penetrated his idle half-attention.

He could recall with eerie vividness the sensation of the blood draining rapidly from his face. He had a sudden fancy that he could actually see himself in some crazy distorting mirror, growing blanched and haggard in mid-air before his own eyes. He could not remember frantically scrabbling among the piles of discarded envelopes and letters in search of the pen. He did not remember his cry of anguish as he recalled that the pen had been almost the last thing Graham had touched before hurrying out to the waiting taxi, jotting single words or brief shorthand notes on letters and bills of the action they required. He had no memory of scribbling the emergency telephone number the newscaster gave for relatives to ring for news of passengers feared to have been on the aircraft.

He could remember falling with a crash into the armchair he had leapt from to get the pen, his legs suddenly refusing to hold him up, and the headlong welter of conflicting thoughts, the reasoning half of him asserting with a deadly finality that Graham must have been aboard the flight while the rest of him howled and screamed in protest that it could not be so. A lunatic certainty that Graham had somehow been delayed and missed the plane seized him, temporarily drowning the dim but insistent awareness that he was doing nothing more than erecting fantasies to keep out the appalling, unbearable truth.

He could not remember making the telephone call to the emergency number he had scribbled, or cursing like a madman when he found it engaged the first twenty times he rang it; yet he could recall with total clarity the moment of icy detachment that descended on him and enveloped him, rescuing him, necessarily, the moment he got the answering tone. That merciful detachment sustained him while the police officer confirmed that a Monsieur Graham Curtis had indeed been among the passengers, and through the man's brief, almost curt, but none the less obviously sincere expression of sympathy, which had somehow been the worst moment of all.

He had no recollection afterwards of how he came to be at

the auberge where he had worked until Graham's unexpected inheritance; but he remembered clearly enough suddenly being surrounded by a crowd of his former regular customers, stunned and tongue-tied but full of a desperate, clumsy, inarticulate pity for the boy: everyone at the auberge had taken to him very quickly after his arrival among them. He remembered his feelings of startled surprise at finding himself somehow transported to the proprietor's own sitting room, crying on the ample bosom of the proprietor's wife, while Nicole the late-shift barmaid clucked and fussed over him and forced some violent drink down his throat. He remembered, ridiculously, becoming unreasonably distraught about the fact that the auberge had been summarily closed for the evening, and trying to insist that they must not lose a night's takings on his account; and being smartly told off by the motherly proprietress.

They filled him with enough drink to get him moderately but not catastrophically drunk, then bedded him down on the premises. He lay awake, half-drunk, rising and sinking in a morass of pain, until just before three o'clock in the morning, at which hour, for no reason that made any particular sense, he decided he must be in his own home, jumped up and slipped out into the night. When he reached home he had made a telephone call and finally dropped into a sleep of physical and emotional exhaustion in the armchair. He had woken, cold, cramped and wondering if it had all been an impossibly awful nightmare, later in the morning, with an insatiable craving for a drink, and went straight out to the auberge. He remembered, guiltily, thanking them far less effusively than they deserved, feeling nothing himself except an unyielding, aching emptiness and loneliness.

The telephone call he had made at three that first morning after had not been to his mother, but to Richard Fitzjohn in England; and it was from that telephone call that his recovery could in truth be said to have begun.

* * *

Richard walked through the door of the auberge six hours and forty-three minutes after putting the receiver of his telephone down, charmed everyone in seconds, and had Stephen walking beside him to his own house in ten minutes. He left the staff and the early morning patrons of the auberge with quiet, sincere thanks that made the women weep and the men fight not to, and with assurances that he, and Stephen himself, would be back soon to express their gratitude properly and sensibly, even as he was propelling Stephen out into the street. Half an hour later he had Stephen sat down at home, talking, at last, quietly, rationally and dry-eyed. He was still talking eight hours later, while Richard sat quietly and let him run on until the poison was flushed from his system. Then, equally quietly and calmly, he gathered him up and took him home to England.

Richard left his parents, who knew Stephen very well and liked him very much indeed, to look after him. He himself flew straight back to Strasbourg, hired a car and drove to Saint-Hippolyte, and set about methodically winding up Stephen's — and Graham's — affairs. He arranged with the post office to redirect mail to his own address; he interviewed the landlord of the house Graham had rented as soon as he had arrived from England nine months before, and terminated the lease. The landlord, who had liked both his tenants and was deeply sympathetic when he heard of the tragedy, immediately wanted to waive the three months' rent payable for premature departure. Richard gently and politely declined his offer.

He gathered up all the mail, and arranged with the landlord and a local removal contractor to have the pair's possessions shipped to Britain at the earliest convenient moment. He settled the telephone and electricity bills, sold Graham's car, and cancelled the newspapers, French and English, that they had on order at the local newsagents. Finally, he found a florist's, commandeered the entire staff and most of the stock, then drove on to the auberge, where he presented the landlady and Nicole the barmaid with the most enormous bouquets of flowers ever seen in Saint-Hippolyte. He sat with the regulars and the staff for an hour, charming every man and woman of them and refusing to allow anyone to pass a centime over the counter. Then, having yielded gracefully to the insistent demands of everyone there that he return, with Stephen, very soon, he waited for a moment when everyone was talking at once, and slipped away. Nicole, who was one of the few who saw him leave, turned to the proprietress, her eyes swimming. So were the proprietress's. "Is he like Stephen and... and p-p-poor Graham, do you think?" Nicole asked. "Is he one of those?" "I suppose so," said the older woman with a gallic shrug. "Must be, I should think."

"Jesus, what a pity," muttered Nicole.

3

For Stephen it was rather like getting back to normal life after a long and delirious illness. The day Richard brought him home he was installed, without fuss or ceremony, in the spare bed in Richard's room, where he had spent so much of the past year of his life, and which he had come to find more familiar than his room at his own home. Richard's parents had always treated him as another son, and dropped back into the same habit as effortlessly as if he had never been away. And, after his lightning trip to Alsace to wind things up there, there was, always, Richard.

On the evening when he got back from Saint-Hippolyte he found Stephen lying on his bed, staring at the ceiling. He padded over and dropped gracefully onto the floor. His head was close to Stephen's, but he carefully avoided getting too close, and made especially sure that he didn't touch him. "How're you feeling, Stevie?" he asked gently.

Stephen rolled onto his side so he could look straight into Richard's light brown eyes, and gave him a very difficult, strained smile. "I'll be all right," he whispered. "Thanks to you. I... I haven't really started to come to terms yet... I still can't really believe it's happened — like that, just normal one minute, and then, bang!" There was a long silence, while Richard delicately devoted his attention to the floor between his thighs. "I could have been on that plane with him, you know," said Stephen, in a low voice that vibrated with horror. "I sometimes wish I had been, you know, Richard. But I don't, not really. And then I hate myself for not wishing I had been, you know what I mean?" Richard nodded gravely, and held his gaze.

"There's nothing for you to reproach yourself for, old chap," he said. "Everyone feels guilty for being the one to survive. He never felt a thing, you can be sure of that. One moment he was flying along. Thinking of you, for sure. The next: well, if there's anything in what the clerics say, he's playing cricket somewhere, and waiting for you, knowing there's all the time in the world. If there's nothing in what they say, he was thinking of you, and then there was nothing at all. The big problem now is you. There's going to be things to do, and they're not going to be pleasant. How do you feel?"

Stephen looked at him in silence for a long time. Then he smiled. It was tentative, uncertain, and a little wobbly, but it was real. After a moment or so, he equally tentatively stretched out a hand and ran his fingers lightly through Richard's abundant shock of white-blond hair. Richard had to fight hard to keep still and betray nothing of the tumult of emotion that the small, almost child-like gesture set off in him. It was the first gesture of physical affection Stephen had offered since Richard's precipitate arrival at Saint-Hippolyte, and Richard's mind worked overtime to decide how best to respond to it.

After a moment he slid an arm under Stephen's neck and let it rest there, taking pleasure from the weight of his head. Stephen flinched for a second, then rallied, and almost shyly nestled his head down, in a tiny motion of confidence, fitting the back of his head into Richard's palm. Richard let his fingers stir very softly in Stephen's hair, and let the small motion continue, soothing Stephen, who closed his eyes and seemed content to remain like that.

They had been like that, like a Rodin group, for twenty minutes, and Richard's arm was going to sleep under the dead weight of Stephen's head. "Have to let my hand breathe a bit, old chap," he said very softly, wriggling his arm free. Stephen lifted his head a fraction of an inch to let him work his hand out from under. Richard stirred his stiffening limbs slightly, and decided to take matters a step further. "Just understand this, Stevie, my lovely," he murmured, keeping his voice soothing. "No one's going to put any pressure on you. You're here for as long as you want to be here, and no strings attached. No one will bother you, least of all me. I shan't touch you, either, unless you want me to. I think you'll want to sleep a lot. Fine. You sleep. Come and go as you please. I've got a set of keys for you. But you're going to have to try to think a bit, love. Like I said, there's going to be things to be done, and you're going to have to do them. Try and get yourself prepared, and tell me when you're ready to talk about them. I'm going to leave you now."

Stephen stirred, rolled towards him, and opened his eyes. "Don't go, Richard," he said softly. "I know what you're talking about, and I think I can talk about them — to you. Stay with me, won't you?"

Richard's heart contracted and throbbed, and all the old desire came flooding back, robbed of none of its power by events. He swallowed hard, and took a firm grip on his emotions. "Sure?"

he said, carefully. Stephen gave him the full searchlight glare of his large grey eyes, and nodded, awkwardly, sideways at him. Then he succeeded in surprising Richard. He slid off the bed and stripped to his underpants in almost a single, sinuous movement. It happened so quickly that he had shot across the room to Richard's double bed, which he had occupied as his own for so long last summer, almost before Richard had had time to assimilate what was happening. Stephen drew the covers up in a quick, fussy, almost prim movement, and all Richard could see was a cascade of dusty-blond hair across his pillow, and a pair of grey eyes gazing at him over the raised ruff of quilt. There was no beseeching there, no pleading, just a serious look of enquiry from a friend in distress. "What was it you said once about a bit of quick-melting blond ice-cream?" said Stephen, and Richard could almost feel the waves of pain and loneliness flowing from him. "Come to me," said Stephen softly. "I don't want... That is... I mean, I can't... couldn't... you know what I mean. But you could come and cuddle me. Please." He sounded like a hurt child. Richard stood up slowly, shed his clothes and slid silently into the bed.

* * *

They lay together for almost two days, chastely, holding each other in a clasp that was passionate yet somehow objective, for all the mounting desire that beset Richard as the memories of the previous summer flooded back to him. He killed the desire, and managed Stephen like a very expensive nurse, soothing him expertly but yielding to none of his own feelings, recognising the oddly sexless urgency of Stephen's needs.

It was Richard's father who roused Stephen from his interlude of automatism and set him back onto a path of practicality that ultimately brought him out of his first, and worst, deep mourning and regression. Mr Fitzjohn was a large, soft-spoken, rumpled man, given to hairy sweaters and aromatic, leather-bound pipes. He watched patiently for the first couple of days, when the two boys hardly left their room, and waited for the first day when Stephen spent any length of time downstairs. Then he made an almost invisible motion with his head to his son, who had been waiting for some such signal and slipped unobtrusively from the room.

"How are you feeling, old chap?" asked Mr Fitzjohn quietly,

taking the pipe from his mouth and waggling the stem gently in Stephen's direction. Stephen raised his head slowly and gazed for a long moment at him. Somehow sensing the goodwill and strength there, he pulled himself visibly together, knowing that he owed a sensible answer.

"I... I'm getting over it," he said slowly, fighting down the stammer that had lately begun to afflict his speech. "I'm... I'm feeling better than I did." He paused to search Mr Fitzjohn's face, and drew strength from what he saw there: concern, but not exaggerated, solicitude, but not sentimentalised, and above all something honest, straightforward, something that positively demanded a firm, undramatised acceptance that life was going on, and was going to go on. He looked steadily at Mr Fitzjohn, understood at last the nature of his loss, and responded. For the first time since he had last been with Graham, not knowing that he was doing it, Stephen smiled.

It was a crucial breakthrough, and the cure proceeded apace from that point onwards. Mr Fitzjohn eased Stephen back to health, treating him with the same uncondescending respect with which he had treated his son from the age of six. He heard the full story of Stephen's relationship with Graham, asked many questions of which none was in the finest degree prurient, and kept his opinions mostly to himself. When Stephen asked him directly for a judgment he gave it placidly, and it was invariably shrewd and worldly, uttered in a tone of cool assessment, and with an almost serious, friendly twinkle, as if to tell him 'It's all right, Steve, I'm on your side.' That was how Stephen took it, and how Mr Fitzjohn meant him to take it. Richard was present at the therapy sessions, sitting quietly on the floor leaning against Stephen's legs and saying little. When they had talked themselves out for the evening he would lead Stephen upstairs and lie with him in bed, holding him gently until he fell asleep, then slipping softly across the room to the single bed to find for himself the relief that he ached to find with Stephen but Stephen couldn't provide.

* * *

"Time for a dose of normality for you, Steve," said Mr Fitzjohn one day later that week. Stephen looked trustingly at him, not really taking in the sense of what he had said.

"Yes," said Mr Fitzjohn briskly. "You've done your mourning, old chap, and it's time to start living again. Your pal'd want that, if he had a vote in the matter. So does Dick, and so do you. There's life going on out there, and you're letting it pass you by. Well, that was necessary for a while. A very short while. You'd been hurt, intolerably as it seemed to you at the time, but it's time to start flexing your muscles. There's another thing, too. You've got things to do." Stephen raised his eyebrows at him. "Dick knows," murmured Mr Fitzjohn, directing a jet of blue smoke at the ceiling. He stood up, smoothed his rumpled pullover, did the same with his hair, and went out with his pipe clamped between his teeth, pausing to ruffle Stephen's hair as he passed. "I'm taking Lydia off for a week or so," he remarked casually as he passed on. "Going off for one of our little jaunts. We're leaving you lads to fend for yourselves. If you'll take my advice you'll start getting out and enjoying yourselves. And start knocking things off that list of jobs." Stephen rose from his armchair to his feet in a single movement, unaware of how graceful he was. Mr Fitzjohn saw it, appreciatively; and he saw for one vivid moment of revelation what Graham Curtis had seen. Graham might have died young, he reflected in that moment's insight, but he achieved something few men do. He had his heart's desire for a time.

"What are these things to do?" asked Stephen.

"Dick knows," repeated Mr Fitzjohn placidly, and left the room in a mantle of blue smoke.

Richard slipped into the room as his father went out. "Come on, Stevie," he said in a carefully normal tone, slipping his arm affectionately round Stephen's waist. "We're going out. Mes parents vont on the piss in Austria, and we're going on it somewhere less glamorous."

"Oh?" said Stephen, feeling a faint inner quiver of pleasurable excitement such as he had feared was dead in him. "Where?"

"Elderton Park Cricket Club," announced Richard. "It's only a week or two till the season starts, and you'll want to bung your name in the availability book." And he bustled Stephen rapidly out of the house, carefully contriving not to give him any time in which to think. He yelled farewells to his parents as they went out of the door, and Stephen unconsciously followed suit.

To Stephen's immense relief there were few people about when the two boys arrived at the cricket ground. They entered the big old pavilion, and Stephen felt a wave of yearning for the recent past break coldly over him as he smelled the familiar odours of leather, whitener, beer and old, faint sweat. Images of Graham tumbled helter-skelter through his mind: Graham taking his arm and leading him through the crush to drive him home after his first match for the club, Graham walking back in, flushed, streaming with sweat but wearing a broad grin of pure contentment after a big innings; Graham sitting at a table, talking, talking endlessly, about everything under the sun, serious but twinkling, picking up his glass occasionally to sip his lager, or glancing up to smile or make some remark to one of the players passing on the way to the bar.

Somehow coming there made Graham's death real and tangible in a way that nothing else had been able to do. Stephen came head on to the realisation that Graham really wasn't going to come back: that he would never see his face again. He halted abruptly a pace or two across the threshold and stood for some moments, absorbing the shock of the realisation. He looked about him, carefully, as if he was seeing the big, airy room with its high raftered ceiling and its masculine decorations and impedimenta for the first time, or as if he had to memorise the exact layout of the place for an observation test later. Richard stood at his side, watching him closely, and a little anxiously. He had known the moment of entry there would be critical, and almost held his breath as he waited to see Stephen's reaction.

And then, suddenly, his fears were relieved. For Stephen, it suddenly became, somehow, much easier to accept. The reality was so stark in this setting that it became, paradoxically, far easier to face and surmount: as if the very nearness of Graham that he felt all about him in this room was itself urging him to pick up the course of his life and accept that an early, indescribably, almost impossibly happy chapter had simply come to an end.

After that it was downhill. The boys went to the bar, where the steward greeted them effusively, and naturally asked how they had wintered. One or two other members were already drinking, and gathered round sympathetically when they heard Stephen telling the steward of Graham's death. Drinks and condolence were proffered liberally, but the men, ranging in age from fourteen to eighty, were so transparently genuine, and so obviously full of concern for Stephen, that it made the breaking of the ice easier than he — or even Richard, generally more optimistic and also more intuitive — had dared to hope.

The turning point came when they had been there for half an

hour. The door was hurled open as if a small depth charge had been detonated behind it, and Bill McKechnie walked in. He tramped in with his customary heavy tread, bawling good evenings in his broad Derbyshire tones, and had reached the bar before his eye fell on the boys. His big, bristling red eyebrows rose sharply as he saw who was there. "Biggsy!" he boomed, and clapped Stephen on the shoulder with a huge red hand, sending him staggering. "Aren't you in France with your partner in crime?" He stared at Stephen for a few moments, then suddenly grinned. "You haven't come back to play for us after all, have you?" Stephen nodded, a little shy all of a sudden, and Bill slapped him on the back again, knocking the breath out of him, at the same time roaring to the steward for pints. "Great, Steve!" he bawled. "I've been at the pair of you to come back, haven't I? Where's his nibs?"

And then they had to tell him, and he became the other Bill, who had helped Stephen in his hour of greatest need, kept a surreptitious but keenly observant eye on his well-being, and looked after him in the most discreet but efficient manner. Beneath the stentorian bawl and the 'hail, fellow, well met' gaiety, beneath the leader of rugby song choruses, the hardest of hard drinking heads, and the great teddy-bear of a man setting his face resolutely against the idea of growing up, there lay a deep and sensitive friend, wise and generous and kind.

Now he became instantly quiet, took Stephen gently by the arm and steered him to a table in the farthest, darkest corner of the big pavilion, jerking his head at Richard to follow. He sat the boys down, got up and went briefly back to the bar to collect the glasses, and returned, looking steadily and observantly at Stephen as he came. Richard noticed that he was walking almost noiselessly. He sat down, and demanded, very gently but in a tone that brooked no argument, to be told the entire story. Stephen told it, glad to be able to do so, for it enabled him to unravel many of his own tangled emotions as he quietly worked his way through the events of the last few months.

When he had finished Richard took up the account, explaining that Stephen was back with him for the foreseeable future, and concluding with his own resolve to come to the club that evening for Stephen to put his name in the book. When the story was finished Bill sat looking keenly at Stephen for some moments. Then he got up, patting Richard on the shoulder as he gathered their glasses. "You did quite right to bring the lad down here," he said, heading for the bar. He returned with the availability book, and thrust it at Stephen. "Here y'are, our kid," he said, still speaking softly, but with no loss of his normal strength of personality. "Stick your name down. You too, Richard — I take it you're still gonna score for us?" Richard nodded. Bill went off again, returned with the refilled glasses, and sat down. He put a big, hard hand gently on Stephen's shoulder.

"I'm not gonna try an say much in the way a sympathy," he said in a soft murmur that was utterly unlike his usual conversation bellow. "There ain't a lot that's worth sayin, an what there is, you know without my sayin it. You had a fine friend in Graham. We all did. But I'll tell you this, young Steve. We all appreciated him a lot better because a you. You brought the best out in him, you made him blossom — I'm speakin as a cricketer, now, as well as a friend. You made him very happy, we could all see that, once we knew what the score was. You took him out of himself, an made him a better pal, a better cricketer certainly, an I'd guess a better man an all. Think about that when it gets hard to bear, our kid. An if there's anything I can do — anything at all, you come to me an you ask, all right?" He sat watching Stephen, who blinked at him through wet eyelashes, too moved to speak. Richard's eyes were moist also. He snuffled loudly, and all three of them jumped, and then laughed. It was a very important moment, because it broke the tension. After that Bill deliberately steered the conversation onto other things, recounting anecdotes about the antics of various members over the winter, and the laughter came more easily, and more often. Throughout the evening he also ensured, without ever making it obvious that he was doing it, that they were left alone by the other players and members who arrived in a steady stream to drink. Richard, who missed very little and was a precocious master of tact himself, conceived an enormous admiration for the skill and discretion with which he did it, so that no one ever actually realised they were being excluded and kept at a distance.

Bill also unobtrusively made sure that Stephen's glass was never allowed to stand empty for more than a second or two, with the result that when the time came for them to go back through the dark and deserted streets both boys were a little unsteady on their feet, and somewhat the worse for wear. Bill saw the fact, understood that his intention had been achieved, and informed them that he was driving them home. They found themselves being propelled into the back of his car, and were very glad of the lift as it had begun to rain — a fine, spiteful, sleety rain that would have made them very wet indeed without appearing to. Bill repeated his sympathy, sincerely but without ceremony, turned round to lean over the back of his seat, and made Stephen promise that he would not fail to ask if he wanted or needed anything. Then he watched while the boys let themselves into Richard's house, gave them a quick bib on the horn and disappeared.

The boys made tea before going rather unsteadily upstairs, and there, for the first time since his return, Stephen gravitated without thinking to Richard's bed. He dropped his clothes in a pile at his feet where he stood, slid down into Richard's bed, and waited, propped on one elbow and gazing levelly at Richard. Richard could sense that something out of the ordinary was afoot, and his heart throbbed and began beating faster as he wondered if it might be what he desired more than anything. It was: that night they made love, fully, firmly and with months of passion cruelly repressed to make up for. It was, Richard felt safe in assuring himself, at least the end of the beginning.

* * *

The first of the unpleasant items for Stephen to tick off his list he had fulfilled some days before: after a great deal of agonising he had managed to steel himself and compose a letter to Graham's parents. Graham had not spoken often of his parents, and Stephen had realised only when he sat down to write to them that he had no idea if they had known of his existence, let alone his relationship with their son. He didn't know, either, if they could have been informed of his death by any other means. Richard didn't know either, so they asked his father. "I think you'll find that the airline will have had a record of his passport on their passenger manifest," Mr Fitzjohn told them. "Which means they'll have informed the Home Office, or the Passport Office, or whoever it is they inform in these cases. He'll have had to fill in details of next-of-kin — you have to tell the buggers your great-granny's favourite colour these days, to get a passport at all. Convince em you're not an illegal immigrant coming in on the night rowing-boat from Bangladesh. Yes, I think they'll have been contacted, Stephen. Poor people," he ruminated. "Some young copper knocking on their door, I imagine."

In the end, after several abortive drafts he produced a long and fairly guarded letter that was tactful and gracious enough to pass the stern scrutiny of Richard and his father. He broke the fact of Graham's death as gently as he could contrive it, saying only that he was a very close friend of Graham's, and devoting most of the text to as sincere and delicate an expression of sympathy and regret as he could put together. He had received, by return, a courteous reply, in dignified, rather old-fashioned English, which gave nothing away about the parents' feelings, or anything to indicate whether they had been aware of their son's nature, or of Stephen's existence, let alone the place he had occupied in Graham's life. Graham's mother wrote the reply, stating that they had already been informed, but thanking him for conveying the news so tactfully and saying that they would be in touch again soon. That had been all, and Stephen, Richard and Mr Fitzjohn between them had been unable to tease any further meaning, explicit or implicit, from it than that.

The second task presented itself early the following week. The plane carrying Graham had blown up over water, and very few identifiable bodies were found, so Stephen was spared the necessity at least of a funeral, and of having to try to identify horribly blasted and charred remains; but the airline announced that it was to hold two memorial services for the dead, one at Strasbourg and one in London. "I can't make up my mind whether to go or not," said Stephen despondently, sitting on his bed the evening of the day they got the news. He was twirling a sock like a propeller in front of him, and staring into vacancy as he turned the matter over in his mind.

"It's not worth it if it's going to upset you all over again," murmured Richard anxiously.

"Well, yes, I thought about that. But I think I... I'd like to go, as far as that goes. Not that I believe in any of their mumbo-jumbo — that was the main reason I fell out with my people, if you remember. But..."

"Well, I don't see that it can do any harm," said Richard reasonably. "Okay, so you're sceptical. So was Graham — you can bet your life he'll be thinking it's a great joke, if he's looking in from somewhere. I know the religious part of it's all bullshit; but if you feel it's a last chance to remember him officially, in public, then go. It'd do you more good than harm in that case. But I really don't see that it matters much."

"But it does matter," argued Stephen, looking doubtful. "I'm not religious, but I can sit through a church service without feeling I've fatally compromised my immortal soul — if I thought I'd got one to compromise. Graham would have felt the same about me — but I'm pretty sure he'd simply have thought 'It's a service in part in Stephen's honour, therefore I go.' It's just that in the first place there's quite likely to be people there who never had a good word to say for Graham when he was alive, and in the second, the fucking church is more than half responsible for the problems Graham and I had to cope with anyway. If the church had been a bit more ready to extend a bit of Christian compassion towards gay people like us the law might never have been as fierce as it is. Then we'd never have had to fuck off to France in the first place, and Graham would never have been on that plane, would he?"

Richard sat and thought about it for a while. Eventually he said "You've got a point about the church. If that part of it sticks in your craw, you'll just have to stay away. But honestly, Stevie, if you want to trace one event to another, you could go on all night, and end up tracing everything back to everything else, all the way back to the big bang or whatever it was. If your aunt had balls she'd be your uncle, surely?"

Stephen glanced up and gave him a quick involuntary grin, which pleased Richard very much. "As for the people who're gonna be there," he continued, "why, they're nothing to do with anything. You're there — if you go — to mourn Graham for yourself. It doesn't matter that much" — he snapped his fingers — "who else is there. If Graham's worst enemy turned up — or Idi Amin and Baby Doc Duvalier for that matter — it shouldn't make the slightest difference to you. You're still there to mourn and do honour to your beloved. It won't make any difference to him who's there and who's not, will it?"

Stephen sat once again in thought for a while. Then he looked up, with an only faintly troubled smile on his fair, regular features. "Will you come with me, Richard?" he asked. "Of course I'll come, my lovely," said Richard. "I wanted to go anyway, on my own account. I liked Graham — nothing to do with what he was for you. He was one of the nicer masters on the staff there, and I liked him. For himself. I couldn't have gone if you'd decided not to, so I'm glad you're going. Now how about putting that sock down, taking off its twin, followed by everything else, and doing some very illegal things with me?"

4

"Dad? It's me. Stephen."

There was a silence at the other end of the line. Then his father's voice came on, sounding a little strained. Stephen thought he could identify surprise, anxiety and a trace of hostility in the voice, but he dismissed the speculation as irrelevant. "I... er... I wanted to ask you something, Dad," he said, a little hesitant himself now that he had steeled himself to make the call. It had been preying on his mind somewhat, and it had taken him a day or two to summon up the resolve to ring the number at all. However, he had done it now, and made himself carry on. "I... I've had some pretty awful news in the last week or so, Dad," he said slowly.

"Oh?" said his father quickly, and there was nothing but concern in the voice now. "What's happened? Where are you speaking from?"

"I'm in England again, Dad. At Richard's, in fact. I... I've come back. The fact is," he went on in a stronger voice, "it's about Graham..."

There was a noise from the other end, half-way between a grunt and a snort, but he pressed on. "He... he was flying back to England to do some business. And... and his plane... his plane... you heard about that airbus? Well, he was on it. He's... he's dead..."

There was another silence. When his father spoke again his voice was different yet again, gentler, and sounding rather stunned. "Oh. Stephen... I'm... I'm very sorry about that. I had no idea. No idea you were back here, to begin with." He paused again, for some time. "We heard about that plane, of course. Well, you know how we felt about your... relationship with him... But I should never have wished this on anyone. I really am deeply sorry, Stephen. What are you going to do now?" he asked after a further pause while Stephen could almost hear the thoughts running through his head.

"I'm not really sure what I'm going to do," he replied slowly, reflecting as he said it that that was nothing more than the simple truth. "I suppose some time I shall have to go on some kind of... of... well, not a holiday, exactly, but some kind of break. Go off to think and get my head back together again. For the moment I'm just trying to get through each day as it comes. Richard's helping me a lot, of course, and his people are very kind. And it's the cricket season next week, and that'll help. I think that'll be good for me. It'll be full of memories, of course, but I think Graham would want me to go back and throw myself into it. I haven't really thought further than that."

"Have you thought about coming home?" asked his father, and Stephen felt sure he could hear a coldness creeping back into the voice. He hesitated, wondering how to say what he knew he was going to say without causing any more pain than he must.

"Well, I did think of it, Dad, yes, of course," he said. "But I really didn't think it would be... well, very wise, I suppose. I mean, I'd have liked to come and tell you, but the way Mother's been... she wouldn't have felt happy about seeing me in the house again, would she? I mean, she more or less told me never to darken her door again, that time I came back after I wrote to you from Holland. She seems to have taken my... the way I am..." He trailed off into an unhappy silence.

His parents' reaction to his elopement the previous summer had been the only real source of sorrow or doubt about his relationship with Graham. He had grown a very long way apart from them during the year or so after he had become Graham's lover, but in the few months before he had made his decision and gone to Saint-Hippolyte to live with him he had begun to feel that his father, at least, was beginning to come to terms with facts, and ready to come to some kind of accord with him. He knew that his mother, on the other hand, was becoming a source of considerable worry to his father. She had been a good deal more unbending in her attitude to her son's desertion first of his religious observance — Stephen had continued to observe long after losing every trace of faith — and then of his family. She had spoken not a single word to Stephen since some time before his cricket tour to Holland and his flight from there to Alsace, and his father's mentions of her in his infrequent letters consistently indicated that her attitude was, if anything, hardening towards him. On his only visit to his parents' home, to which he had just referred, she had been pointedly out of the house, and his father had sadly made it clear that it was not by chance.

Stephen allowed these reflections to run at radio speeds through his mind before picking up the thread of his conversation with his father. "Anyway, Dad, the long and the short of it is that I thought it would probably do no good for me to come home — at least for a while, until Mother's... well, for a while, anyway — and quite possibly it might do a lot of harm. So I didn't. But I... I've missed seeing you. I wanted to talk to you, I did, really..." He broke off, and mentally admonished himself. It occurred to him that he very often, indeed nearly always, somehow ended up sounding as if he was pleading when he spoke to his father, and the thought was followed instantly by the further one that that had been the case for a very long time. He shook himself and continued. "Anyway, the real reason I'm ringing is that there's a memorial service for Graham — well, I mean, of course, it's for all the passengers and the crew of the plane — in London, next week; I'm going, of course, and I wondered..."

He let the sentence drift into nothing, and there was another long silence from the other end. "I wondered if you'd like to come," finished Stephen, more strongly as he got it out.

His father's voice sounded a little subdued when he answered. "I... er... It's good of you to think of us," he said at last. "But I'm not really sure... Will you let me think about it for a short while?" he said after a little thought. "Give me a chance to consider?"

"Of course I will, Dad," said Stephen, feeling rather relieved. "But you don't have to let me know until next week. The service isn't until next Thursday. You don't even have to let me know at all, I suppose, come to that. I mean, you could just turn up. But there'll be a lot of people there, and if you want to meet, well..."

"There's another difficulty," said his father slowly.

"Mother?"

"Er... well, yes," was the reluctant reply. "I'm not at all sure how she'll react to the idea. I'm afraid I'm pretty sure she won't come herself, you realise that, don't you, Stephen?"

"Yes, of course I do," said Stephen, beginning to feel distressed and a little angry. The last person his father seemed to be thinking about was Graham, who was, after all, the most important figure in the matter. "But do you have to mention it to her at all?"

"Stephen," said his father, with a weary sigh, "I'm afraid you have a tendency to judge others by your own standards. Things like that — simply not mentioning something when it happens to be unpalatable, or to suggest inconvenient consequences — may be your way of going about things, but it most certainly isn't ours. Of course I shall have to mention it to your mother. I wouldn't dream of not doing so even if it might be practicable to avoid it. But I'm a little anxious about her reaction. And — I'm afraid I must be completely candid with you about this, Stephen — if I feel that it may hurt her in any way for me to raise this matter with her, well, I'm afraid I simply shan't do so."

They talked on for a few more minutes, a rather chilly, sterile conversation, both of them feeling awkward and slightly embarrassed in each other's presence, even only down a telephone line. Richard was waiting and watching, concerned for his friend, as Stephen put the receiver down. Stephen turned to him with a frown, half puzzled, half irritated. "No?" said Richard.

"God, I wish he wasn't so bloody pompous," growled Stephen. "Pompous and... and..." He sawed the air with his hands in frustration as he sought for the word. "And self-righteous," he said, finding it. "He always was, and he doesn't seem to be changing." He related the gist of the conversation, and Richard, who could not quite keep a faint smile of half-amusement from crossing his face, tut-tutted gently in sympathy.

"Why can't some people tell the difference between lying and being diplomatic?" Stephen demanded crossly. "Christ, he's talking like someone who's been cheating on his wife, and then goes and confesses to her when it's all over, to ease his own conscience, and all he's really doing is passing the bloody burden from himself to someone else. As if there's some kind of absolute, inherent virtue in telling the truth, for its own sake. Jesus! It doesn't make it any more right, or sensible, to tell people certain things, just because they're true, does it?" He shook his head despairingly as he considered human silliness.

"Well, no, it doesn't," assented Richard mildly. "He could come to this do and say he'd been to London on business, and everybody's happy. You are cos he's come, he is cos he's had an excuse — no, not an excuse, an opportunity — to see you, which he clearly wants to do, and your mother's not caused completely unnecessary distress. But he's entitled to have his own point of view, isn't he? I mean, I agree with you about this religious business. Always seems a bit daft to me to get so het up about something you can't be sure is real that it upsets your relationships with people you know are real. But he's obviously sincere about it, and it ain't quite fair to damn him just because it doesn't fit in with what you want, is it?" He took the sting out of the mild reproof by giving Stephen a naughty wink, and a lazy, sexy smile. Stephen glowered into space for a few seconds while he thought about it; then his face, too, relaxed into a faintly grudging smile. "You're right as usual," he admitted, shaking a fist at his friend. "It must get boring being right all the time, mustn't it? Specially when you've got a hot-head like me to deal with." Richard grinned at him, and he grinned back, a genuine grin this time, full of the deep liking that had extracted it from him.

"Anyway, the upshot of it is," he said, "that he wants time to think about it, and he'll let me know."

In the end his father took the easiest road out. He didn't ring back, and he and Stephen's mother didn't attend the memorial service.

* * *

A couple of days before the service another letter arrived from Graham's parents. It was very short and to the point, suggesting that as a special friend of Graham's Stephen might care to meet them before the service. Stephen telephoned to tell them he would be glad to, and then spent the intervening period worrying about the encounter. "S'pose they don't know he was gay," he said, confiding in Richard that night. "S'pose they just think I'm some pal from the cricket club or something."

"Well, you are a pal from the cricket club," said Richard in surprise, looking up at him from where he was lying lazily on his bed. "You don't have to be ashamed of being gay to recognise that there's no point in ramming the fact down people's throats. If they raise the matter, talk openly about it. If they don't, you don't. Cross your bridges when you come to them, and stop worrying, that's my advice." Stephen threw himself down beside him and started playing with him, comforted and relieved as always by his friend's good sense. But he still looked forward to meeting his lover's parents with great apprehension, and lay staring into the darkness long after Richard, relaxed and satiated, had stretched like a cat and dropped instantly into a deep and peaceful sleep. Eventually, lulled by Richard's light snore, he fell into a shallow and troubled sleep of his own.

* * *

They spotted Graham's parents immediately, waiting at the agreed point outside the great church, and Stephen's heart sank at the sight of them. The father was shortish and stockily built like his son, but with a high-bridged nose and high cheekbones that Graham had lacked, giving him an austere, even slightly arrogant look. He also had an impeccably trimmed head of distinguished silver hair and moustache, and an unmistakably military bearing. Stephen remembered, with a sudden searing bolt of almost physical pain, that Graham had mentioned, on one of the rare occasions when he had spoken of his parents, that his father had been something stratospheric in the RAF. "Literally and metaphorically," as he had put it. The mother was taller than her husband, good-looking in a well-groomed and expensively-tailored way. Even while they were still a good distance away the boys could see clearly a lot of Graham's features in her. They exchanged apprehensive glances. "Better get on and get it over with," muttered Richard, not looking forward to the interview. They forced their way through the early arrivals at the church.

As it turned out, their apprehensions were unfounded. The Curtises spotted them edging through the milling people and came forward to meet them immediately. Richard dropped back a pace. Stephen, gulping slightly, offered his hand to the woman first. "I'm Stephen Hill," he said, anxious to get his word in first. She gave him a very rapid head-to-foot appraisal, but she did it so quickly that there was no time for it to give offence before she was giving him her hand. Her handshake was firm and brisk, two firm, sharp pumps, rather masculine. But she softened the effect by a brief, taut smile. "Elizabeth Curtis," she said formally. "How do you do?" Her voice was educated rather than county, and the smile looked genuine. "My husband," she added, stepping aside to allow her husband to offer Stephen his hand. He gave Stephen a brief, hard grip, almost whiplashing Stephen's hand off. "How d'you do?" he barked, and he, too, bestowed a fast up-and-down look on the boy from slightly bulging blue eyes.

"How do you do?" said Stephen, keeping his voice even. He turned to gesture Richard, waiting politely to be drawn into the group. "This is Richard Fitzjohn, a friend of mine and Graham's. He's here to give me some moral support, but he's here on his own account too. Graham taught him, and he was a good friend."

Richard, who was never to be seen in anything other than tee-shirts and trainers, and who only ever shed his jeans to put on shorts, was immaculate in an icy white shirt, black tie and navy blazer, dark blue slacks with razor-blade creases, and black town-shoes that glowed with polishing. Stephen could see immediately that he made a very good impression on the Curtises. He had no idea whatever what impression he himself had made. He soon learned.

"You were Graham's special friend, Stephen," said Mrs Curtis, turning elegantly back from Richard. She saw various different expressions chase each other rapidly across his face, and smiled, a little less tautly than before. "Yes, we knew," she said softly. "Or rather, we felt fairly sure. He never confided in us, about that or anything else. He was a very self-sufficient man. But we were meant to know: we were provided with the necessary information. I hope he was happy."

Stephen swallowed, moved more than he could ever have imagined he might be by such an unemotional little speech. "He was," he said. "I... I think he was very happy. No. I know he was," he ended, more firmly. "I'm very sorry," he added, feeling very conscious of the inadequacy of the words. He shot a quick side-long glance in the direction of Graham's father, and saw that he was being appraised again, piercingly. The man saw that his obser-vation had been noticed, and took a smart step forward. "You're a cricketer, I believe?" Stephen nodded, too surprised to speak. "Mmmm. Graham talked of you. Said you were an off-spinner. Good to see that in a boy your age. Dying art, I'd have said. Good to see I'm not entirely correct." He paused, and his prominent blue eyes misted very slightly. "He loved his cricket," he resumed, staring through Stephen into some mental picture from the past. "More than almost anything else. He wasn't a man of strong pas-sions, or a boy for that matter. But cricket he loved." Stephen thought he could have had something to say about the strong pas-sions, but he wisely refrained from saying it.

After that they found that they naturally paired off, Gra-ham's father, oddly, gravitating towards Stephen and talking about cricket, while Mrs Curtis talked quietly to Richard, and was unob-trusively charmed as they talked of Graham's gifted teaching and his love of France. Before long she was speaking quite naturally to the quiet, somehow reassuring young man of intimate and per-sonal aspects of her son. "He was quite extraordinarily self-possessed — even as a boy," she found herself telling a perfect stranger. "He was... not secretive... but he made very certain that he kept the entire emotional side of his life completely to himself. We never knew what he was thinking, or feeling. Just occasionally he would become passionately concerned about something or other: he once half-killed a boy at school — a very much older and larger boy, we found out later — for bullying a friend of his. But for the most part, he contrived to live his own life, quite separate from us and the rest of the family..."

"...remember the first time he played for the Vine First Eleven... He was sixteen. Drafted in at the last minute, someone taken ill. I happened to be at home on leave, and damned glad I was. Wouldn't have missed it. Scored seventy-three in an hour and a half, and held onto a scorcher at cover point. Never saw him on a Saturday or a Sunday after that..."

"...I've seen them together, and I've got no doubt whatever that they were happy. Blissfully happy, deliriously happy, I might say, if I'd read the wrong kind of literature and acquired a fondness for clichés..."

"...course, we began to wonder if he might be... of the kind to prefer other men, but we never knew for certain. I feel sure that that was to spare us any possible distress. But I do wish he'd felt he could confide in us. I wish he'd known that we wished him only happiness, from whatever source he found it..."

"...amazing how much he taught me — I don't mean in class, though he was a brilliant teacher there, too. I mean, the amount of information he had stored up, about every subject that ever cropped up... there was more to it than that, though. It wasn't only information, or even mainly. It was... I don't know, culture I suppose. He introduced me to so many things: good food, music — he was very fond of classical music, you know..."

"...startled when he declared that he was going to teach. Never wanted him to follow me into the service. Saw from the outset that he was too... too thoughtful for that. Got his mother's brains. More than me, by a long chalk..."

"...getting over it pretty well, I think. I'm doing all I can, and I've got a very wise father and a mother with a bedside manner that would be worth a fortune. And the cricket is starting very soon, and I think that will be the best tonic of all..."

"...time to go into the church, I think. Perhaps we can squeeze a drink in afterwards..."

"...be delighted..."

* * *

They went into the vast church together, but separated once inside. Graham's parents wished to sit alone for the service, and said courteous goodbyes to the boys just inside the doors. Richard and

Stephen set about finding a familiar face among the crowds that had by this time gathered. After interminable edging and easing through knots of chattering people, Stephen finally caught sight of Bill McKechnie's battered features, and they barged through the crush as if to a long-lost brother. Bill, looking surprisingly at home and comfortable in a dark suit and tie, led them with an efficient mixture of tact and brute force through the milling multitude to where the cricket club had annexed a couple of pews. The dozen club members and players who had turned up waved and grinned.

Before the boys went to squeeze in among the others Bill grabbed them for a moment. "We're all goin back to the club after," he said in an oddly subdued version of his usual conversational bawl. "Thought we'd have a private do of our own after this show's finished. You'll both come, a course?" The boys assented immediately. "Good," said Bill. "It won't be anything special — just a small private remembrance of an old pal, you know?" He looked down on them and smiled, an uncharacteristic, shifting smile in which sadness and his usual mischievous twinkle were strangely mingled. "Course, it's gonna be a piss-up, really. But I don't s'pose Graham'da minded that, do you, our kid?" he added, looking very closely at Stephen.

Stephen smiled, a slightly guilty smile. "I think he'd have approved thoroughly," he admitted. "But we're supposed to be meeting his parents after the service. We said we'd have a drink with them...

"Okay," said Bill, leading them back to the cricket club pews. "Maybe we'll all come. Otherwise, you go and have a drink an a chat with em, an we'll find a boozer somewhere an wait for you, if they wanna be alone with you. I'll fix it. You can trust me to be tactful."

"I know we can," said Stephen. He felt a sudden surge of affection for the hulking, ugly, kindly Bill. It found expression in a beautiful, sad, lost smile, in which admiration had a large part. He never knew how appealing it made him, so he never knew either how it brought a lump to Bill's throat that threatened to choke him for a moment. Nor did he know that Graham's mother, watching the little scene curiously from her seat, saw the smile and understood a great deal about her son that had been hidden until that moment. But Richard saw all these things, and his heart swelled alarmingly as he reflected on the fact that he was now the recipient of that smile, beneficiary and custodian alike.

"Okay," said Bill, giving the boys a conspiratorial wink as he shepherded them into their seats. "By the way," he added, turning back and bending low to murmur to them. "You're both okay for the match on Saturday, are you? You're both selected." They beamed him simultaneous grins, unable to help it. Then they turned to each other and exchanged slightly guilty looks. Bill saw, and understood, both, and paused before striding off to gather in the remains of his party. "He'da wanted it this way," he said softly. "Don't feel guilty about it." Then he was gone, leaving Stephen still reeling under the impact of the great wave of love that had engulfed him, and Richard, cooler, feeling none the less an immense admiration for the man's sensitivity and perception — qualities he was well equipped to judge, being possessed of both in good measure himself.

They sat waiting for the proceedings to get under way, looking interestedly about them at the appointments of the great church, and studying the still thickly flowing crowds of mourners curiously in search of familiar faces. "Hey!" whispered Richard a few minutes later. "There's Jack Page. And Inky Knight. And Bill Williams and Killer Collins... Half the school's here. Half the staff, anyway. Haven't seen any of the blokes yet. Hey! There's the HM. They must've called an extra half-holiday, I should think. Can't be enough masters to go round, with that lot here."

Stephen craned his neck and watched the school contingent as they made their way up the aisle, clearly scanning the packed pews for known faces. He saw the sudden broad smile of recognition dawn on Jack Page's face as he spotted Bill McKechnie, Colin Preston and the rest of the cricketers. He saw Page immediately jab a bony elbow into the ribs of Inky Knight, head of the chemistry department, and watched as the entire group of masters swung round in a well-ordered phalanx to descend on the remaining empty seats in the cricketers' enclave. Several of them paused to greet Stephen and Richard, and one or two, Stephen felt half-sure, lingered to offer him sympathetic glances before passing on to their seats. He saw Bill take a moment off from directing traffic to lean sideways and whisper in Jack Page's ear; and he saw Page nod vigorously. Then he glanced rather uncertainly in Stephen's direction.

Stephen saw a very uncharacteristic expression pass over Page's face, distinctly apprehensive, even a little shifty. He understood clearly that the man was remembering how he had been in part responsible for Graham's troubles the previous year, ending in his discreet but rather precipitate departure from the school staff. But Page had made amends as best he could, and Stephen felt no animosity. He smiled and raised a hand in an amiable wave, and Page's face immediately cleared. He grinned and waved, and made his way to a space in the row behind. He bent over to whisper in Stephen's ear as he squeezed along the row. "See yew later, at the club," he said. "I'd like a chat, if you're willin."

"Of course," hissed Stephen, risking a crick in his neck to twist round and whisper back. Page nodded and passed on.

The headmaster also looked directly at Stephen, and gave him a serious, austere look, which just turned into a brief, cur-tailed smile before he passed on, parting the crowds in his customary majestic fashion, like an angular heron picking its way fastidiously through a mob of chattering sparrows. Stephen managed to re-strain the bitter, ironical smile that rose unbidden, and stared seriously back for an instant before the man went out of sight. "Hypocritical bastard," he muttered to Richard, who gave him a worried glance. A moment later the service got under way.

*　　*　　*

The headmaster was waiting for them, however, an hour later as the crowds streamed out into the mild Spring sunshine. "Stephen," he said, materialising beside the boys. "I wanted to say to you per-sonally how very sorry I am." He waited.

Stephen, tall though he was, had to look up at the man. He stared into his face, momentarily at a loss. The headmaster's di-rectness had had the unexpected effect of temporarily defusing Stephen's deep and contemptuous bitterness towards the man he blamed above all others for Graham's downfall. It didn't take long for it to find its way back to the surface, however. "I don't see how you can be that sorry," he said icily. "I'm surprised you could find the gall to turn up here, frankly. It was your action in sacking him that drove him to France in the first place, and if he hadn't been there he'd never have been on that plane." He caught a motion out of the corner of his eye, and saw Richard, visibly wincing, slipping away a few paces to wait out of earshot.

The headmaster was not a shirker, and for all his air of slightly chilly aloofness he was a man of honour and some moral courage. He looked quizzically down at Stephen for a moment, then cleared his throat and said "I can understand your taking that attitude,

Stephen. But I was in a difficult position. I liked Graham, personally, very much — as almost everyone did. I had the greatest respect for him professionally, as a teacher, and I recognised his great personal integrity. I also made it abundantly clear to him that his private sexual nature was of no concern to me. But when I was faced with a potential scandal which would have affected every boy at the school, to say nothing of my staff and the school itself, I had very little choice in what I did. In fact I had no choice at all. I hope that you will come to understand that some time. But there was nothing personal in it: I should hope that my presence here was sufficient indication of that. Please accept my deep condolences." And with that he gave Stephen a slightly frosty, but obviously sincere smile, and passed rapidly out of sight amongst the clearing crowds of people.

Richard, who had been hovering anxiously on the fringe of earshot, came up quickly, and a little breathlessly. "Stevie, you didn't...?" He left the question unasked. Stephen gave him a faint, rather rueful smile. "No, I didn't bite him," he said. There was a curiously adult and equivocal look about him. "He's got more guts than I'd have credited him with. It took some pluck, to come and face me like that. I've got a feeling I misjudged him, you know." The worried expression on Richard's face cleared and was replaced by one of relief. "You do have a bit of a way of doing that, old chap," he said gently. "You can sometimes be a teeny-weeny bit hasty in your judgments, you know. I'm not criticising you. Wouldn't dream of it. It's the way you are, part of your strength. But just sometimes you do tend to be a bit..." He sought for the word. "A bit... rigorous. A bit uncompromising. Almost pitiless sometimes."

Stephen turned and stared at him. After a moment his expression relaxed, and he laughed. Richard's heart jumped as he realised that it was the first time he had heard Stephen's old, natural laugh since they had been in Holland together on the tour last summer. "I know what I'm like," said Stephen, giving his friend a fond smile that caused several passing mourners to stare briefly before turning to friends and making comments. Neither boy noticed. "I think I need someone like you, Richard," Stephen went on. "You're too good for me, but I need you. You calm me down. Graham did, too. I've had an idea."

"Oh?" said Richard. "What's that, then?"

"I think," said Stephen, reflectively, speaking softly but clearly close to Richard's ear, "it would be a very good idea if, after this do at the cricket club, you took me back to your place and fucked a bit of sense into me."

Richard stared at him for some moments in mingled disbelief and delight. Then he said "You've got a deal, partner," Suddenly, the world was back to normal.

5

They found Bill and the cricketers waiting in a thirsty-looking group at the foot of the huge sweep of steps up to the front doors of the church. Then they looked about anxiously for Graham's parents. After a search they found them talking gravely to a number of other mourners in the lee of a vast pillar. They hovered nearby until the little group broke up and the Curtises were left alone. Then they approached diffidently, wondering if the earlier atmosphere of warm comity had survived the lengthy, rather cold impersonality of the service.

It had. In an unrehearsed swap of partners, Richard was promptly annexed by Graham's father, while Stephen ran back to ask the cricket club contingent to kill an hour in a nearby pub, then returned to walk beside Mrs Curtis as they went purposefully, led by Mr Curtis, to a small and semi-deserted restaurant and wine bar down a nearby back-street.

There Mr Curtis quietly took control of the proceedings, piloting them to a secluded table in a remote corner of the subterranean restaurant, ordering with no more than perfunctory reference to the boys or even his wife, and opening the conversation with the arrival of grissini and a bottle of Barolo.

"Tell us about Graham," he said without preamble as soon as the waiter had left them. "Tell us about the last year or so," he elaborated. "We didn't see very much of him," put in his wife sadly, toying with her glass.

And so the boys, hesitantly at first, then with gathering confidence under Mr Curtis's tactful management, told the Curtises the full story of the last two years of their son's life. When they had talked themselves to a standstill the four of them sat, all by some common instinct devoting their attention to their plates for a few minutes, almost as if in prayer. Graham's father broke the moment. He looked up, patted his lips briskly with his napkin, and said quietly, "Thank you. Thank you very much indeed." Everyone looked up then, and the table became animated again. He went on, a little awkwardly, "I'm glad to have heard the account of my son's final year from such close and devoted friends, who had his interests so much at heart." He looked at Stephen, and said, "And I'm glad he was lucky enough to find someone as loyal and steadfast as you, Stephen, if I may say so. He might have done almost infinitely worse. He could hardly have done better."

The words, unforced and without a trace of affectation, made Stephen blink rapidly from sudden emotion. He could think of nothing to say except a whispered "Thank you." Richard, who had very quickly conceived a great liking for Curtis senior, and was also privately, and a little guiltily, admiring his distinguished looks, smiled from simple admiration at the generosity of the words. He was thus a little flustered when his own turn came. "And you are equally lucky in your own friend here," Mr Curtis went on. Turning to Richard he said "You've been a tower of strength, my boy. You seem to me to have acted in the most conspicuously honourable fashion throughout these dreadful episodes." He hesitated. "I'd have liked to have had you serve with me." There was nothing to be said in answer to that. Richard dropped his head to conceal the deep flush of pleasure the words brought to his face.

Mr Curtis, who had managed men expertly for many years, broke the tension by courteously gesturing to the waiter and ordering coffee, with brandy for himself and his wife; and the emotion of the moment was gently and painlessly relieved by the boys' faintly panic-stricken requests for glasses of lager instead.

An hour and a half had flown by, and there was little more to be said. They emerged into the street, blinking in the bright sunlight after the subdued lighting of the restaurant, with the boys gladly promising to go to visit the Curtises in Sevenoaks very soon. Then they stood in silence outside the restaurant and watched as the Curtises walked briskly down the street until they turned a corner out of sight. Mrs Curtis turned just before they disappeared and gave them a brief, almost curt, wave of her hand. Mr Curtis did not look back at all.

The boys looked at one another. "That was a lot easier than it might have been," said Richard slowly, feeling the lump in his throat that had been there since Mr Curtis's tribute gradually subsiding. Stephen looked at him steadily for a long moment. "He was right about one thing," he said at last.

"What was that?"

"You're just about the best friend anyone could have, Richard," Stephen said very quietly; there was an undercurrent of feeling, and passion, in his low voice that made Richard's pulse quicken. Without saying any more they began walking briskly in the direction of the pub where the cricketers were waiting.

* * *

Several of the party were already frisking on the fringe of tipsiness when the two boys arrived. Bill McKechnie saw them first and was at the bar before they had got through the door. "Have a drink, lads," he said, already shoving pints of lager at them. "How did it go?" he asked, tactfully staying at the bar in order to ask out of the hearing of the rest.

"Very well," they said in chorus. "They're very nice people," said Stephen. "I wonder why Graham never talked about them much."

"You never know people till you live with em," murmured Bill, and smiled as the boys leaped simultaneously to the Curtises' defence. "True, though, lads," he said quietly. "You've seen these people for an hour or so, when they're at their most vulnerable and subdued. I'm sure they were every bit as nice as you say they were. An probably they are like that. But the scope for misunderstanding between parents an sons is about the longest measurable distance in the world. Cept the scope for misunderstanding between husbands an wives. Any case, maybe it was just something Graham was a bit private about."

"But they said he hardly saw anything of them in the last couple of years," said Stephen, feeling a deep and painful sense of shame on behalf of his dead lover. Bill looked at him kindly, but very levelly. "That's something you've learned then, Stevie, our kid," he said softly. "There's always things you don't know about someone, however close you may be. You think you know everything there is to know about em, and one day they go an do summin, an you hear yourself sayin 'Well, I'm buggered, I'd never a said he'd do that', whatever it was. 'Him, of all people.' Well, I got a fair idea how close you an Graham were, an here he is, still capable a surprisin you now. It's a little quiet gift from providence, you know, son. Or maybe a little quiet hand grenade, just to keep you on the qui vive — you know, if you pull the pin out in a moment

53

a carelessness, you blow yourself to buggery — an your mate, as well."

The boys stared at him. "How's it a gift, not ever knowing someone?" asked Stephen. They both waited curiously for the answer, because this conundrum was too deep even for Richard. They were also looking with a new, and rather surprised, respect at Bill. They had known very well his great kindness, and that there was vastly more to him than he liked to let the world see, but the present face of the man, worldly, a little distant and wise, was a novelty.

"Very simple," said Bill. "It's a very wise little gift. Priceless. It stops you from ever gettin any ideas a takin people for granted. That's something everybody does, unfortunately. So if nature, or providence, or whatever, can contrive it so that the first few times you do it with the special person, you pull out the pin, an end up a few seconds later sittin on your arse fifteen feet distant with a surprised look on your face, well, that's a pretty useful thing to have around the house, I'd say. Wouldn't you?" And he laughed, picked up his pint, drained it, bought refills for all three of them, and led the way back to the others at the far end of the room.

The first person Stephen's eyes fell on when they arrived in Bill's wake was Jack Page, who had clearly been invited to join the cricket club's private act of remembrance. Stephen murmured in Richard's ear, and went straight over to Page. Richard, still smiling to himself over Bill's pearl of wisdom, sat a little apart from the group, demonstrating far more clearly than he had intended that he wanted to be alone with his thoughts, and reflect on the day's events so far.

"You wanted to talk to me, Jacko," said Stephen.

"I did, my boy," said Jack Page. he was a lean, ferret-like Welshman, all sinew and tough as whipcord, who taught German to the lower forms at Stephen's old school, but devoted most of his time, and all his energy and passion, to the school's rugby. "I wanted to tell ewe," he went on in his broad Ebbw Vale brogue, "ow sorry I was that ewe never made it into the First Fifteen last year. But mainly I wanted to say that we're lookin for a decent loose-ead in the Old Boys' side this year. Chris Perkins as gone off to the States, God elp im. What sort a rugby e thinks e's gonna find there Lord only knows. But anyway, we're left with a vacancy, an bein as ewe were the natural choice to step into the spot in the School XV last year, well, there ewe are, lad. Fancy it?"

Stephen thought about it, and grinned with pleasure. After

all the drama, trauma and bitterness of his departure from the school near the end of the previous year, he was profoundly surprised to find how gratifying it was to be asked back into the fold — which was what Jack Page's offer amounted to. "Yes, please, Jacko," he said excitedly. "I'd love to play. I haven't given a thought to rugby lately," he said, thinking back over the previous winter. "We watched the Five Nations on the box, of course," he added. "And we went to watch one or two games at Strasbourg, but that was about all. Yes. Yes, please. Put me down. What's the sub?"

"Oh, don't worry about the sub yet awhile," said Jack Page dismissively. "Better get yourself sorted out with a job an all before you bother your ead about that."

"But I don't need a..." began Stephen, and then stopped abruptly in mid-sentence. For the first time since the headlong turmoil and anguish of the day of Graham's death, it occurred to him that he might be wealthy. He found himself wondering if Graham might have left him money. He had no idea, but it struck him with great force that it was highly likely that he had left him some of it — probably quite a lot. The reflection was followed closely by the further thought that if he hadn't inherited something, he would indeed need to start thinking about finding some source of income, and soon, at that. It was an unpleasant thought, and wiped the smile off his face for a moment.

He quickly suppressed both thoughts, however, as unworthy, on the day he was doing official honour to his beloved friend; but they kept creeping back, insidiously, into his mind, at odd moments throughout the remainder of the day. For now, though, he resolutely dismissed them to the dark corner of his mind where such stark, undeniable thoughts dwelt, and chattered excitedly about rugby with Jack Page until they were all ready to head for the station and go home to the club.

* * *

As soon as they were all back in the clubhouse, Bill marshalled them all in front of the great picture windows that made up most of the pitch-side wall of the building. He organised drinks, and then called for silence, on the principle that if he left it any later half the mourners would be too drunk to remember whose memory they were honouring, or to keep quiet for a minute in any case.

"I'm not going to say much", said Bill when everyone had stopped shuffling their feet and all was quiet. "We all had a fair ration of sanctimonious unction this morning. But I think you'd like to show your respects for our old friend Graham Curtis by standing in silence for a few moments and remembering him when he was with us. I'd like to think he passed some of the happiest hours of his life out there in front of us, and here, among his friends. He was a good friend, at that: there aren't many of us here who weren't at some time or other the recipients of his kindness, his common sense and his generosity of spirit. He was also, I don't need to remind you, a very good cricketer, a very good one indeed. You'll remember that the last time he played on this ground he scored his first century for the club — and speaking for myself, I don't think he'd have asked for any better way of being remembered. So now I ask you to lift your glasses and drink to the memory of our friend and fellow cricketer, and then to stand silent in his honour."

He lifted his own pint of lager and murmured "Graham Curtis," followed by everyone else. There was a sudden choking sob, instantly stifled. Richard and Stephen, standing side by side at one end of the line of cricketers, shot hasty glances at each other, each thinking it must have been the other; in fact it was Colin Preston, one of the younger members, who had, more or less unwittingly, been responsible for some of Graham's problems the previous season. Stephen felt a momentary spasm of irritation flit through his mind as he identified the breaker of the silence; but then a more indulgent mood chased it away. He could feel no animosity towards anyone in that company today. He blinked a couple of times, conscious that Bill's unpretentious words had touched him as none of the loftier pieties of the service that morning had managed to do.

They stood looking out across the ground, which was looking at its best. The outfield was lush and deep green, awaiting its final close mow before the first games of the season the coming weekend. The square in the middle was pristine, mown close and showing a much lighter green, but as yet free of scuffed, bald spots, holes dug by fast bowlers' feet, old stump-holes and patches of grass seed. There was no tracery of faded white lines from earlier games, no spikemarks, no red streaks on the tracks where the ball had landed, and no cracks from summer droughts. The trees round three sides of the ground were putting out a first few tentative buds, and the little stream that ran beside the pavilion and then skirted the ground for two sides was in full spate, chuckling noisily to itself, and clearly audible inside the pavilion as they stood in silence.

When the minute was up Bill lifted his glass once more, and drained the three-quarters of a pint remaining in it in a single prodigious draught, to cries of "Bravo!" Then he came quickly across to Stephen and Richard and swept them off to the bar. "If you wanna stay, lads, stay by all means, an welcome," he murmured. "But don't hold it against em if there's a bit a less-than-solemnity goes on now. They're good Englishmen an true, an as such they're not ready for any sorta open display of emotion yet. Now lemme get you a drink."

They protested that he had not so far that day allowed them to buy him one, and he growled at them, seizing their glasses anyway.

After they had stood chatting quietly with Bill for a few minutes more he drifted away to circulate round the other groups of two and three. Seeing them alone, the others gradually came up and offered their condolences to Stephen. Some did so shyly, such as Colin Preston, who was feeling acutely embarrassed by his earlier betrayal of emotion, and sidled selfconsciously up to offer a whispered mixture of regret, apology for his thoughtlessness the year before, and what they thought was certainly genuine sadness. Stephen looked steadily at him, saw the pain and misery in his eyes, and forgave him internally on the spot. He murmured a few words of comfort, and Colin went away, obscurely impressed by the boy's bearing and his new air of adulthood, and feeling a lot better.

Jack Page, by contrast, marched briskly up carrying three pint mugs of lager in one hand, looked curiously at Stephen, gave him and Richard one of the mugs apiece, and spoke briefly but straightforwardly about his former colleague. Stephen responded in kind, and he strode off in the same self-possessed way as he had approached, to talk rugby with Preston, Don Parker and one or two other luminaries of local club sides. By the time they felt that they had done their duty, and everyone had come to offer sympathy in one way or another, they had been at the club for an hour and a half, and both were beginning to feel a little drunk. A few of the younger ones had taken bats and balls out: all four nets were in use, there were close- and deep-catching practice groups dotted about the outfield, and Stephen and Richard were left alone in the pavilion.

"D'you remember me saying something about fucking a bit of sense into me?" said Stephen, shooting a quick glace round and whispering into Richard's ear. Richard nodded, flushing slightly in anticipation. "Come on, then," whispered Stephen, gesturing with his head. "Let's go, shall we?"

They glanced round the building, checked the team lists for the coming weekend, when the club played its first fixture of the season, and slipped away. They found Bill, and thanked him soberly and sincerely for conducting the small private commemoration so delicately and sensitively, and finally told him of their intention to slip away quietly. He nodded seriously. "Probably makes sense," he said. "Things can only go one way from here, an that's downhill. You slip off, an I'll see you both on Saturday. It's here, at home to Boston Ramblers — they're a lovely crowd. Wanderin sides all give you the best games a cricket. One-thirty start. Don't be late. See you then. Take care a yourselves now."

They went, waving to anyone among the practice matches who saw them going. Twenty-five minutes later they were in Richard's bed.

*　*　*

They got out of bed lazily, hours later, and only because pangs of hunger were gnawing insistently at them and would not be stilled. They made themselves a generous snack meal downstairs, watched television with little interest while they ate it, and then suddenly gave the set their full attention as the news report turned to the memorial service that morning. They watched the report minutely, hoping to see themselves or someone they knew, but there was no such treat for them. When the news was over they scanned the programme details, found nothing that could compete with their own bodies, and went back to bed.

It was while they were lying side by side on their backs, sated, sticky and pleasantly tired from their exertions, that Stephen turned their desultory conversation to the thoughts that had suddenly assailed him earlier that day, while he had been talking to Jack Page. He turned lazily onto his side and propped himself on an elbow so that he could see Richard's face as he talked.

"D'you think he may have left me something?" he said, and

promptly wished he hadn't mentioned it. "Not that I..." He floundered, feeling a strong sense of embarrassment to be discussing such matters. Richard understood, and swiftly moved to dispel his doubts.

"There's no need to be worried about it," he said, stroking Stephen's thigh. "You were bound to think of it some time. I imagine," he continued, looking thoughtful as he returned to the original point, "it rather depends on whether he made a will or not. Did he, d'you know?"

Stephen didn't: Graham's will had been so much an afterthought when he had made his last visit to Chancery Lane that he had forgotten about it after leaving the solicitors' offices, and never subsequently remembered to mention it to Stephen.

"Oh well," said Richard, feeling signs of arousal under his hand and preparing for more immediate matters, "I dare say we can find out easily enough. Let's ring those lawyers he went to see tomorrow, shall we?"

"Mmm.. okay" murmured Stephen, rolling on top of Richard and slipping his tongue into his mouth.

As it turned out, events overtook their vague notion, because when they eventually left each other alone for long enough to get out of bed late the following morning they found a number of letters on the mat, forwarded from the post office in Saint-Hippolyte in accordance with Richard's instructions. One of them was from the solicitors. They looked at each other expectantly; but as it happened the letter answered none of their questions, simply requesting Stephen to make contact with them as a matter of urgency. He rang them after breakfast, with Richard perched beside him trying to work out what was being said at the other end from Stephen's contributions. Since these were mostly excited monosyllables he didn't have much luck.

"Yes," said Stephen. "Yes... Yes, I see... No, I didn't... Yes, I can, of course. When? ... Today? ... Oh, right... Yes, I understand that... Yes... Right. Thank you very much... Who do I ask for, please?... Mr Guilfoyle, right, yes I've got that... Yes, I've got your letter here with the address... Fine. Thank you very much... I'll see you at two o'clock then... Bye."

Richard raised his eyebrows eloquently at him as he put the receiver down. Stephen hugged him and twirled him off the ground. "I've got to go and see them today," he said excitedly. "He said Graham did make a will, and — you'll never guess!"

Richard thought he could make a very fair guess, watching the rapid succession of conflicting emotions passing across Stephen's face. There was sadness there, every time a memory of Graham himself came into his mind. But there was excitement too, a deep, powerful throbbing kind of excitement, which communicated itself immediately to Richard. They knew each other very well, these two, and in certain moments of stress or high emotion they barely needed words to communicate. Richard found himself feeling as if he was looking down into a very deep well, funnelling down into a darkness so profound that he couldn't even imagine such blackness, let alone what might be at the bottom of it. It was a giddy, unpleasant feeling, and he strove to force it back into whatever cage it had escaped from. But he was still very aware of having distinctly mixed feelings about what he had privately already made up his mind was going to turn out to be Stephen's immense good fortune — or at least, he heard part of his mind murmur, his immense fortune.

He had to force himself to lift his eyes to meet Stephen's, and some of the lights were instantly extinguished in Stephen's own. "What's the matter?" he asked, acutely sensitive as always to every small cloud that passed over Richard's countenance, and immediately concerned.

Richard gave him a brave and not very successful smile. "Nothing," he muttered. "Nothing at all. What did they tell you about Graham's will? You said I'd never guess."

Stephen looked anxiously into Richard's pretty face, still anxious. But he answered, with most of the excitement gone from his voice. "Well... it's... I don't know... it's good news...," he said, feeling faintly foolish, and somehow guilty.

Richard gave him a wide, open smile; Stephen never knew what an effort it cost him to make it. "That's marvellous," he said, but inside he trembled. He experienced a sudden vertiginous sensation of bottomless nausea, as if a tangled knot of maggots was trying to unravel itself in his stomach.

Stephen was by now seriously worried. He grabbed Richard by the shoulders and held him at arm's length, gazing intensely into his light brown eyes. "Richard!" he said, almost shouting. "Please. Please tell me. What's the matter?"

Richard stared emptily at him for a few agonised seconds, then suddenly pulled himself free of Stephen's grip and wept. There was no sound, his shoulders didn't shake. He simply stood there with tears flowing from his eyes and sliding down his cheeks, his eyes all the time fixed on Stephen's face, indistinct and fragmented by the fast-flowing sheen of tears.

"Richard!" cried Stephen in horrified amazement. "RICHARD! What is it? What's the matter? For Christ's sake tell me!"

Richard stood there, tears still sliding astonishing copiously out of his eyes, for a few moments longer. Then he took a couple of paces forward, hurled his arms around Stephen and buried his face in Stephen's shaggy dusty-blond hair. Stephen could feel him shaking — it was too violent to be mere trembling — all over. He wrapped his arms round him and held him in a fierce bear-hug, managing to reach up to stroke his hair as he held him.

After quite a long time the violent shivering quietened down, and then stopped completely. Stephen stayed exactly as he was, frightened to move or do or say anything in case it should bring on another fit. As he hadn't the slightest idea what he had said or done to start the attack off the first time, he didn't know what to avoid doing or saying this time. He held his beloved friend tightly, wondering frantically in his mind what he could have done. He rocked Richard gently for some time, consciously doing anything he could think of to soothe him. Eventually Richard raised a hand and tentatively stroked the back of his hair. Stephen felt a bolt of relief shoot through him that would have been more appropriate if he'd just reanimated a corpse, he thought.

He relaxed his hold on Richard for a moment, backed away a few inches, and got a look at Richard's face. It was flushed, blotchy and stained with tears, but some of the wild, hysterical panic had ebbed out of his eyes, to Stephen's vast relief. He risked asking a question, still holding Richard loosely. "Can you talk a bit now, sweet?" he said very gently, tensing himself to grab him again if there was another outburst.

Richard trembled again, just once, and gasped aloud, violently, as if expelling a vast breath of poisoned air from his body. Then his entire face seemed to sag. "Let me sit down, will you," he said, and his voice sounded as tired as he looked.

"Of course," said Stephen.

Richard went into the living room, walking wearily, as if he had been filleted. Stephen followed him into the big room and sat tentatively down beside him on a sofa, taking care not to touch him, for he had a sudden instinct that it would break the calm that Richard had reached with such apparent difficulty. "Tell me what the matter is," he said gently. "Please try and tell me. It's some-thing I've done or said, I know that, but please tell me what it is. I don't know what I can possibly have done to hurt you, but you've got to tell me, otherwise I can't put it right, whatever it is. Tell me, my lovely," he went on, keeping his voice low and hypnotic, and unthinkingly using Richard's own favourite endearment.

Richard looked up at him at the sound of it, and sketched a watery, grisly spectre of his usual bright grin.

"It was when you said I'd never guess what Graham had done in his will," he said tremulously, and Stephen could see his lip trembling. "And then... then you said it was good... g-good news..."

"Yes," he said, mystified. "But how could that upset you like that? Please tell me. I wouldn't hurt you, Rich, you of all people. I know I'm not good enough for you, but you're the best friend I've got, and I wouldn't hurt a... a hair on your head, not for the world. So what have I done?"

"Well, I could guess," snuffled Richard. "I can. He's left you the bloody lot, hasn't he? That's why I got upset. I couldn't help it..." He broke off, and a single giant sob pulsated its way right through him and out of him. Stephen, still groping helplessly for understanding in darkness, did the best thing he could have done: he sat silent and waited.

"That m..m..means you'll be rich," snuffled Richard. "I mean seriously rich."

"Eh? Well, I s'pose it may do," said Stephen. "I dunno how much Graham had, not really. Or how much of it I've got. There's some kind of tax, or death duties or some such. They were waf-fling about them on the phone. But yes, certainly it means I'll be pretty decently off. I shan't have to fuck around looking for some god-awful bottom-of-the-heap job, anyway. But why, for Christ's sake, did that make you go off into a fit of the vapours like that? Christ, I'd've thought you'd be as pleased as a guinea pig with one tail, knowing we'll have enough cash to blow, do what we like instead of working for a bloody living. I don't get it."

Richard had another attempt at a smile, slightly less damp and correspondingly more successful. "But that's what set me off like that," he muttered. Stephen shook his head. "Sorry, sweet," he said. "I still don't get it."

"Well, I thought you'd be off," said Richard. "I thought you came back to me because you needed me to help get you over... over Graham... But I didn't think you'd want to stay with me now you'd got a lot of money. I knew I couldn't come first with you. I always accepted that. I always knew you'd go off to Graham as soon as he called you; and I could bear it once. But twice... I thought about it all happening over again, and... and I couldn't bear it. I saw you going off to look for another Graham, and..." He sat back, gazing at Stephen through a fresh film of tears.

Stephen stared at him, aghast. The impact of what Richard had said hit him so hard that for some moments he literally couldn't speak. He sat for a while, feeling certain that he was going to be physically sick. Gradually he fought down the waves of nausea, which reminded him horribly of his single experience of sea-sickness. Eventually he regained speech. "Jesus!" he breathed. "You thought I'd do that? You thought I'd do that to you? To you? Jesus Christ, Rich. I said I knew I wasn't good enough for you, and I'm not. I know that. But there's a difference between not quite measuring up to somebody else's standards and being an absolute copper-bottomed bastard. How could you think I'd do such a thing to you? Why, that wouldn't be just cruel. That'd be bloody treachery."

He sat back, breathing hard. After a moment he shifted along the sofa and threw an arm heavily across Richard's shoulders, which were still heaving spasmodically. "Rich, my dearest," he said earnestly and very emphatically. "I don't know how much money I've got, and I've no idea what I'm going to do with it, but you'd better remember this one thing, or you and I'll have a little fight. Whatever I do with that money, there's only one person I intend to do it with, and only one that Graham, bless him, would want me to do it with, and that, my lovely, is you."

6

The building in Chancery Lane was a tall, thin relic of Victorian London, looking uncomfortable and squashed between two shiny new cubes of glass and steel. The staircase within was narrow, dingy and twisting. They puffed their way as far as the fourth floor and then had a rest. "If it goes up any further we'll need crampons and an ice pick," gasped Stephen.

"Oxygen bottles," said Richard.

"A couple of Sherpas," suggested Stephen.

"We'll need the Union Jack to plant at the summit," said Richard.

Fortunately they spotted the nameplate of the firm of solicitors they were looking for, and pushed into the tiny reception area, tittering.

The area was just about large enough for the two of them to lean on the highly polished wooden counter. A busy girl looked up and asked them their business, and a few moments later they were sitting in a surprisingly spacious and airy office, being greeted by one of the sharp operators in person. "Mr Hill," said Mr Guilfoyle, raising his eyebrows a little as he saw how youthful his new client was. "I'm Stephen Hill," said Stephen, still a little out of breath, and thankful to drop into the chair to which the solicitor motioned him. Richard drew up another, and they ranged themselves before the enormous desk, looking around them interestedly.

The office was in remarkable contrast to the building that contained it. It was sparsely furnished with ultra-modern designer furniture, there were several Paul Klees on the wall which, Richard informed Stephen afterwards, were either originals or very high-class reproductions indeed. There was the big desk, which was almost bare except for a large personal computer, a calculator, three telephones, an intercom and a single, thick grey folder. The only other things in the room were a grey metal shredder, another computer terminal on a table on its own, and a large and impregnable-looking safe set deep into a recess in an internal wall. Richard smiled in pleasure at the ascetic room. Stephen glanced about in disappointment: of the dusty leather-bound and gold-blocked legal tomes and yellowing, dog-eared papers bound in red ribbon for which he had been hoping, there was not a sign.

He turned his attention to Mr Guilfoyle himself, who, after shaking hands with the two of them, was sitting with a polite expression of mild amusement as he studied the two very different reactions to his sanctum.

"Not what you were expecting, Mr Hill?" he said pleasantly.

"Nunno," said Stephen, colouring a little as he realised that his covert survey of the room had not gone unnoticed. "I was expecting — well, law books and old papers and suchlike."

Guilfoyle grinned, a youthful, human grin that caught them both by surprise, and brought involuntary grins in response. He was an athletic-looking man in his early thirties, with immaculately groomed dark hair, penetrating blue eyes and a very expensive suit. Stephen found himself wondering if he was a cricketer. "Not today's style," went on Guilfoyle in the same pleasant tone. "No quill pens, either, I'm afraid. The law library's down on the first floor."

"You must keep fit working here," ventured Richard.

Guilfoyle grinned again. "It keeps me in trim for weekends," he said.

"Cricket?" asked Stephen hopefully.

"Sailing," said the solicitor with a regretful smile. "And golf — though that's part of my professional duties, really. Now then," he went on, deftly turning them to the matter in hand. "First of all, I have to ask — forgive me..." He left the sentence hanging in mid-air and offered Richard a courteous nod of acknowledgement.

"I wanted to bring a friend with me," said Stephen, disconcerted. "He's got eleven times as much brain as me. I thought he might understand more of what you said than I shall."

"All right," said Guilfoyle. "But I'll do my best to make it all easily understandable. Before we proceed, I must ask you for some form of identification — I mentioned it when we spoke on the telephone this morning, you'll recall."

Stephen produced his passport from the pocket of his blazer — the boys had discussed the matter and decided that their smart school blazers would be the most appropriate things to wear. Guilfoyle inspected the passport, subjected first the picture inside it and then Stephen's face to several seconds' intense scrutiny, then nodded briskly and slid the document back across the desk.

He opened the grey folder, which, Stephen observed with a further pinprick of regret, was very new and sharply creased. "This is Mr Curtis's will..."

* * *

"... so," said Guilfoyle smoothly three-quarters of an hour later, "I'll advance you a reasonable sum to cover your everyday living expenses now. Since you've agreed — very sensibly, if I may say so — to allow us and Mr Curtis's accountants — and Mr Westwood's before him, as a matter of fact — to continue to manage the estate for you, that concludes our business. Very satisfactorily for all concerned, I think we can say. So, unless you have any further questions..." He waited; but both boys were too stunned by what they had been told to have any thought to spare for questions. They shook their heads, a little dazed. Guilfoyle watched them with an understanding smile. "Good," he said after a moment, seeing that they had nothing to say. "Well, if you'll wait here for a moment, I'll go and arrange a cheque. Would..." He paused, looking thoughtfully at Stephen and calculating swiftly. "Would a thousand be a reasonable sum for the time being? You will, of course, as I said, be able to draw on the estate fairly shortly, but we can advance more if you think it necessary. But..." He pursed his lips and left it at that. Stephen goggled at him, not sure whether he was more dumbfounded by the prospect of having a thousand pounds of his own or at the offer of more, with its implication that a thousand wasn't enough.

"Oh!" he said, pulling himself together. "I... er... a thousand will be fine," he went on. He felt a sudden, almost irrepressible urge to jump up and perform several cartwheels across Guilfoyle's very expensive carpet, or perhaps, he thought inconsequentially, he might stand on his head.

He suppressed the urges with an effort, watched with great amusement by Guilfoyle, who was wholly unaccustomed to this kind of response to his professional services, and thoroughly enjoying the contrast with his more usual kinds of client.

"Yes," said Stephen, feeling a little more himself after a few moments' quiet. "A thousand will be wonderful."

"Good," said Guilfoyle. "If you'll just wait here, I'll only be a few minutes. And then, if you'd care to, perhaps we might — ah — permit ourselves a small celebration of your good fortune." He shot a dazzling inch of white cuff and consulted a Patek Philippe wristwatch. "Yes, I think I can spare half an hour. Will you allow me to buy you a drink?"

Stephen stared at him. "Er... aren't we... aren't I... shouldn't it be me buying you one?" he said in surprise.

Guilfoyle turned on his way to the door and smiled. "You're a very wealthy young man, Mr Hill," he said. "I think you'll discover that among the benefits that status brings in its wake is the fact that other people, mostly less wealthy than you by some orders of magnitude, are most anxious to spend their money on you, rather than the other way about. I'd only advise you to be very careful which ones you allow to do so." And with that he disappeared.

* * *

An hour later the boys stood gazing at each other, in a state of considerable emotional shock that left them unable to think of anything sensible to say, and more than a little dazed, on the pavement outside the very expensive wine bar to which Guilfoyle had led them. The solicitor had considerately done most of the talking as they sipped a grand cru Burgundy that was wholly wasted on them, had offered a few last bits of advice, presented Stephen with his card and instructed him to telephone at once if he later thought of any questions he wished to ask, congratulated him once more on his good fortune, and returned to his office in a glow of pleasure in his work that came very rarely to a sharp operator such as himself.

"Golly," said Richard at last. It summed up perfectly what they were both feeling, and neither felt the need to say more. Then, suddenly, moved by an identical feeling, they both laughed, at first normally, then wildly, uproariously, and finally almost hysterically. Passers-by stared at them in astonishment as they side-stepped them, wondering if they were drunk or escaped from some home for the mentally ill, as people do on seeing anyone laughing aloud in a public place.

When the fit at last subsided, leaving them doubled up and clutching their sides in pain, they looked at each other and wondered what to do.

"The first thing I'm going to do," said Stephen, "is to get a taxi back to the station. Bugger the underground!" This started them off again. When the second attack had subsided, they waved frantically at a passing taxi, and went home.

* * *

They had no chance to discuss their startling afternoon on the train home. When they arrived at Euston in their ceremonial taxi the evening exodus of commuters was in full swing, and they watched in dismay as train after train filled to capacity and beyond. Staring at people with their heads pressed at impossible angles against windows, Stephen was struck by a sudden thought. "Hey, Rich," he yelled at the top of his voice, startling several dozen *Evening Standard* readers out of their semi-stupor and into freezing, yet furtive, glances of disapproval. Richard, trapped by three fat men and a bevy of secretarial beauty some yards distant, cast him a despairing look. Stephen gestured frantically, and Richard fought his way through the press to his side. "I've just realised," crowed Stephen

— though he prudently lowered his voice as he thought about what he was saying. "I'm bloody rich, aren't I?" he hissed into Richard's ear. "Let's go and get first-class tickets."

Richard nodded and grinned, and they struggled off the platform, up the ramp and through the teeming concourse to the ticket office.

A sad farce followed. Realisation came to Stephen — as such realisations always come — at the worst possible moment, when they had at last reached the head of the long queue and Stephen had ordered the first-class tickets importantly, only to be reminded by the more thoughtful Richard that they already possessed ordinary tickets. He promptly asked to amend his requirement to paying the difference, but he wasn't quite prompt enough for the clerk, who had already run full first-class tickets through his machine, and was less than pleased to be told that they were no longer wanted. The lengthening queue behind them tut-tutted and grumbled and went for short walks of impatient exasperation.

The clerk, who couldn't care less if the entire queue missed their trains and got home late, or whether they ever got home at all, eventually agreed to accept the difference between the ordinary fare and the first-class, and thrust two laboriously hand-written tickets at them through the slot below his security glass. It was at that critical moment that Stephen was struck by a sudden thought. His hand flew to his mouth, but the thought was so appalling that for a moment he was left at a loss for words. As soon as he thought he could speak again he turned to Richard, who was eying the queue behind them uneasily. "I say," he hissed in Richard's ear. Richard looked anxiously at him, detecting the incipient panic in his voice. "What's up?" he demanded. "Look, for Christ's sake pay up and let's get out of here. This lot'll fucking lynch us if we make them all miss their trains." "Yes," hissed Stephen, "but that's just it. Have you got any loot on you?"

Richard stared at him in gathering horror. "Loot?" he queried blankly. "What d'you mean, loot? You've got..." The words dried in his throat as the appalling truth dawned on him. "Oh, Christ!" he said, and it came out as almost a sob. "Jesus. It's only a cheque, isn't it? Oh, help." He fumbled frantically in his pocket, and produced three pound coins, a fifty-pence piece and a few coppers. "That any good?" he asked in a desperate whisper. Stephen seized the coins from his friend's hand, nodding eagerly. Unfortunately he fumbled in his haste and they managed to drop all the coins, which rolled off in all directions, chased by both boys and a dozen or more of the increasingly enraged would-be commuters behind them, who were by this stage rapidly approaching a state of mutiny — probably homicidal mutiny, reflected Richard bitterly as he darted, sweating profusely, in crabwise, stooping pursuit of an apparently motorised five-pence piece, ending up grovelling miserably at the highly-polished feet of a military-looking gentleman who surveyed him from on high with intense, moustache-twitching disapproval.

They managed eventually to track down most, at least, of the errant coins, and pooled their resources, not daring even to consider the possibility of not having quite enough as they added the last few pence together. They found that they had the required sum with eleven pence to spare, heaved vast, simultaneous sighs of relief, and, at last, took their tickets, thrust the clattering collection of coins under the grille to the frowning clerk, and escaped.

"Fuck me!" breathed Richard as they hastened away from the near-homicidal queue. "I never want to have to go through anything like that again. They'd have just about been ready to tear us limb from limb if we'd taken any longer. What about a coffee?" he suggested as an afterthought.

"What with?" asked Stephen, who was beginning to quiver with internal laughter. Richard saw him shaking, and started to laugh himself.

They halted, counted their last eleven pence, and gave it, with ill-suppressed explosions of laughter, to a puzzled wino, who stared at them through watery eyes and an alcoholic haze and thought he had identified kindred spirits. Then they charged down the ramp, forced their way aboard the first train going to their station and found their way to the first-class section. When they reached it they found that it was so full that they had to stand in conditions almost as cramped as those that had sent them on their ill-fated mission in the first place. For the duration of their half-hour journey the remainder of the weary, squashed and hideously uncomfortable passengers devoted a great deal of speculation to why the two good-looking and smartly-blazered boys among them persistently doubled up in convulsive laughter every time they managed to catch one another's eye.

* * *

By the time they got off their train they were weak to the point of falling down, from a lethal combination of high excitement, emotional shock, hysterical laughter and the delayed-action effects of nearly half a bottle each of very good Burgundy. They tumbled off the train and emerged in the forecourt feeling slightly sick, but otherwise in a high, and slightly drunken, good humour.

"Cricket club?" suggested Stephen. "We can borrow some money there — specially with this cheque to borrow it against."

But Richard demurred. "No," he said quietly, the hilarious mood of the last hour evaporating as they found themselves left behind by the galloping crowds and able to think calmly once more. "He said you oughtn't to flash your money about, didn't he?" he went on, alluding to some of the good advice the sharp operator had offered Stephen in the wine bar. "No point in telling the whole world you've come into money. No, my lovely," he said, "Let's go home for a minute. I'd kill for a cup of tea. And I know where I can lay my hands on a bit of cash, too. Dad always leaves me with an emergency reserve — sort of float, in case there are any bills they've forgotten, and so on. I can raid that. They wouldn't mind, in the circumstances. Besides, you can pay the cheque in tomorrow, and then draw some in a day or so's time, so nobody'll ever be the wiser. Then we'll go to the club. How's that sound, sweet?"

"It sounds fine," said Stephen tenderly. "You're a good chap, Rich. Don't ever let me forget that, will you?"

Richard stared at him for a moment. Then he smiled, a sexy, lascivious smile which Stephen recognised very well. They set off for home at a fast walk, and didn't make the cricket club that evening.

* * *

The next day was Saturday, and they were both up early, having been in bed for fifteen hours, and asleep for much of the time. Stephen left Richard cooking breakfast while he trotted into the town centre to pay in his cheque at the solitary Saturday-opening bank. He watched the bored girl behind the security glass closely as he handed over his cheque, and was deeply disappointed when she stamped the slip and returned the stub without a glance. So much, he thought, for being rich, wondering if a cheque for a million would have brought a trace of animation to her face. He giggled to himself as the thought suddenly popped into his head that he was glad he preferred boys. He walked cheerfully out of the bank, never knowing that while his cheque had not done a thing to raise the bored girl's temperature, his sudden chuckle and his very fair looks had done a great deal. She watched him all the way through the revolving door before returning to the paperback she had out of sight beneath her counter.

When he got home Richard had made a huge breakfast, for which they were both more than ready, having fallen straight into bed when they had got back early the previous evening. They wolfed it, then set to an eager assessment of the cricket match to come that day. Richard had thoughtfully included Stephen's cricket bag among the things he had brought back with him after his deck-clearing visit to Saint-Hippolyte, and Stephen had found some solace during the hardest part of the previous week in pressing his flannels, cleaning and whitening his pads and boots and meticulously cleaning the face of his bat. He sat with it now, remembering his last birthday but one, when Graham had presented it to him on one of his clandestine visits to his flat in the town.

He stroked the creamy, silky-textured blade, and suddenly bent forward and kissed it fondly. "Lots of runs from you this season, my darling," he whispered tenderly. Richard, who knew the bat's provenance, turned his head away, too moved for words. But Stephen saw the movement, and looked up, instantly concerned. "There's three things I want for today," he said softly. Richard raised his eyebrows. "I'm going to get a hundred today," went on Stephen. "For... him. And five wickets — for me. And the third thing I want," he added, very tenderly, "is you. For you. We've got time. You're my banker. I may not get the ton or the wickets, but I can have you, if you're willing." Richard looked down at the mug he was drying up, and finished polishing it as if it was ceremonial plate. He put it carefully back in its place in a cupboard and hung the tea-cloth equally carefully on its peg to dry before he raised his eyes again to look into Stephen's.

"I love you, Steve," he said simply.

* * *

Stephen came so close to his extravagant target that they reckoned afterwards that it counted as achieved.

The news of his loss had gone round the cricket club long since, and everybody was very kind to him when he and Richard sauntered up to the clubhouse an hour and a half before play was due to start. They gathered round him and made a fuss of him, telling how glad they were to see him back in the fold. The players had also put two and two together about Stephen's relationship with Richard, and once the necessary homage to Graham's shade was over, the two of them came in for a certain amount of ribaldry. But, in marked contrast to the unpleasant, prurient rumour-mongering that had caused Graham and Stephen such distress the previous year, it had the virtue of being open ribaldry, of much the same rough and ready kind as everybody else got in equal measures, and as such was robbed of offence.

"We're throwing first," said the Boston Ramblers captain ruefully as he strolled back to the pavilion with Bill after the second and third elevens had been chased out of the bar and seen off to their away matches. Don Parker and his partner disappeared into the dressing room to pad up. Bill ambled across to the scorebox, where Stephen was watching the lights come on in the various boxes on the scoreboard while Richard, inside the box, flicked switches, sharpened pencils and hunted for moth-eaten cushions to mitigate the worst effects of his and his colleague's hard chairs. "Yeah, all okay," shouted Stephen. "All showing zero."

"Get your pads on, Steve," said Bill, dropping a heavy arm across his shoulders. Stephen looked at him in surprise. "Number three," said Bill, on his way back to the enclosure. Stephen and Richard looked at each other, and smiled. It was a gesture typical of Bill: kind, generous but yet unobtrusive; and quite clearly intended as a last small tribute to Graham's memory. First wicket down had been Graham's regular position. Stephen popped into the scorebox and drew Richard into the cobwebby darkness of the far corner. They gave each other a hard, hurried embrace amongst the paper sacks of Surrey loam and a broken wheelbarrow that people had been meaning to repair for twenty years. Richard kissed Stephen softly as he prepared to dash back to the dressing room. "Get that hundred, my lovely," he whispered. "For me, as well as him." Stephen turned back, his eyes gleaming in the semi-darkness, and gave him an affectionate peck on the cheek. "I'll do my best," he said, and was gone.

A few minutes later, promptly at one-thirty — Bill was a martinet about starting games on time — Don and his partner walked out of the dressing room, looked up into the sky to accustom their eyes to the unseasonable but welcome mild sunshine, and walked briskly to the wickets.

Don's partner was a newcomer, who had moved into the area over the winter. He was a batsman with a prodigious reputation, who opened the batting for a Minor County side and had averaged eighty-odd for it over the past five seasons. He was a lightish-brown West Indian, very big built but on the portly side, and had a fondness for enormous floppy white billycock hats. On account of his colour, his spherical tendencies and his hats he was known as Paddington Bear, usually abbreviated to P-B. More than half the side had no idea of his real name.

The Boston Ramblers' opening bowler was fearsomely quick, but his great accuracy was feared more. It was not at all funny to go in first and face a barrage of ferociously hostile inswingers, all on or about off stump and on a full length, interspersed with the occasional villainous ball that pitched on the identical spot, but fizzed and lifted, or, occasionally, sheered the crucial half-inch away to the off, while the predatory ring of slips and gulleys licked their chops and grinned evilly.

Don Parker, like most cricketers, was superstitious, and his little foible took the form of an intense dislike of facing the first ball of an innings. Accordingly Paddington Bear settled into his negligent, rather two-eyed stance, leaning on his bat as if he was trying to push it into the ground like a stump, and waited for the first ball of the season. The bowler licked his fingers, did a little stuttering movement with his feet, then settled into his run. It was not very long, but rhythmical and economical of energy, which had enabled him to bowl unchanged many times throughout an innings. He leapt gracefully into a perfect delivery stride that reminded some of the old men sitting in deckchairs in the enclosure of Ray Lindwall, the middle-aged ones of Dennis Lillee, and the young ones of Michael Holding.

The ball was prodigiously fast; but for once the bowler's line strayed a little, and it pitched a fraction of an inch outside Paddington Bear's leg stump. He didn't bother with a backlift at all; just moved the bat in a short arc, with a kind of short-armed motion, and without any effort at all flicked the ball slightly backward of square-leg, over the row of very tall, newly-budding poplar trees on that boundary, and out of the ground.

There was a howl of delight from the pavilion enclosure, followed by a stream of white-clad figures running round the boundary to find the ball. They were beaten to it by a small boy, who lobbed it back to square-leg, waiting for it with a rueful grin on his face. "I wouldn't mind bettin it's the first time he's been pinged for six first ball of a season," he grinned to Bill and the others as they stopped in their rush to find the ball. "First time I've ever seen such a thing," said Bill delightedly. They decided to turn their mission of assistance into a stroll round the boundary, but stood watching in great curiosity to see what form the bowler's reprisal for such an outrageous assault would take.

"Betcha he drops it short," said Alan Hood, Bill's vice-captain. "Nah!" said Bill. "Waste a time on this strip. Like bowlin on Christmas pudd'n. No, he'll try an york him, you see."

Bill was right. The bowler, furious though he was at being treated in so dismissive a manner, was nonetheless far too good a cricketer to waste a delivery on a gesture of outrage that, on that pitch, would have been stillborn. The next ball was even faster than its predecessor, and had the advantage of not losing any of its sting by contact with the deadening pitch. It speared in lethally at the roots of Paddington Bear's middle and off stumps, low and swinging just the right amount. It was a beautiful ball, the perfect response of a very good cricketer indeed to an act of outrageous disrespect.

Paddington Bear watched the ball closely, as if inspecting a form of bug hitherto unknown to science, and, at the very last moment, dropped the deadest bat in the county on it, killing it stone dead in his blockhole. In its way it was a still more magnificent stroke of batsmanship than the six the ball before, and the players walking round greeted it with a roar still louder than for the six. Like the six, it was played with such masterly ease, and such total lack of any conspicuous effort, that everyone on the ground knew they were in the presence of a cricketer a class above almost anyone else there, except, probably, Don Parker.

For the next twenty minutes they watched in deep appreciation as Paddington Bear treated them to a short but champagne-quality exhibition of batsmanship. On a pitch which made scoring runs at least as difficult as bowling penetratively, he scored 47, taking runs all round the wicket, and not missing a single chance of scoring. It was a masterpiece of an innings, and when he was out, caught on the backward point boundary attempting to square cut a six to reach his fifty, he was cheered from the wicket to the dressing room, including by the opposition. "Sorry, Bill," he said in his pronounced London accent as he threw his bat down and dropped heavily into a deckchair. "Can't seem to stop playin these risky shots." Bill laughed. "We'll forgive you this once," he said. "But see that it doesn't happen again. Good luck, our kid," he went on, addressing Stephen, who had risen lithely from his deckchair and was just setting off to the wicket, adjusting his school XI cap. Stephen turned and gave him a faintly apprehensive smile. "Just play your own game, kid," said Bill. "No hurry. An don't try an square cut any sixes, or it's jugsville for you, like him." He jabbed an elbow in Paddington Bear's ribs.

Stephen grinned. "They ought to be pretty well softened up," he said mildly, and walked briskly out to the middle, where he played without a trace of PB-style flamboyance but very well indeed, hitting bad balls mercilessly, scampering singles so fast that they turned into twos and left Don Parker, who was twenty years older than Stephen, complaining and asking the umpire to call a cardiologist. At four o'clock he wanted seven for his century. Bill pursed his lips, for he hated teams that batted on when they were in no trouble; but he decided to give Stephen five minutes or so to make his hundred. Next ball Stephen, tiring rapidly, tried to whip an innocuous half-volley on leg stump through mid-wicket. The only fate it deserved was to be retrieved from the hedge by the perspiring mid-on. As it was, he played it a fraction early, got a leading edge, and spooned up a dolly of a return catch to the bowler, who was so surprised that he dropped it, tried again, juggled it, dropped it again, and caught it triumphantly and in unprintable relief as it bounced a foot upwards off his knee. Bill declared, and they came in with a far more than respectable 227 on Richard's board for the loss of two wickets.

Stephen came off beetroot-red, sweating like a carthorse and grinning in triumph at the best score, and by far the best innings, of his life. He swerved away to the scorebox, anxious, like every youthful batsmen who has just made his best score, to feast his eyes on the story of the innings in the scorebook, as if the sight of the neatly-pencilled figures somehow confers a greater degree of reality on the thing. Richard greeted him ecstatically, and made extravagant and physically improbable promises of the reward he planned for that night. They went happily into tea.

After that the game was all anticlimax. Boston Ramblers, though a very fine batting side, could make little headway against such an unlooked-for target, on a difficult pitch against first-class bowling, and were eventually dismissed in the last over of the final twenty, at ten past seven, for a score of 166 which was far more creditable than it appeared. Stephen bowled twenty overs without a break, and was rewarded with three wickets. He bought the mandatory jugs, mentally hugging himself when Bill asked in an undertone if he could afford it, and that night Richard faithfully delivered all but the most impossible of the rewards he had promised.

The following day they played away to Hemel Hempstead, old friends and rivals. Stephen was retained at first wicket down and hit a very fast 67, hitting three balls over the poplars beside the Grand Union Canal beside the ground, and one clean out of the ground, over the road and, via a vast plate-glass window, into the bar of the Heath Park Hotel, frightening several customers so much that they had to drink several additional pints to calm their nerves. "Jugsville," called Bill ominously from the boundary, wagging an admonitory finger in Stephen's direction.

They won that match, too, by a narrow margin. Hemel Hempstead were friendly and hospitable as usual, but they got back to their own clubhouse in time for a drink. When they got there they found that there had been a telephone call, asking Bill to ring a number. Stephen happened to glance his way as he was talking into the phone, a big finger stuck in his other ear and the receiver shielded from the surrounding hubbub, and saw his face suddenly cloud over. He couldn't hear what Bill was saying, but he managed to catch an occasional word. "...sorry to hear... yes, please pass on... really am very... of course..." Bill saw the enquiring look on his young face as he came away from the phone. "Bad news?" said Stephen, ready to sympathise.

"Not good," said Bill soberly. "Old John at Malton. You remember John? Ran the boozer where we went on tour? Just after you came to the club, wasn't it?" Stephen remembered it perfectly. The tour was one of the sweetest moments of his life. It had been in that pub that he had lost his virginity, delightfully and delightedly, to Graham Curtis, at that time his French master at school.

"Seems John's been canin it a bit too heavily," said Bill sadly. "His quack's just read him the riot act, an told him he's gotta lay off the shandy, pronto, an get outa the booze business to boot. Parently his liver's got about six months to live if he carries on layin into the stuff. Funny, that," he mused. "Ida said when he finally kicked the bucket his liver'd have to be beaten to death, but there it is. Anyway, he's sellin the hotel, an goin into retirement. It won't be the same tourin there without him. Poor ol Fred's cryin his heart out in the bar, John said. He's just been told." Stephen had a vivid mental vision of old Fred, the eighty-five-year-old barman at the hotel, and was suddenly filled with a deep, sorrowful emptiness at the passage of loved things. He was growing up this year, he reflected sadly.

"Will we still go on tour there?" he asked Bill.

"Shouldn't think so," muttered Bill. "Not now. Have to find somewhere else, I think. Always best — when a publican you're very fond of moves, it's never the same after, an you're always makin comparisons, an they're always to the new man's detriment. We're booked for Holland again next year, but I dunno what we'll do about this year. I was gonna start makin the arrangements soon." He clumped over to the bar to tell the others.

Stephen sat sipping his lager, thinking back in a mixture of memories of his first tour with the club, some very sweet, some now become very sad. And as he sat thinking, an idea came into his head. He sat bolt upright as its ramifications crowded into his mind. Then he went in search of Richard, finding him chattering among a crowd of younger players. He forebore to interrupt right then, and passed on instead to the bar, where he bought himself a pint, insisted on getting Bill one, and waited until Richard was free.

As soon as he saw Richard detach himself from his group and look about he called him. Richard came over, and saw instantly that Stephen was bursting with something to say. "What's up?" he said anxiously.

"Are you ready to go home?" asked Stephen, draining his glass.

"Can be," said Richard. "Why? What are you cooking up?" he asked shrewdly — he was very familiar with all Stephen's moods and expressions.

"I've just had an idea," said Stephen, "and I think it's a corker."

"Okay," said Richard. "Let's go."

7

"It's a good idea," said Richard as they lay in bed that night. "But it'll cost us a bit to get there. You'll have to wait until that cheque of yours has cleared. And if I were you, I'd ring that solicitor, what was his name? Guilfoyle. Ask him if you really are in control. You don't want to go barging in only to find you haven't got any real power."

"I'd already come to the same conclusions myself," said Stephen.

For the next few days he possessed himself of such patience as he could muster. In the strong glow of pleasure induced by his fine start to the season and his growing awareness of his powers, he spent hours in the evenings hitting the cover off the ball in the nets at the club, occasionally varying the procedure by tossing his off-spinners ever higher and slower, to the delight of Bill McKechnie, who relished the prospect of going into matches with one of fewer than half a dozen genuine slow spin bowlers in the entire league.

Every morning they walked into the town centre, where Stephen pushed his plastic card hopefully into the hole in the wall at his bank and swore vividly when the machine announced that his balance remained at its normal level. On Thursday morning, however, he at last saw the wonderful, almost unbelievable legend displayed in bright green numerals: for the first time in his life he had a balance at the bank in four figures. "One thousand, no hundreds and sixty-three pounds," he crowed. "And forty-eight pence," he added. He executed a short highland fling on the pavement, watched in astonishment by passing shoppers. Then he dashed into the bank, brandishing his cheque book. Richard tut-tutted affectionately to himself, removed Stephen's card from the slot in the cash dispenser, where Stephen had forgotten it in his triumph, and followed him into the bank at a more sober pace, grinning.

"Crikey!" said Stephen in some dismay as Richard held the little plastic card in front of his eyes. "Did I leave it there? Sorry, Rich."

"No need to apologise to me," said Richard, feeling a bright glow of pleasure all the same in the automatic, unthinking acceptance of belonging to himself that Stephen's casually-spoken words implied. "I'm not your keeper. Though I sometimes think you need one," he added. But he took the sting out of the words with a grin.

"How much shall I take out?" asked Stephen, making firm mental resolutions to be much more cautious in his handling of his new-found wealth.

Richard considered. "I shouldn't think we can possibly need more than about fifty quid, can we?" he said. "Say a hundred, to cover sudden emergencies. I've got about forty, so you only need to take out sixty."

"No," said Stephen quietly. "You're not spending anything on this trip, Rich." Richard opened his mouth to protest, but Stephen cut him off ruthlessly. "No," he repeated. "This one's on the house. You can spend some of your own money later on, but not now. This is the first thing we've spent any of this money on, and I want it to be on me. On Graham," he added, seeking to explain the importance it had suddenly assumed in his mind that he should use their little excursion as a means of repaying Richard for his innumerable kindnesses while paying a last homage to Graham at the same time. Richard understood, and accepted the gesture with his usual grace. Stephen considered Richard's suggestion as he stood in the queue, and, when he reached the window, wrote a cheque for a hundred and fifty pounds, counting the sheaf of ten- and twenty-pound notes with relish and also, not quite able to help himself, a little ostentatiously before folding it firmly and slipping it into his trouser pocket.

"You wanna be careful, son," said a smallish, very tough-looking man with a drooping moustache, wearing clothes liberally spattered with the detritus of the building site. "There's an awful lot a people'd mace you for a fiver in this town. It ain't good policy to show off your wealth, what with hard times an all." Stephen looked up at him in alarm. He saw the grin of understanding on the man's face, and flushed. Then he found the grace to smile, a little shamefacedly, and offered the man a word of thanks. He kept a hand in his pocket, fingers curled reassuringly round the wad of notes, all the way back.

They went triumphantly home, drank a last mug of tea, then Richard carefully eased his mother's small, cherry-red Volvo out of the garage. There was one nasty moment when he almost eased it into the side of his father's vast BMW. When he had got over the bout of jitters that this induced, he asked Stephen to get out and see him out into the road.

"Christ, that was a near thing," said Richard with feeling as he got back in the car after closing the garage and locking it. Stephen studied him as he put the car in gear and pulled away from the kerb. Once in the open road he regained his confidence, and they set off at a lively speed for Bognor Regis, which Richard's father's road atlas told them was the nearest place of any size to their destination. "Would he have gone berserk?" asked Stephen.

Richard pursed his lips as he thought about it. "No," he said eventually. "I don't think so. He's a very tolerant and reasonable man. So he never goes berserk, as such, about anything. But I think scratching the paint on the BMW's probably just about the one thing that would take him as near to berserk point as he'll ever get. He loves that car. You'd think he'd given birth to it himself. I've got a theory that he wanted to be a racing driver when he was a kid, and never quite got over it. The way he drives that bloody great thing I sometimes think he still thinks he is a racing driver. Anyway, hurting the car is just about the one thing in the world I wouldn't want to have to confess to when they got back. Almost anything else, short of burning the house down, I could face him over. But that... that would cost."

They drove on in a comfortable silence, which Stephen broke by asking if he could put the radio on. Richard turned his head very briefly, and bestowed a look on him that was seven-eighths made up of fathomless love and affection and one-eighth genuine, very slightly irritated puzzlement. Stephen caught the look, but couldn't read it, and looked a little puzzled himself. "Honestly, Stevie," said Richard. "When will you learn that you don't have to ask my permission to do things? Don't you know by now that you can treat anything of mine as your own? You don't have to ask. Not ever."

Stephen glanced at him, still puzzled. "Only being polite," he said defensively. "I don't want to take you for granted, Rich. You of all people."

"There's taking for granted and taking for granted," said Richard, trying and failing to get past a lorry rumbling along at twenty-eight miles an hour. "The wrong kind you'd never do to me, I know, and the right kind I want you to do. Understand me?"

"I think so," said Stephen, not understanding at all, but loving his friend and wanting to please him by saying the right thing.

"Well, put the radio on, then, and remember," said Richard finally.

Stephen switched on the radio, and twiddled the knob until he found Radio Three. He had never had much interest in classical music until Graham had taken him to his first ever orchestral concert in Geneva. Listening to the Orchestra of the Suisse Romande, with Graham to talk knowledgeably about the music in the interval and after the concert, had made a very deep impression on the boy, and given him a taste for music that he had never suspected.

He had taken every opportunity since that evening to listen, and was acquiring knowledge of the subject rapidly. He suspected that half the appeal was the opportunity it afforded him to indulge in unsentimental memories of the kind, loving friend who had introduced him to it.

The car was filled with the thunderous glories of the last movement of Sibelius's second symphony. Stephen immediately felt a prickling of tears behind his eyes. Sibelius had been one of Graham's favourites. Richard knew that, shot a quick, anxious glance sideways out of the corner of his eye, and saw Stephen's wet eyes. "Graham loved this," said Stephen, and Richard relaxed and was glad, because his voice was steady and level, the regret in it contained and unhysterical. The symphony came to its majestic end a few minutes later, and, unexpectedly, Stephen chuckled. "What's up?" asked Richard.

Stephen laughed again. "We used to play a game," he said. "We used to select cricket teams made up of composers from all the various countries — French composers, Russian ones, English, Viennese, and so on. Sometimes we'd pick a team of violinists, or pianists — you know the kind of thing. Anyway, he always used to say that Sibelius should be umpire, because no one would ever argue with someone with a bald head that size, would they? And then he'd always say 'Mendelssohn, aged eleven, is scorer.' It became a kind of catch-phrase of his." His eyes softened at the memory of a silly game played in innocent fun, and the stocky, attractive man, hard, combative but at the same time gentle and affectionate, with whom he had played it.

There was only one way the conversation could possibly go after that, and they selected cricket teams, to an accompaniment of Schubert piano sonatas, all the way to Bognor Regis. There they stopped and asked their way, having to stop half a dozen people before they found one who knew the obscure hamlet for which they were heading. Eventually, however, they found someone who not only claimed to know the way but also sounded as if he really did. They followed his directions on their road atlas, and drove off again. Half an hour later they came to the village they were looking for. Squarely in the very heart of it was a green that might have been lifted from any one of a thousand tourist guides, complete with thatched cottages, a sprinkling of rather larger houses in the style of Queen Anne, and some lofty trees putting out their first green dusting of foliage. Richard parked the car at the side of the road along one side of the triangular green. The boys got out and looked across the green to where, as picturesque as all its archetypal Old England setting, stood Stephen's pub.

They stood looking at it for some minutes on end, trying to assimilate the fact that Stephen was its owner. But the realisation wouldn't sink in. The idea that he actually owned this beautiful piece of picture-postcard English heritage was somehow more difficult to take in than the knowledge of vast sums of money.

It was a very large pub, two storeys high, of authentic Tudor half-timbered construction, all angles and corners, with tall, decorated Elizabethan chimneys at each end. It had been beautifully maintained, and gleamed in brilliant white paint to emphasise the irregular black ship's timbers that criss-crossed it. To one side there was a large car park, covered with heavy orange gravel, with high sleeping policemen across the mouth to prevent its users from entering and leaving too fast and churning the gravel into tyre-ruts. In front of the building was a wide paved area, fenced off by a low fence of pointed white wooden palings. The area was gay with small white tables and garden chairs, topped off by big umbrellas in ice-cream colours. Everything looked in immaculate repair.

Behind the great building they could see the tops of a lot of ancient trees swaying in the constant breeze from the south. As they stood in the mild spring sunshine they became aware of a sound, faint but not distant, and never fading, always there behind the birdsong. It took them a moment or two to recognise it as the murmur of the sea, which lapped the south coast less than a quarter of a mile away beyond the pub. "Well," said Stephen, and suddenly realised that he was speaking in a hushed whisper. "We shan't get anywhere just standing looking at it, shall we?" he went on in a normal voice. "Let's go and have a pint of my beer, shall we?"

* * *

They sauntered across the short, springy grass on the triangular green, across the road, and through an opening in the wicket fence. They saw that the pavings beneath the tables were scrubbed, and that there wasn't even the suspicion of moss peeping between the big irregular slabs. They paused there for a moment to look up at the large, tasteful sign. "The Crown Hotel," murmured Stephen to himself. It had a ring to it that none of the dozens of Crown Hotels he had seen and drunk pints in up to that moment had ever had. He repeated it, twice more, rolling the words in his mouth and savouring them. Then they moved on, halting again before the wide, low front door to admire the massive timbers of the frame, and the equally enormous oak door, studded with huge, star-headed nails blackened by time while the timbers of the door itself had become bleached almost white.

They inspected the narrow flower beds that ran along the front of the building, showing little signs of flowers that early in the year, but neatly tended, with no stones visible in the rich black soil. Some kind of creeper was trained round the whole of the great doorway, and there was an old-fashioned boot-scraper to one side. They looked at the board above the lintel, and read the white lettering on the black paint, hoping to see Stephen's name there, but the notice informed them only that one Thomas John Whitfield was licensed to sell beers, wines and spirits. They looked at one another, finding, somewhat to their surprise, that it needed an effort of will to push open the heavy door and enter their own property. "Let's go," said Richard.

Stephen turned the big wrought-iron ring that was the door handle, and lifted the heavy latch. "I say," he said. "Look at the keyhole. The key must be like the one to the Tower of London." They looked at the huge keyhole, and both conceived an instant desire to see the key that fitted such a hole. It must indeed, Richard thought, be a titan among keys.

Inside there was a second door, of ordinary construction, across a yard-wide space of dark red tiles. The tiles had been worn away in the middle by the feet of several centuries. They opened the inner door, and found themselves in a long, low-ceilinged bar. There was no one about, but they noticed immediately that the room did not have the unpleasant odour of stale beer and smoke common to many pubs. By contrast, this room smelt sweetly of flowers, furniture polish and, overhanging all, the faint but pervasive aroma of the smoke of old wood burning.

Looking about them curiously, the boys headed for the bar, examining its highly polished surface approvingly. The floor was mostly polished parquet blocks, except for a large area at one end, which was paved with the same red tiles as they had seen in the air-lock between the two doors. The woodwork of the pillars and canopy above the long bar was old, of high quality and very well looked after. On the broad shelf behind the bar a vast array of bottles, optics and glasses winked and shone in the soft lighting that, even at just after eleven on a fine spring morning, was necessary to illuminate the low room. They leaned on the bar, in no hurry to start drinking, and content to look about and take in the atmosphere of the place.

When they had been leaning easily on the bar for two or three minutes, a large red-faced man with dark hair going grey and a rather magnificent handlebar moustache appeared from somewhere. "Morning," he said agreeably. "Pleasant one, at that." They noticed that he made no attempt to apologise for having kept them waiting, and concluded that hurry was not endemic to the way of life in so remote and rural a spot.

"Morning. Could we have two pints of lager, please?" said Stephen politely. The man automatically reached up and took two mugs hanging on hooks beneath the carved canopy above the bar. "Which one would you like?" he asked, gesturing along an immense row of pump handles. "Oh," said Stephen, looking in some dismay. "I didn't notice you had so many. Er..." He wandered along the bar, astonished to see so many different varieties of beer on sale.

"We're a free house," said the man, making conversation. "I doubt if you'll find a wider choice of beers in Sussex." They settled for Kronenbourg. Stephen suffered a sudden lapse into his recent past, and pronounced it in the French manner. "Oh. Sorry," he apologised as he heard himself. "I spent a while working in a bar in Alsace recently," he explained. "They make this stuff there. Just slipped back into the habit, I suppose. Have one yourself?" he added, to cover his mild embarrassment at having sounded appallingly affected, as he thought he probably had.

"That's very kind of you," said the man amiably. "I'll have fifty-pennorth." He took a large wine glass from the back shelf, where it was evidently reserved for his own use, and pulled himself a small beer from one of the bitter pumps, which were even more numerous than those for lager.

"*Un galopin*," said Stephen happily, remembering.

"Sorry?" queried the man, wiping his extravagant moustache.

"Oh, nothing," said Stephen. "They call that — a little beer, in a wine glass — a *galopin* in France."

The man seemed glad of some company to chat to early in the day. They discovered that he was Thomas Whitfield, the manager of the hotel, and Stephen decided to risk a direct question.

"You don't own it, then?" he said, hoping so direct an approach was not inviting a rebuff. But Whitfield didn't seem to mind.

"No, no," he said. "There's an absentee landlord somewhere in the background. I haven't the slightest idea who he is. Some shady billionaire in the Cayman Islands, I shouldn't be surprised." Stephen smothered a titter by turning it into a paroxysm of coughing, while Richard discovered an infinite fascination in the toes of his trainers as he fought to suppress his emotions. The landlord noticed nothing, and went on talking. "We're run ostensibly from a firm of lawyers in London. We never see anything of them. They send someone to go through the books once a quarter, they pay the VAT man and authorise repairs and so on. I'll tell you lads the truth, I wouldn't have it any other way. The owner, whoever he is, is obviously ready to make sure the place is kept in good order. I've spent a small fortune on this place in the three years since I took it over, and there's never been the suspicion of haggling. That's practically unheard of these days. The way most tenants have to fight to get a replacement toilet roll out of the brewers, it makes me very glad I landed here. I reckon I can say without blushing, I've got the smartest pub in Sussex here."

A rapid conversation went on in facial expressions, at the end of which Stephen, on receiving an affirmative from Richard, said, hesitantly, "We... er... we haven't quite been playing fair with you, Mr Whitfield."

Whitfield, who had observed the unspoken exchange and been puzzled by it, put down the glass he had been polishing and leaned across the bar, sensing suddenly that something of some substance was afoot, and prepared to take a more intense interest. "How d'you mean?" he said, a little tensely.

"This firm of lawyers you deal with," began Stephen. "Are they...?" He named the sharp operators in Chancery Lane.

Whitfield narrowed his eyes and looked very closely at him. "Yes," he said softly after a very long, difficult pause. "But I'm very curious how you might know that." There was a distinct undertone of hostility, or, at least, of suspicion, in his voice now.

"It's as I said, Mr Whitfield," said Stephen, weighing his words carefully. "We haven't played fair with you. But I'm going to now. I'll lay my cards down. The man who the solicitors represented was a Mr Westwood. He was a very old gentleman, a retired doctor. He lived in London, more or less as a recluse. He died last year, and left everything he owned, including this hotel, to... to a very close friend of mine. That friend also died very recently — he was killed in an air disaster — the plane that blew up over the Channel, you probably heard about it." Whitfield nodded and made a rumbling sound in his throat, which Stephen took to mean both that he had heard of the disaster and that he was waiting for Stephen to continue.

"That friend of mine, in his turn, left everything he owned — to me," Stephen finished simply. He waited in silence, curious to see how Whitfield reacted. There was a momentary awkward silence. Then Whitfield said "I'm sorry. I'm very distressed to hear that." There was another, very long pause, while he subjected first Stephen, then Richard, to an intense and unashamed scrutiny. When he at last spoke it was slowly and quietly, as if he was uncertain whether to take what he had heard seriously.

Richard, watching him, could almost hear his thoughts: that it was an almost impossible chain of coincidences that had brought a mere boy to ownership of his haven of affluent and interference-free comfort; then the reflection that it was still more unlikely that Stephen could know such details, let alone present them in so self-assured a manner, unless he was speaking of something that he knew very well. Promptly on the heels of this thought he observed the first tremors of anxiety on his own account. Worries about new brooms wrote themselves loud and clear over his face. Finally he saw a determined expression wipe out all its predecessors, and waited, certain that he was about to ask for further cards to be laid on the table.

He was right. "I have to accept what you say," he said slowly, considering. "It's pretty unexpected, as I dare say you can imagine. I'd have thought you were a couple of silly kids taking the piss, but for the fact that you were able to quote the name of the lawyers, and you gave the details like someone who was speaking from knowledge. But I can check in thirty seconds if I'm in any doubt about your bona fides, can't I?"

"Please do, by all means," said Stephen, "if you'd feel more sure of us. Here's the man to ask for." He slipped his fingers into the hip pocket of his jeans and passed over the card that Guilfoyle had given him. "Do ring him," said Stephen earnestly. "Please. It'll make it much easier for us to talk if you know for certain you can trust us to be who we say we are." Whitfield stared at him for some seconds, a long, hard, concentrated stare. Then his face cleared, he nodded, and said "Good enough." He went to the telephone at the far end of the bar, turning the card over in his fingers as he went. They couldn't hear what he was saying, but they could see him nodding, and once or twice he turned to look back towards them. After a short conversation he disappeared through a door in the rear wall of the bar. He was gone for some minutes, during which the boys looked at each other and wondered if they were doing the right thing. Then Whitfield came back, looking at them with considerably more respect. "Well, Mr Hill — I take it you're Mr Hill," he said, addressing Stephen, who nodded and smiled as pleasantly as he was able. "Well, yes, I spoke to your Mr Guilfoyle, he confirms every word you've just been saying, and — you asked me to check you to feel sure, so I did. I looked in our books, and his name's mentioned in some of the correspondence. I'm satisfied — satisfied that you're who you say you are. So I'm talking to my boss. What I'm wondering is, are you satisfied?"

Stephen was about to speak, but he hesitated, feeling very distinctly uneasy. He wished they hadn't approached the matter in the way they had, which was beginning to seem more and more underhand with every moment that passed. Whitfield, taking his hesitation for doubts about what answer to give, went on speaking. "I mean, Mr Hill, you can imagine, it's a bit of a shock to stand chatting to a couple of casual customers and then suddenly to find that you've been talking to your employer. Especially — I hope you won't mind me saying this..." He paused awkwardly, flushing a little. Stephen took pity on him.

"Especially since he's only a bit of a kid," he said, with a grin that took any possible sting out of the words. "Of course I understand that, Mr Whitfield. I also think we — sorry, I — owe you a very profound apology. For the way we handled it. It was more than unfair. It was mean and underhand to come in incognito like that. But I can only promise you that we weren't trying to catch you out in anything. As I'm sure you can imagine, I'm very new to this sort of thing — I mean, I've never owned anything, let alone something like a pub. We wanted to come down and look at the place, for a specific reason, which I'd like to tell you about, in a bit. But we thought if we just walked in and said 'Hi, we're the owners', it would look so... so cock-sure and conceited that we... well, we thought we'd just come in and have a look. Then, if we liked what we saw, well, okay, fine, we could open up, as we have done. If we didn't like what we saw, well, then we were just going to walk out again, and the plan I've got would never have happened.

"But I'd like to say one thing right from the start. We are happy with what we see — aren't we, Rich?" He turned for support from his friend, who nodded seriously, but otherwise indicated that Stephen should continue to be spokesman. "You're doing fine," was the message that passed between them, once again without the necessity for words. As before, Whitfield observed the unspoken communication. Whitfield had been appointed by an agent who had in turn been appointed by Guilfoyle, and was not surprisingly a very shrewd man. He had already begun to place the two young men — kids, as he would have thought them in almost any other conceivable circumstances. He waited to see what Stephen had to say next. "We're very happy," went on Stephen. "And we're not going to come storming in here interfering in all your arrangements, changing things for the sake of changing them, or to impress our personalities on the place. You know the pub, the business, the area and the people, we don't know anything about any of them. You're a publican. Less than a year ago I was a schoolboy. My knowledge of pubs amounts to drinking in them, and a few months working as a barman in France. As far as the books and the finances are concerned, if Guilfoyle and his friends are satisfied with the way you run the show, fine. He doesn't strike me as a man very easily satisfied, and I shouldn't dream of poking my nose in.

"As for the place itself, well, it's about the nicest pub I've ever been in. It's beautiful, it's been kept wonderfully, and it'll be perfect for what I've got in mind. But before I go on to that, I'd like to ask you three things. Okay?" Whitfield nodded, watching Stephen's face with a considerable respect dawning on his own.

"Okay," went on Stephen, glancing once again at Richard for further reassurance, and receiving it. "First: do you feel better for what I've said already?"

"Yes, thank you, Mr Hill," said Whitfield slowly. "I do. I must admit, I was beginning to get a little anxious, when you started talking about schemes and plans. But you've been very generous in what you've said." Stephen wondered if he had really heard a faint emphasis on the last word, and would have liked to ask Richard if he had heard it also. But that was impossible, so he nodded and went on.

"Good. Second: can I persuade you to drop the 'Mr Hill', and call me Stephen. Or Steve. Everybody does. Besides —" he added shrewdly, "I'm hardly old enough to be called Mr yet, am

I?"

This time Whitfield stared at him for a second or two, taken aback at hearing his own thoughts so exactly enunciated. Suddenly he laughed. "You're nobody's fool, however old you may be," he said. "Steve it is. Everybody calls me Tom."

"Okay," said Stephen. "And this is Richard. Richard Fitzjohn." The other two shook hands across the bar. "The third thing," said Stephen, "is, can we have another drink, please? My glass has been empty for fifteen minutes, and I'm getting thirsty. Two more of the same for us, and whatever you fancy for yourself, er, Tom."

So Tom Whitfield busied himself pulling pints, having one himself this time. A few other early customers drifted in — it was still not yet mid-day — and he served them quickly and efficiently, while Stephen grabbed the chance to ask Richard how he was managing. "You're doing great," said Richard very quietly. He gently ran his fingers of the hand that was hidden from Tom and the newcomers by Stephen's body up and down the curve of Stephen's bottom. Stephen stiffened immediately, and suppressed a desire to writhe with pleasure. Richard kept on stroking him until Tom, having disposed of the customers' wants, returned hastily. "Now then," he said, "may I know what this plan is of yours? Not that I'm prying, of course," he added hurriedly. "But if it concerns the hotel..." "Of course," said Stephen. "It's to do with cricket. You see, our club have got a bit of a problem with our tour..."

"You a cricketer?" asked Tom, a gleam coming instantly into his eye.

"I certainly am," Stephen responded warmly, and the enthusiasm was plain in his voice and face.

"I'm a hundred-and-two per cent, clinically-certifiable cricket lunatic myself," said Tom. "To my unfortunate wife's unending despair, I'm afraid. I turn out for the local side whenever I can. They're all regulars here. They'll be in tonight, as it happens: they hold their selection committee meetings in here on Thursday nights. Pity you can't be here to meet em. They're a nice bunch."

"I was coming to that," said Stephen. "We were going to ask if you'd got a room."

"Rooms?" queried Tom, poker-faced.

Stephen gave him a solemn look for a moment, then replaced it with a cat-like grin. "Room," he corrected. Tom blinked, just once, then said "Room it is. You can have your pick. We don't do much residential business this time of year. Twin beds, I take it?" he said with considerable delicacy.

"How big are the doubles?" asked Stephen, twinkling.

"Not big enough," said Tom, once again poker-faced.

"Twin beds it is," said Stephen. He hesitated, watching Tom's face, which Tom was carefully keeping stolidly neutral. "Is this going to be a problem here?" Stephen asked in the end. "I mean, I let you have it with both barrels like that because you were going to have to know. I don't like being secretive about myself, and I've no intention of being. But is it likely to be a problem for you — with the cricket club, or the customers? I'm only asking so we know what we've got to be prepared for. We don't keep secrets; but we don't stuff anything down people's throats — if you take my meaning," he added with a saucy grin. Tom grinned a little uncertainly back. Richard chuckled.

Tom considered the question for a while. "It's nothing to me," he said levelly. "I've got no problem with your... with that kind of thing. Live and let live, I say. I don't think you'll have any trouble with most of the customers, either. The young ones, especially. They won't give a damn, or very few of em will, anyway. One or two of the older inhabitants might be a bit shaken. This is purple Tory country, remember, and we've got more than our fair share of Colonel Blimps. The Costa Geriatrica, this is. Full of retired people, and a lot of em pretty set in their ways. They won't — ah — they won't exactly offer you a twenty-one gun salute, if you take my meaning. On the other hand they most likely won't bother you too much. But what kind of reception you get will rather depend on how you present yourselves, d'you see what I mean? I mean, they're not the sort to see — er — gay people as the younger element do... on the other hand, they're a rather reserved breed, given to keeping emselves to emselves. If you don't... sort of brandish it in front of em — stuff it down their throats, as you yourself put it... well, they'll probably make retired colonel noises at me when you're not here. But that'll be all there is to it, I should think." He paused, considering another aspect of the matter. "Can I tell em about you being the owner of the place?" he asked.

The boys looked at each other and thought about it. "I don't see that it matters," said Stephen judicially. "I don't see any reason why not," he said. "Yes, tell em, if you like."

"Okay," said Tom.

"Now then," said Stephen, glad to have disposed of business

matters for the time being, "what's the cricket like round here?"

And so between them, by a simple decision, taken in a few casual words and forgotten in a few moments once they had fallen to talking cricket, they set in motion a chain of events that was to have momentous consequences for all of them.

8

"You'll be comfortable here," said Tom, waving a hand expansively and standing back to allow them to precede him into their room. "Best room in the house. It's the biggest, and it's got the best view. There's very little traffic comes past the green here, so you won't be disturbed by noise if you want to have the windows open. I'll leave you to get settled. See you later, I hope?"

They assured him that they would be in the bar later, and he withdrew. They sat down on one of the beds, and found that it was deep, soft and comfortable. Richard bounced up and down a couple of times, then got up and went across the uneven, convex floor to the windows. There were two big casements, looking out across the little green. He threw both open to their widest extent and leaned out, breathing the sweet, chilly spring air. Then he examined the windows. "Mmm," he mused. "They're modern. Made of some kind of plastic, by the look of it. Double-glazed, too. But they're very well made. Made up to look as much like the real thing as poss. Must've cost a bomb."

"Like everything else about this place," said Stephen.

"Yes," said Richard, looking more closely. "They've been made to fit in with ye olde worlde image. But they fit their frames perfectly, and the frames have been specially made to fit the irregularities of the hole for them. Very clever."

They spent a quarter of an hour exploring the room. Then Stephen lay spreadeagled lazily and luxuriously across his bed, his eyes following Richard as he moved about. Richard, suddenly conscious of the silence, turned, and immediately saw the expression in Stephen's eyes. They were slightly moist, which Richard shrewdly divined as signifying that he was thinking about Graham, but there was another look in them, too, one with which Richard was intimately and happily familiar. He went over to the bed, sat down in the curve of Stephen's stomach, and caressed him, stroking gently up and down the inside of Stephen's thigh. "What are you thinking?" he asked gently.

"Just wishing none of this had happened," murmured Stephen, worming himself across the bed to fit his long, slim body round Richard's behind, and making a faint gurgling sound of appreciation at the caress. "And then..." he went on, "and then... I can't actually be sorry about anything that brought you back to me. Or me back to you. Whichever," he concluded, almost absently, dismissing the puzzle as too difficult to solve, or too trivial to be worth solving. "I'm terribly sorry about Graham," he went on after a long silence. "I don't think I shall ever stop mourning him. Seeing this place, and thinking what he could have done with it, has brought it all back home to me again. But I'm just as glad — in a way — that he was the means of bringing us back together. He... I... Oh, hell! You know what I mean, I expect."

Richard nodded. "I think so," he murmured, slipping out of his shirt.

They made love with all the old urgency, then again, languidly and peaceably. There was the usual horseplay in the shower. Richard burrowed in his holdall and jumped into the big glass cubicle brandishing a soap in the shape of an enormous, purple-tipped phallus. "Saw it in that sex-shop down by the Harp," he cried, jumping on Stephen and thrusting it energetically at his backside. Stephen yelped, swung round and pushed him off, eying the huge thing in alarm.

"You big coward," spluttered Richard, fondling the soap lasciviously. "Big strong boy like you wouldn't be worried by a little rapist like me, would you?"

"Only if he tried to escape," gasped Stephen. He hurled himself on him, wrestled the soap out of his grasp and did his best to stick the swollen, purple-red end into his mouth. Eventually they called it a draw, tidied up the shower cubicle and went downstairs to the bar laughing.

They chatted with Tom over a leisurely drink, then decided to have a look at the village. They strolled off, looking interestedly about them. The high street was an ordinary enough affair, with the usual shops and amenities of a large village in a prosperous area. Crooked streets ran off it to both sides, turning very quickly into narrow, twisting lanes between high walls of ancient dark red brick, ivy-covered and stained with the grime of time. They followed one such lane half a mile into open ploughland, then cut across the fields when they came on a green 'footpath' sign to the church and village centre.

Back in known territory, they slipped into the cool half-light of the fourteenth-century church, where they admired the font, the choir stalls and rood screen, and a young man in a cassock who came out of a door in a great hurry, stopped to say "Good afternoon" courteously, and then, his hurry, whatever it had been, forgotten, spent half an hour showing them over the church, of which he was clearly very proud.

Eventually he remembered his errand and said a hurried goodbye, blushing prettily as he hastened off down the long nave and out into the mild sunlight. "Yum yum," murmured Richard appreciatively, watching him until he was out of sight. "I could get religion in a place like this..."

"D'you think he'd ever shaved?" asked Stephen, gazing speculatively at the vast oaken door through which the young man had disappeared.

"Not for very long, if he has. D'you think he was wearing anything under that robe?" said Richard, rolling his eyes and letting his tongue loll out. And, seeing Stephen looking urgently about, "What's up?"

"Looking for a bucket of water," said Stephen laconically. "Ow," he added as Richard punched him hard in his ribs. "That hurt."

"Serves you right," said Richard, giggling. "For being po-faced."

"Well, what about you, then?" retorted Stephen indignantly. "Fancying clergymen. Under-age clergymen, too, for sure. You can probably go to prison for a hundred years for that."

"No," jeered Richard. "That's only the armed forces." "I bet you're not allowed to do it with someone in orders," said Stephen. "I bet there's some Act of Parliament — the Ecclesiastical Jurisdiction (Buggery with Parsons) Act, 1467, section 1: 'no person shall lust after the body of an ordained clergyman between the hours of Matins and Evensong, on pain of six hours in the stocks, castration with a rusty breadknife and a year's enforced subscription to the Jehovah's Witness's Gazette.' What do you think he would have been? Some sort of trainee vicar, I s'pose."

"Curate or something, I expect," said Richard vaguely. "Or a verger, maybe."

"Yes, that'll be it," agreed Stephen. "Actually, I'm on the verge myself," he added, trying to keep a straight face but in fact giving vent to an explosive giggle.

"Honestly," groaned Richard, "it's hopeless trying to take you anywhere. I mean, Christ, all the candles are likely to go out, or we'll get struck by lightning or something." His effort at keeping the laugh out of his voice was little better than Stephen's. They turned towards each other, and suddenly the intense quiet and the twilit atmosphere of the place got through to them. They quietened abruptly. Stephen took his friend in his arms in a firm, passionless embrace, resting his head against Richard's cheek.

They stood like that for some time, allowing the deep cool of the ancient stones to seep through them. It was Richard who broke the silence. "Don't leave me," he said in a small, scared voice, and Stephen was surprised, and a little chilled, at the deep fear that was clearly audible. While he was still trying to think of an adequate reply Richard spoke again, in the same voice, like a frightened child. "I couldn't bear it, Steve. I coped last time, because I knew it was going to happen. You remember I said to you that night, I knew you'd let your little blond bit of peaches and cream go without a memory when Mr. Someone Else came back to claim you? You remember I used to call him that back in those days, before I knew who he was?" Stephen nodded his head against Richard's cheek.

"You remember I said I'd find the right person?"

Stephen nodded again.

"Well, I wasn't being honest with you," went on Richard, twisting Stephen's fine dusty-blond hair anxiously in his fingers. "I knew I'd already found him. But I couldn't stand between you and him, you know. He'd been there first, he had prior claim. So I convinced myself that it was nothing but a short affair between you and me, that would be soon finished, and that I'd get over it. It didn't work," he finished with a gulp. "It nearly broke my heart that morning you walked away in the hotel in The Hague. Please don't make me go through that again. I... I couldn't stand it a second time."

Stephen stood for a long time without answering, holding him gently and motionlessly. Finally, he said, "I won't leave you. Not till you tell me to clear out."

"I... I'll never do that," said Richard in a whisper into his ear. "Do you know, I... no, I can't say that." "Say it," commanded Stephen in a whisper.

"No... no, I daren't..."

"Say it," he repeated, in a tone that brooked no refusal.

"When you... when I heard the news, about Graham, I mean... Do you know what the first thought that ran through my head was?" His voice had diminished until it was barely audible.

Stephen stood there for some moments. "I think I could make a fairly shrewd guess," he murmured. "But I don't hold it against you. I understand."

"I... I... I was glad," whispered Richard, with horror in his voice. "I was actually glad. I pushed it away, the same moment, but it was there. Just for that one instant, it was there. I was glad, I tell you. Glad he was out of the way, so I could fight to get you back and have you for my own. Isn't that the wickedest thing you ever heard in your life?"

"Richard, Richard," murmured Stephen, rocking him gently in his arms. "I know what you meant. I know you never held any grudge against Graham. I know you couldn't help feeling something like that go through you. I'd have felt exactly the same. And I know you didn't mean it. So will you now stop worrying about it? Please?"

"Okay," came a low, muffled murmur, and Stephen felt suddenly better. "But don't go away from me again, right?"

"Right," said Stephen, feeling at that moment a more profound love, a simpler affection than he had ever felt for his friend before. "I'm not going anywhere. You don't have a second chance very often, and I'd be the bloody fool of all time if I didn't jump at this one. You're stuck with me, old chap."

"Good," said Richard. He wriggled out of Stephen's arms and blew his nose vigorously. "Come on," he said, in almost his natural voice. "Let's carry on, shall we?" They left the church and stood for a moment, blinking in the contrasting bright light outside, before heading back down the rough track that led from the church front door to the village and the high street.

They wandered through the rest of the village, seeing what there was to be seen, and ended up at the small, bright cricket ground, tucked neatly between a lane of stockbrokers' cottages with apple trees leaning over the impeccably repaired fences on one side, and a huge farmhouse and its complex of outbuildings on the other. They examined the short, springy turf of the outfield, then strolled to the middle. "Bloody good nick," muttered Stephen approvingly, stooping and pressing a finger into the hard, firm track, mown so close as to be almost white in its lush green surround.

"Got somebody who knows what he's up to here." He trotted to the scuffed, piebald but beautifully remade area where one of the wickets had been pitched in a recent game, measured out his short, casual run-up, and hopped in to bowl an imaginary off-break. Then they moved on to look at the pavilion. It was small but immaculate, gleaming in very fresh white paint. So were the sightscreens at each end, they noted, the person responsible for running the club rising rapidly in their estimation with each new revelation of competence and devotion.

"Know what I smell here?" said Stephen, shading his face and peering through the big armoured glass window in an attempt to see the interior of the pavilion.

"Money," suggested Richard.

"Quite right. But there's something else, too. There's somebody here who loves this club. And knows what he's doing, too."

"Very kind of you to say so," said a voice. They both jumped almost clear of the ground in their surprise. A moment later the owner of the voice appeared round the corner of the pavilion wheeling an old-fashioned wooden wheelbarrow laden with sacks of loam and marl, tools and a besom of whippy birch twigs.

He was lean and very tall, with a creased face burned dark even in the early spring by exposure to wind and daylight. His hair was grey, but he looked formidably fit. He could have been any age from forty to seventy-five. He set the barrow down and looked down on the two boys curiously. "I take it you're cricketers," he observed. "Judging by the comments you were kind enough to make." He said no more, content to wait for them to reply.

"We are," said Stephen, who had to look up at the man despite his own six feet plus. "New in the district. Tom at the Crown told us about the club. We were just having a look round. I..." He hesitated. "I hope we weren't being a nuisance," he said a bit lamely. "We haven't been anywhere we shouldn't. Only had a quick glance at the table."

"And welcome," said the man. His voice was a curious mixture of educated and rural burr. Richard found himself thinking of Bernard Miles. "Once I heard what you were saying I wasn't worrying about you. Only we have occasional bits of trouble with some of the youngsters." He surveyed them again, then stuck out a huge, thin hand at Richard, who happened to be nearer. Richard took it, and promptly winced at the bone-crushing grip the man gave it. Stephen did the same a moment later.

"Brett," barked the man in his strange voice. "Everybody calls me Alfie." The boys introduced themselves. "Found the Crown, have you?," said Alfie. "You'll be comfortable there. Knows how to run an inn, Tom." They looked at each other unconsciously. The faintly archaic usage sounded perfectly natural in Alfie Brett's mouth. He lifted the barrow and moved easily towards the table. They ambled along beside him in a comfortable silence. Politeness or reserve had kept the question unspoken, but they were both aware of it, hovering in the mild, crisp air between them. Both were wondering if they should give some account of themselves. He solved the problem for them as he reached the wicket at the pavilion end and set the barrow down gently, off the mown square.

"You'll be the young owners that turned up out of the blue, I suppose?" he said, and smiled faintly at the twin looks of surprise that appeared simultaneously on their faces. "You don't keep many secrets for very long round here." His smile broadened as he proceeded to explain. "Young Blundell was in for a half-pint earlier this morning, and Tom was saying about how his employer had turned up as large as life, and how he looked like..." He stopped speaking, and the smile widened still further into a grin.

"How he looked like a schoolboy?" hazarded Stephen, with a faintly whimsical edition of the same smile.

"Ah, that's roughly the size of it," assented Alfie. "But he allowed you were pleasant, polite lads. Took him by surprise, of course. He's been running the inn according to his own ideas for a good many years now, and it came as a bit of a shock to have his absentee landlord turn up, and have to wonder if he was old enough to be served in the bar to begin with." He laughed softly. "Still, he said you seemed to like the way he's handled the place. He's well-liked in the village," he added apparently casually, but watching them closely as he said it. They looked gratefully at him, appreciating the delicacy with which he had offered them a hint. Alfie, who missed little, saw the appreciation, and acknowledged it in his turn with a curiously gracious nod and a half-bow. Then he laughed softly again, and set about some delicate repair work to a badly damaged patch of the crease where some bowler's front foot had created a miniature dust-bowl. They watched him working, his long, bony fingers as gentle as a surgeon's with trowel and miniature fork, soil and seed.

They kept him company for better than an hour, much of it in silent admiration of the skill and care with which he went about his work, sometimes picking up titbits of the life of the village, and telling him a little about themselves. At length he announced that he was finished for the day. They kept him company while he replaced the tools in an impregnable-looking extension at the back of the pavilion. They walked back across the field towards the cottages in the lane behind the far sightscreen, and there Alfie took his leave of them. "I live in the last house," he said, gesturing up to where the cottages, and the lane, petered out. "Last one that hasn't been bought up by townsmen," he murmured.

The boys ventured a question. "Me?" he said softly. "I was born here. Born, bred, and lived here most of my life. I've seen this village change, I can tell you. But I'm not going to," he added, and his smile was bright with intelligence. "I'm not that kind of ancient-leaning-on-a-scythe village bore, as I'm sure you're relieved to hear." He chuckled.

"Have you... er... been here very long?" asked Richard, curious to know how old the man was.

"You mean how old am I, but you're too well-mannered to ask direct, don't you?" said Alfie in his disconcerting way. Richard blushed, and he laughed again. "I'm seventy-two next birthday." He chuckled again at the expressions of surprise on their faces. "Aye," he went on. "And still turn my arm over for the first XI, and score my five hundred runs a season. Used to be a thousand every year, but I'm a bit short of wind for the quick singles these days. Like to take my runs in fours as far as I can nowadays. You'll see me about, if you're planning to spend much time here. I dare say you'll turn out for us from time to time?"

Stephen assented brightly. Alfie looked at Richard. "Not play yourself?" he asked.

"Scorer," said Richard, blushing for no reason that he could have explained. "I'm no good at games of any sort."

"But he keeps a beautiful neat book," put in Stephen, not wanting his friend to go unacknowledged. The old man looked down on them from his great height, saw the small gesture of loyalty for what it was, and did it the honour of a friendly smile. Then he said an abrupt farewell, turned and strode off towards his cottage, his long, bony arms swinging vigorously by his sides. On their way back to the Crown the boys said little, each being occupied with his own thoughts.

That evening they met a number of the cricket club, who gave them the undemonstrative welcome that is the hallmark of the freemasonry of cricketers all over the world. The boys left them for a while to drink with Tom at the bar while they held their short selection meeting; and their welcome became markedly more effusive after they had extracted a brief summary of Stephen's playing form from Richard while Stephen was paying a visit to the gents'. Just before the end of the evening Stephen broached the matter that was uppermost in his mind. "The main reason we came down," he began, "was to see if there was any chance of fixing up a short tour round these parts at short notice." He explained the difficulty that had arisen over John in Malton.

The local players looked interrogatively at each other. Scraps of paper were produced, and questions fired back and forth among themselves, at the boys and into mid-air. After a lot of scribbling, crossing-out and semi-coded discussion the captain of the local First XI looked up at them over his glasses and said "I think we could rustle up five games for you, if you like." They looked at each other in triumph. "That'd be great," said Stephen, elated, and dashed off to the bar to buy a round.

When he returned with the drinks on a tray he found them busily reducing the mass of bits of paper to a single sheet with lists of names. "We're okay, so that's one game you've got, for certain," announced the captain, chewing his pencil. "If any of the other possibles can't get a side up, we could put up a pretty good President's XI, as well. That's two certainties. I play for Brighton Brunswick occasionally, and I'm sure I can roust out a goodish side for you there. They're good drinkers, too. Worthing'll turn out, no sweat. That's four. I can talk to a few people in Portsmouth..."

"I could talk to some people at Southampton Uni," contributed another of the players. "I played for them in the UAU till the year before last."

"Right," murmured the captain, alternately gnawing and scribbling. "What about the duchess?" he added, glancing up at another of his team. "You know the estate manager, don't you, Les?" The other man nodded and jotted a note in a small pocket diary. "Duchess of Norfolk," added the captain by way of explanation. "Up at Arundel — only five minutes up the road. They might put out a side from the estate for you."

The talk went on, with Stephen and Richard getting more and more enthusiastic, as well as slightly drunk, until Tom came hovering and asked if they wished to continue behind closed doors, the while delicately making it apparent that he would prefer to close. "Okay, Tom," said the captain in mock annoyance, defusing it at the same time with a wry grin. "We'll let you get to bed. Anyway, Steve, you can tell your people they've got a certain four fixtures more or less when they want, and probably five. That do you?"

The two thanked him and the others brightly, and they said their goodnights amid general satisfaction. "We've got a touring side next Tuesday," said the captain as the cricketers were moving off gradually towards the door. "Monday, Wednesday and Friday as well, as a matter of fact. More than half our matches are in mid-week," he added in explanation. "Holiday area. Point is, we're a bit short on Tuesday, I happen to know. Wouldn't like to turn out for us, would you?" he went on, looking at Stephen. "Good," he added, seeing the answer in Stephen's face before he had opened his mouth. "I'll bung you down. Scorer too?" he asked, glancing at Richard, who nodded and smiled. "Right," repeated the captain, busily jotting in his diary. "Leave a phone number with Tom, eh? Case it rains, or whatever, okay? Numbers, I should have said," he added, just a fraction too hastily, and Richard, who had had less to drink than Stephen and was a little more alert, observed a rapid sequence of glances being exchanged among the local team. Stephen, who had noticed nothing, was assuring him that they would leave a number, however, and he left it at that. Since it always takes a cricket team — or even half a cricket team — a minimum of a quarter of an hour to pass from the inside of a pub door to the outside (though a great deal less going the other way), it was almost midnight when they finally called goodnights to Tom and went rather unsteadily upstairs.

* * *

The drive back the following morning was uneventful, but they were both feeling very pleased with their day's work. Richard occasionally felt a momentary frisson of unease when he thought about the small current he had sensed at the end of the night; but he quickly marked it as nothing more than the kind of curiosity that they were quite used to at their own club, and by the time he eased his mother's car into its slot in the garage he had dismissed it from his mind.

The next day was Saturday, and they had an 11.30 start at

their own ground. Stephen disappointingly ran himself out before he had scored, but made amends by capturing four wickets, including a tenacious opening batsman who occupied the crease in the manner of Trevor Bailey, and a ferocious hitter of the ball who replaced him. He also held a fine catch low down to his left at cover point, so he ended his day in a pleasant glow of satisfaction that was enhanced by the knowledge, which he and Richard had been hugging jealousy to themselves all day, of the news they had for Bill after the game.

The match ended in a nerve-racking draw, with the visitors scrambling byes to the slips in a desperate effort to pinch the last half a dozen runs for an improbable victory, and Elderton Park hurling caution to the winds as they tried everything possible, and quite a lot that wasn't, to take the last wicket. In the pavilion afterwards Stephen buttonholed Bill and took him aside to an unfrequented corner of the long bar. "I've got some news," he said, waving frantically to Richard to join them.

"What's up then, Biggsy?" asked Bill, half-turning to get their glasses refilled.

"It's the tour," said Stephen triumphantly. "I think I've fixed us up with a replacement, if you're really going to go ahead and cancel Yorkshire."

Bill stared at him. "Replacement?" he said blankly. "You've fixed up... How d'you mean, you've fixed up a replacement?"

They told him excitedly, Richard coming to Stephen's aid when he got carried away by his own cleverness and adding small explanatory footnotes to the confused narrative.

At length Bill thought he had unravelled the tale and made some kind of sense out of it. "Let me see if I've got it straight," he said, brushing beer off his big moustache and bawling to the steward for refills. "You've been down to Sussex-by-the-Sea this week, stayed at a hotel where the local cricket team have their selection meetings, and fixed up five matches for us if we want them. That's right so far, ain't it?" They nodded.

"Okay," Bill went on. "Well, it was a very kind thought, Steve, and I don't say we can't do something about it. But let me have more details. For a start, I'm curious about how you know this place. You go on holidays there, or summat?"

"No," said Stephen, straining to keep a straight face and repress the bubbling surge of internal laughter that was seething to burst from him. "I'd never been there till the day before yesterday.

But I went down to have a look at the hotel, and the rest of it just, sort of, happened."

Bill still looked puzzled. "But why should you go down 'just to have a look at a hotel' in a place you've never been to before?" he asked.

"I own it," said Stephen quietly.

Bill's involuntary intake of breath was so vast and so rapid that he inhaled a large quantity of lager, promptly choked on it and had to be thumped on the back to get it all up out of his windpipe again before they could go on. "You — ach-wah-prrrrp — you own it?" he spluttered, scarlet in the face and gazing at Stephen through streaming eyes. "What? This hotel? What are you givin me?"

"No, honestly, he does," put in Richard, pounding Bill on the back again as he hawked and spluttered once more.

"Graham left it to me," said Stephen quietly, his own fit of exuberance safely under control now. Bill gradually regained his composure. The flush ebbed out of his face and his eyes stopped watering. "Now come on, lads," he said, glancing round to see that no one was taking any special notice of them. "Just run it by me once again, so I know I've got it right." Eventually, after many steadying gestures and occasional questions from Bill, they managed to explain the sudden and dramatic change in Stephen's fortunes. When they had finished Bill gazed at him in some amazement. "So Graham suddenly became a millionaire," he ruminated, "and then never had time to enjoy it... Poor sod. And now you've inherited, and you're the rich man of the club, eh?"

"Something like that," assented Stephen, absurdly pleased at Bill's way of putting it.

"What's it like in that part of the world?" went on Bill. "All old fogeys — 'Disgusted of Tunbridge Wells' an all that, I s'pose?"

"Well, Tom — that's the manager of the hotel — says it's the Costa Geriatrica," ventured Stephen.

"Aye, I can imagine," grinned Bill. "All authoresses in tweeds lookin like Margaret Rutherford, an retired officers. Lieutenant-Commander Rottem-Soxe, RN (retired), eh?"

"Something like that," they agreed, grinning.

"Well," said Bill. "I don't see any good reason why we shouldn't give it a go. It's a nice part of the world, and by the sound of it your boozer's a bit of all right. You really are serious?" he added, looking a little doubtfully at Stephen. Stephen nodded and assured him eagerly that he was. "Well, okey-dokey, then," said Bill. "I'll talk to some of the others, and the Tour Committee, and then maybe we'll put it up to the full club Committee. But it's very generous of you, our kid. I mean that. Thanks." It was an apparently perfunctory expression of gratitude, but it was all Stephen needed; and he said far more in the way he ruffled Stephen's hair, and in the smile he gave both boys before lumbering across to some of the other seniors to consult them about the unexpected development.

Stephen and Richard wandered off and joined some of the youngsters in a lively replay of the final overs of the match. It was a couple of hours later when Bill found them playing killer on the dartboard with half the side. "Well, our kid," he said. "Your idea seems to be pretty popular. We're calling an extraordinary committee meeting for Monday night to discuss it. Meanwhile, you'd better call Rottem-Soxe an tell him it's firmin up, okay, Stevie? Then he can start puttin the first few ideas in train."

"Your wish is my command, O king," said Stephen, and went back to the darts match feeling as happy as he had felt since Graham died.

9

Over the next few weeks the two of them spent their weekends at cricket and most of their weekdays in Sussex. Richard's parents came back bright and faintly tanned from their holiday, and had to be taken to the Crown for a welcome-home dinner with champagne. The boys quickly made themselves popular with the younger element in the village. This was in part because the cricket club took to them whole-heartedly. Stephen made a fairly vast difference to the playing prowess of the local side. Richard scored for the club, and both of them made great efforts to avoid giving any impression of being pushy outsiders. They did their utmost not to rock any long-serving local boats or to put any local noses out of joint. Both felt their way into the local atmosphere gently, almost gingerly. Stephen made a conspicuous point of being a model player, accepting his captain's instructions without question, and never succumbed to the temptation to make reference to the considerably grander standard of cricket to which he was accustomed at weekends.

There was a great day at Elderton Park when Bill drew the boys aside and informed them that Stephen's name had been mentioned as a possibility for the Hertfordshire side in the Minor Counties Championship later that season. Down in Sussex the following week it was Richard who let the fact slip in conversation, in passing, almost absent-mindedly, and this did Stephen a great deal of good among the players, who crowded round him and demanded to know why he had been hiding his newly-enhanced light under a bushel, while all the time thoroughly approving the fact that he had done so.

Their popularity in the village flowed also from the fact that the Crown was the only public house, and as such featured strongly as the main social centre for the village. The fact that they used the pub as ordinary customers, treated it, its traditions, and the staff and customers alike with the greatest respect, meant much to the villagers, and the related fact that they studiously allowed, even encouraged, Tom to continue to run it as he had always run it counted for still more.

One night they were lounging in the bar, idly watching Tom cleaning up before sitting with them for their by-now customary after-hours drink with him. "I s'pose they all know we're gay, don't they?" said Stephen out of the blue. He spoke casually, more for something to say than anything else. They always stayed in the same room together, they were inseparable, neither of them was ever seen with a girl or heard to mention girls, generally or specifically, and in all they had become so accustomed to their relationship attracting no untoward interest that either of them would have been astonished to discover that it was the cause of any comment at all.

"Oh, yes," said Tom absently, wrestling with a gas-bottle nozzle that had developed a fault in the course of the evening. "Most of em assumed that from the first coupla times you stayed here after the selection meeting. Always goin upstairs together and so on. Never talking about girls. Oh yes. People aren't blind, you know."

"But no one's bothered about it?" said Stephen, more alertly. He had sensed, rather than heard, a note he didn't quite like in Tom's voice — or, at any rate, he thought he had. He raised his eyes at Richard, who gave him an almost imperceptible nod, indicating that he thought so too. He was looking faintly perturbed, and Stephen, who had a profound respect for his friend's acuity, straightened up and began to take more interest in Tom's reply.

In fact, Tom said nothing at all until he had persuaded the gas nozzle to behave itself. Then he straightened up; but his eyes remained firmly directed at his hands as he rubbed them briskly together to remove the grime he had gathered in his exertions with the fitting. At length he examined his hands a last time, assured himself that they were clean again, and, rather reluctantly, they thought, looked once more in their direction.

"It's... it's like this," he said slowly and, they both thought, a little uncomfortably. "Amongst the youngsters, you're all right. There's no problem there. Sure they know about you, and they don't care. They think, most of em at any rate, that it's your business and no one else's, and that what you get up to in your room at nights has nothing to do with anyone or anything else. That goes for most of em, as I say. Most of the others, the older ones, well, they may not approve, as such, but they'll turn a blind eye rather than make a fuss about it, I think, as long as you leave things much as they are. You've made yourselves pleasant, in fact you've gone out of your way to make yourselves agreeable. You haven't come sweeping in here making a lot of changes for the sake of the thing, as most of the older ones, at least, feared you would. It's just..." He tailed off unhappily. "It's just one or two of them," he went on. "One or two that have got some sort of... of thing about... er... your sort..."

"Like who?" said Stephen, bridling.

Tom shifted awkwardly. "The Major, I suppose?" murmured Richard gently, feeling rather sorry for Tom, who had always made it abundantly clear that he liked and accepted them completely.

"No," said Tom quickly. "No, oddly enough, the Major's one of your supporters. He's seen it all before, he's said, more than once. In the army, I imagine. No, the old Major's on your side. He's often put in a tactful word when... when... people have said the odd thing, you know. He's tried to take the wind out of their sails."

"Who, then?" demanded Stephen, a steely note creeping into his voice. Richard put a hand softly on his forearm, shaking his head slightly. "Give him a chance," he murmured, so softly that even Stephen only barely heard the words.

"Do you really want me to say?" asked Tom, looking steadily at Stephen.

"Yes," said Stephen, and it came out almost as a snap. "No," said Richard softly at the same moment. Stephen rounded on him, his eyes wide in surprise to find opposition coming from such an unexpected quarter. "Don't we?" he said, very puzzled.

"Richard's right, if you want my opinion," said Tom. "If I tell you — and I will, if you do, really, want me to, it'll make for unpleasantness, without doing any good."

"I only want to know who thinks he's got the right to dictate to me about my private life," rumbled Stephen. "I shan't go hitting him on the nose or anything."

"No, I know you won't do anything like that," agreed Tom. "But you wouldn't be able to keep your feelings to yourself, Steve. I know you pretty well by this time, and you must know yourself, too. You know you're not the kind to have that kind of information and not say anything. Next time the people concerned come into the bar, you'll be on the attack, giving em opportunities to say something, and then you'll tear into em, and there'll be a thoroughly unpleasant scene, which will probably end in them stamping out and not coming back, losing us trade and making waves in the village that we can well do without..."

He paused, choosing his next words carefully, then continued. "I wouldn't have anything to say about this, except for the fact that no actual good would come of it. The people I'm thinking of aren't the kind to come round with argument or persuasion. You wouldn't make them think any differently. All you'd do would be to... what's the bloody word? Polarise, that's it. You'd polarise the feeling in the village, very probably stirring up much worse trouble for yourselves in the process. Several of the ones who're more or less on your side might well change over to the opposition if they thought you were trying to ride roughshod over the feelings of people who live here."

"Huh!" snorted Stephen, getting angry. "It's okay for them to ride roughshod over our feelings, then, is it? But I'm not to utter a word of retaliation, in case I hurt their tender feelings. Is that it?"

"No, Steve," said Tom, still speaking carefully. "No, it's not that at all. It's that — this is only my personal opinion, you understand, but you asked me to speak — it's that all you'd get out of it would be the self-satisfaction of telling these people what you thought of them. You won't actually get any good out of it. And even the satisfaction would be pretty short-lived, if I'm any sort of a guesser. Because they'd simply up and go to another pub for their drinks, taking others with them more than likely. There would be a nasty smell, and some of the unpleasantness would spill over into areas where you've got no problems at the moment — like the cricket club, for example. See what I mean?"

Stephen didn't, but Richard did. "Stevie's not the sort to offer the soft answer that turneth away wrath," he put in gently, with an affectionate glance at Stephen. "He prefers the old-fashioned direct method. 'Fuck you and the horse you rode in on', and all that. But in this case, Stevie, I think Tom's right. There's no earthly point in stirring up a hornets' nest unless there's any actual advantage or benefit going to come from it. In this case, you'll just cause a row, which no one can win, and that's all."

Tom nodded, looking earnestly and seriously at Stephen. "That's my feeling, as I've said," he said quietly.

Stephen looked from one of them to the other in some frustration. Then he saw Richard's light-brown eyes fixed on him, widened slightly in concern and anxiety, and his face softened abruptly. "All right," he said, and chuckled. Richard breathed a deep sigh of relief, and the tension ebbed out of Tom's face also. "All right," Stephen repeated, "I'll be good. But if I promise — to both of you, cross my heart and hope to die and all that — that I won't go storming into these people, will you at least tell me who they are? After all, I may not go and hit em on the nose, but at least I'd like to feel sure I'm not wasting friendly overtures, or betraying confidences, to people who are my enemies. Surely that's reasonable, isn't it?

"Fair enough," said Richard. "But promise me — promise, Stevie, promise me — that you'll keep your hair on, and not go chucking em out of the pub, or putting acid in their beer or something."

Stephen laughed, a proper, full-bodied laugh this time, and all three of them relaxed. "All right, Rich, I promise," he said, still laughing. "Though I must say, I reckon you'd be better at scotching em than I would anyway. I'd never have thought of putting dope in their drinks. Sugar in their petrol tanks is more my line."

"Okay," said Richard. "Who are these nasty bastards, then, Tom?"

"It's mostly one man," said Tom, still rather reluctantly. "Pat Gibson. He never lets a chance get past him without declaring that it's a disease that ought to be cured, or some gibe about AIDS, or something of the kind. It's him and his circle of pals, mainly. Plus one or two of the yuppies. Right-wing types to a man. But they shouldn't worry people like you. They see life in primary colours, and you're too big to be bothered by people like that, I should hope."

"Mother Thatcher's chickens," grinned Richard, looking a shade anxiously at Stephen now that the names were out.

To his surprise Stephen's frowning face had cleared, and he was smiling. "Pat Gibson, eh?" he murmured, more to himself than to the other two. "Well, that's no big thing. I won't go to him if I need a tooth out, though, eh?"

"He wouldn't pull it," said Tom, grinning in his relief at seeing Stephen's own. "He's been saying how he's looking forward to having you knock on his door in agony with an abscess some night, and what a pleasure it'd be to tell you he wasn't going to risk catching AIDS if you bit down on his fingers. Loudly."

"When's that bastard ever say anything other than loudly," said Stephen with a chortle. "Oh, well, if it's only that crush that we've got to worry about, I'm quite relieved. I never did like that loud-mouthed cunt of a dentist, and as for the yuppies, well, as you say, they're not worth working up a sweat over. Maybe I'll just happen to leave my Labour Party card lying about some time. That'll annoy em. Still, thanks for telling us, Tom. It's as well to know who your enemies are. At least you know where you stand with your enemies. It's your friends you have to watch," he added cynically. "Come on, Tom, stop trying to polish the stamp off those glasses and come and have a drink."

* * *

Rather to Richard's surprise, Stephen faithfully observed his promise not to provoke trouble with the local dentist and his cronies. He did occasionally derive a malicious pleasure from stirring up argument over politics when the despised yuppies were in attendance, taking particular delight in dropping odd references into such conversations to the vast extent of his own wealth. On one such occasion he ostentatiously sent Tom down to the capacious and munificently stocked cellar for a bottle of the most expensive champagne in the house, paying for it by lugging a huge fat wad of twenty-pound notes out and tossing several of them carelessly on the bar, and then swigging it from the bottle in front of the astonished and outraged young city types. The tormenting was almost spoiled, because he was quivering so much from internal laughter and excitement that he almost squirted the wine straight back out of his nose; but he managed to contain himself sufficiently to set the bottle down, grin insolently round the glowering faces, and stroll unconcernedly outside before collapsing in convulsive paroxysms of laughter round the back of the hotel. Richard and Tom caught each other's eye and simultaneously shook their heads sadly. But Richard, at least, was having difficulty in concealing his own grin, and ceased trying when the infuriated young high-flyers stamped ungraciously out of the bar.

* * *

At last, one Sunday midway through a fine, sunny June, the great day arrived when Elderton Park were to arrive for their hastily rearranged tour.

Stephen and Richard had driven down very late the night before, after the league match on the Saturday, both in high spirits from anticipation, excitement at the prospect of showing off Stephen's splendid pub to such men as Bill McKechnie, who were dedicated drinkers but very discerning all the same about the quality of the pubs they favoured with their custom, and from Stephen's triumphant seventy-odd that day, batting at first wicket down, which he had, that season, made his own exclusive property.

They burst into the bar ten minutes before closing time, and Stephen, impetuous as always, talked ninety-nine to the dozen about the impending visit of his friends, and bought a round of drinks for everyone in the bar — having checked first and established that neither the local dentist and his circle nor the young City broking element were among those present. It was the start of a very happy week, with not the slightest foreshadowing of the calamity that was waiting to happen. The first chance steps towards accelerating catastrophe came, unseen, in the midst of the best fun of the week, and Stephen's greatest triumph.

* * *

Bill brought a strong side down on the Sunday morning, with almost all the regular First XI and a handful of close contenders. They all admired the hotel unequivocally and, having sorted out room-mates and made the acquaintance of Tom and some of the regulars, got the week under way in fine style with a hard-fought victory against a strong Worthing side. That evening they celebrated the start of the tour in the usual manner, wreaking great devastation on Tom's beer supplies until five in the morning. ("I'll have to ring round for extra deliveries first thing," he muttered to Stephen, watching the consumption in great satisfaction, and some awe.) Monday's game was against the local side, with Stephen playing for the village to strengthen the batting. The fine form he had shown all season did not desert him. He took three of his erstwhile teammates' wickets, including Don Parker's when he was well-set and looking very menacing on 49. He then led a valiant onslaught on the Elderton bowling in pursuit of a very stiff target of 284, scoring fluently all round the wicket for a very fine 81, and surviving all manner of sledging from his friends in the process. When he was out the village were within striking distance of the total, and they failed in the end by the narrowest of margins, the last wicket going down with the villagers eight runs short. He lost count of the jugs he had to buy in mock chagrin afterwards.

On Tuesday they had no fixture, so they consulted the local paper to find a cricket match within driving distance, then piled into cars and roared off to Brighton for the day. Tom's frantic efforts to secure extra deliveries paid off while they were watching cricket, and they accounted for a good deal of them in the evening.

On the Wednesday they enjoyed a fine win against a very strong Brighton Brunswick side, and were then cast into anxiety when the sky clouded over and a very heavy shower of rain fell for an hour and a half in the evening. The following day's game was the highlight of the week, against the President's impromptu XI. Stephen had eavesdropped assiduously and shamelessly at every opportunity, and had been able to warn them that the local club had taken the match very seriously. They had borrowed the cream of the surrounding clubs' players and assembled a tremendously powerful side, including four current Minor Counties players, two batsmen, a very quick opening bowler and a leg-spinner of prodigious gifts, who until two years before had regularly taken his hundred wickets for Sussex. It was the game of all games that they were anxious to play without interference by the weather.

Their apprehensions were unfounded, however. Thursday was a little overcast, but bright and warm, with enough of a breeze off the sea to keep the players cool.

The President's side batted first, and racked up what was, even on a small ground, the colossal score of 362 for seven. "Christ," said Bill as they sat in the dressing room after the declaration. "We'll have to go some for this. Only good thing is, they got em so bloody fast they've still left us time to get em. You'd better be anchorman, Don," he added to Don Parker, who was putting his pads on unconcernedly in his corner. "Need at least a hundred from you, mate." Don smiled easily. "Hundreds won't come easily against that attack," he said. "But I'll see what I can do." He pulled his cap on and strolled outside to accustom his eyes to the light. Bill meanwhile turned to Stephen. "Present for you, our kid," he said, tossing a large brown-paper bag across the dressing-room into Stephen's lap.

Stephen opened it curiously. His face broke into a wide smile of delight. Richard watched, wondering what it could be. Then he smiled, equally delighted for his beloved friend, as Stephen drew out a new cricket cap, bright in the club's colours. He stripped off the cellophane wrapping and unfolded the cap with fingers that trembled slightly. Then he jumped up and bounded across to the mirror to try it on, too pleased to speak.

"Hope it's the right size," said Bill, pleased at the happiness in Stephen's face. "Been intending to give you your colours since the first month of the season, but we had to order a new stock."

"Oh, Bill..." mumbled Stephen, still too overcome to say anything. He choked slightly as he went back to his seat to resume padding up. "Now's your chance to earn it, too," added Bill drily. "You won't have many better chances. You're first wicket down as usual. Play your own game, but be careful. Bloody careful. You won't have faced any bowling better than this in your life, so have a good look at it before you try anything fancy." Stephen nodded, his beam of gratification replaced instantly by an expression so serious as to be almost grim. "I... I shan't let you down, Bill," he said earnestly. "All right, son," said Bill. "I know you won't. Okay, lads," he went on to his team as a whole, "let's go for em."

It had never been more vital to get off to a good start. The spirits of the Elderton players, watching anxiously from the neat little pavilion enclosure, initially went up like a rocket. Paddington Bear, on whom words of caution were a sheer waste, propped himself on his bat to await the first delivery from the Minor County quick. It was a very fast half-volley outside off stump, and he let it go by, to a chorus of 'Well left!' and 'Steady, P-B' from the spectators. The second ball was on a better length, but wider. P-B stepped easily across to the pitch of it, and drove it effortlessly through square cover for four. The third ball was a big in-ducker, but started a shade too far over towards leg stump. P-B straightened up and flicked it high over where square-leg would have been, into the hedge for six. He blocked a bullet-like yorker, ran the fifth ball perfectly between third slip and gulley for four, and waited to see what the bowler, astonished and infuriated by turns at such cavalier treatment, would think up for the final ball of the over. It was the fastest ball so far, a fraction short of a length, dead straight on middle stump. P-B hit it on the up, clean over the pavilion for six more. The roar from his team-mates exploded while the ball was still airborne.

Don Parker played sedately through an accurate over from the much more ordinary opener at the other end, taking a comfortable two and thrashing the last ball handsomely through extra-cover for four, to another roar from the pavilion, where everyone was feeling much better already. Twenty-six for no wicket, and only two overs gone.

But alas for their dreams of effortless victories. Their spirits, having gone up like the rocket, within seven balls had come down again like the stick!

The crack fast bowler was a cricketer of great experience, and he had seen often enough what could happen to a bowling attack put to the sword by a batsman like Paddington Bear. For his second over he carefully re-paced his run, adding ten yards to it and pausing several times to turn and glare ferociously at Paddington Bear. Then he fiddled with his field, while P-B leaned on his bat handle and yawned ostentatiously. Then he came hurtling in, leapt like a salmon into his delivery stride — and bowled a high, slow-medium donkey drop, pitched up on middle stump. Paddington Bear's eyes widened as he watched the ball lolloping through the air towards him, unable to believe his luck. He stepped out to it and launched an on-drive at it that would have sent it in the wake of his last shot, over the pavilion. Unfortunately for him, it was a perfectly concealed leg-break. It turned the perfect amount to elude his ferocious drive, but not too much to miss the flashing blade altogether, flicked the outside edge and was swallowed without difficulty by the ecstatic wicket-keeper with a howl of "Yeeeee-haw! Beauty, Colin!" out of his mouth before he had even got the ball safely under control in his gloves.

There was a short, electric silence. P-B stood for a moment, all at sea outside his crease. He turned to look back at the jubilant wicket-keeper and slips. Then he turned back to stare at the bowler, and finally walked off, shaking his head in disbelief. He paused, however, as he drew level with the bowler, raised his bat to his shoulder and aimed it like a rifle at the grinning bowler. "You bugger," he murmured, and resumed his long walk back to the dressing room amid a chorus of "well batteds" elicited as much by his gesture of sportsmanship as by his batting itself.

Stephen walked out to the wicket feeling more nervous than he had ever felt since his first few games for the club. He was not normally a nervous player, but receiving his club cap, the feeling that he was on trial by both clubs, and the extraordinary performance that was needed to win, or even make the scores respectable, weighed heavily on him. Richard, who was scoring alone, sat in his wooden box, stroking himself in a vain effort to reduce the tension that gripped him and the anxiety for his friend to do well, and offered up a small prayer.

Don Parker came to meet Stephen and offered a word of advice to see himself well-settled before worrying about scoring. The advice was unnecessary, but it did have the valuable effect of calming his nerves a little. He took guard, and played out the rest of the over, delivered off the bowler's normal run, very fast but with little movement. And the first ball of the next over, disaster struck again. Don Parker, as reliable and safe a batsman as there was in amateur cricket, got a ball that hit a greasy spot and never got more than an inch above the turf. It skidded underneath his immaculate defensive stroke, and hit him squarely in front of all three stumps. He hardly bothered to look up to see the umpire's finger raised, walking off with his eyes closed in anguish. Stephen quaked, and waited.

There followed a scrappy period in which neither side gained any further advantage. And, somewhere in the course of it, Stephen made a momentous decision. He waited for a bad ball.

Watching from the pavilion, the others sat up and took notice. For several overs Stephen and his partner had played doggedly, fending off the good balls and ignoring anything that did not demand a stroke. Then, without any visible cause, Stephen changed his approach. He threw caution to the wind, and launched an onslaught that would have been worthy of Paddington Bear himself. The ace quick bowler, who was, perhaps, beginning to lose his freshness, sent down a fast half-volley on off stump. Stephen flayed it through extra-cover for four. He then gave four of the remaining five balls of the over the same treatment. The last ball he steered wide of gulley for a single.

From that point on he farmed the bowling assiduously. Wickets fell, but he remained, and the longer he stayed the fiercer his hitting became. He stopped showing the county bowler even a semblance of respect, and treated the assortment of stock bowlers brought on at the other end with lordly contempt. When twenty overs had been bowled the score stood at a miserable 48-2, with Stephen on 13, most of them grubbed. After thirty overs he and his partner had added eighty-six, of which Stephen had taken seventy-nine. After 31 he was on 99. The first ball of the 32nd over he flicked disdainfully off his legs through mid-wicket for four, and thus achieved his first century, for the club or for anyone. The entire fielding side applauded. In the pavilion his team-mates went to the lengths of putting down the cans they had thoughtfully brought from the Crown in order to give him a roaring ovation that lasted a full minute. In the scorebox, Richard wept.

After this, it was almost over. Having reached his hundred in a kind of trance of deadly concentration, he now stepped up both his scoring rate and the risks he was willing to take; and when he was finally bowled playing over the top of a long-hop from sheer tiredness, for 168, his side needed under a hundred to win. They got them without difficulty, the fielders being by now so leaden-footed from the leather-hunting they had endured that the run-rate if anything actually increased after Stephen's departure. As for Stephen himself, when he trailed into the enclosure, bone-weary but in a state of elation unlike anything he had known, Bill picked him clean off the ground, swung him round in a crushing bear-hug and planted a huge kiss on each cheek, Russian style, before charging off to find him a can of beer. The others pounded him on the back until his shoulders ached fiercely. Paddington Bear threatened to put bromide in his beer if he intended to try to steal his reputation in such cavalier fashion. And after sinking his first can without a pause, Stephen allowed someone to press another into his hand, then slipped away to the scorebox to dry Richard's eyes and be alone with his lover and his triumph, on the most glorious, joyful day of his life.

* * *

Back in the Crown a couple of hours later the celebrations were well advanced when a member of the President's XI, who had been in conversation for some time at the bar with Tom, threaded his way through the press and asked Richard if he might have a word somewhere quieter. Richard was a little surprised, wondering what the man could want to say to him in private, but he was quite glad to escape from the hubbub and the smoke for a few moments, so he followed the man outside to the car park.

"What can I do for you?" he asked.

"I'm a reporter," said the other man. "For the local paper in Brighton. I've been talking to the chap behind the bar, and he's told me a very surprising thing."

"Oh?" said Richard suspiciously. "What was that, then?"

"Don't get worried," said the journalist. "It's a story I think would be of interest locally. He said this pub's actually owned by the boy who got the hundred today. He also said that he's only nineteen or twenty. I think it would make a very interesting story locally. Maybe we could get up some sort of advertising feature to accompany it. But there's no need for that if he'd rather not. The story's interesting enough in its own right."

Richard stood in silence for a moment, thinking rapidly. "Why are you speaking to me?" he asked. "I'm not his keeper, you know."

"No," said the journalist, watching him closely. "But I thought I'd have a quiet word with you first, to see how you thought he might react to a suggestion. I understand you're a... very good friend of his."

"Well," said Richard slowly, mentally cursing Tom for a loquacious ass, and wondering how best to squash the man without merely arousing his interest further. "You can ask him, I suppose. But I don't think he'll be very interested in publicity. I'd better get back," he added, and turned to head back inside. The reporter moved quickly, however, and caught him by the arm. "If you're worried about the gay aspect of it, you've no need to," he said. Richard swung round on him, his eyes gleaming. "Don't lose your wool," urged the reporter quietly. "I'm gay myself, and I know he wouldn't want to make a splash about that round these parts. But I would like to do a straightforward story about his owning the pub, how he came to acquire such a place at his age. That sort of thing."

"As I said," muttered Richard, very angry indeed, "you'll have to ask him yourself. But I don't think he'll want a story." He turned away again, and this time went quickly back into the bar before the man could ask him anything further. The reporter, however, stood for some moments after he had disappeared, considering.

Inside Richard was fighting his way through a densely packed circle of players, in the middle of which Stephen, already slightly tipsy, was animatedly discussing the weaknesses of the current England Test squad. At last he managed to seize Stephen's elbow and signal frantically to him to come away for a moment. Stephen, mistaking his motives, smiled to himself and followed him through the door into the accommodation part of the hotel, still clutching his pint glass.

Richard breathed a deep gasp of relief when they got into their room. He sat down heavily on one of the beds and rapidly repeated his short conversation with the journalist. Stephen looked thoughtfully at him. "I don't know," he said. "I don't see what harm it can do, do you? Be good for the pub, anyway, wouldn't it? And I don't see how we can stop him writing his article if he wants to, can we?"

"I don't like it," said Richard, not quite knowing why his hackles were up as they were. "But I do know that that bloody idiot Tom's blabbed about us — being gay, I mean. This reporter said he was gay himself, so he wasn't planning to make anything of that side of it. But I don't like getting mixed up with newspapers. Once they get hold of something they never let it go, and there's no end of grief." "Well," said Stephen mildly, after thinking about it, "I can't very well refuse to talk to him. That'll only make him more curious. I'll talk to him if he really wants to, and try to make it so boring that he won't think it's worth reporting in the first place. If he insists, well, I'll tell him the bare minimum. Thanks for letting me know," he finished, putting an arm round Richard and kissing him fondly. Now come down and have a drink, my sweet." Richard, with deep misgivings, had little alternative, and went.

* * *

The last match of the tour was, almost inevitably, something of an anticlimax. Elderton Park made it five straight wins for the week, despatching Bognor Regis in convincing style. Bill and his men departed in the small hours of Saturday morning to get ready for their league match later the same day, feeling well satisfied with their impromptu substitute tour. Stephen and Richard went with them, in bubbling high spirits which effectively neutralised their hangovers.

* * *

The story appeared in the following weekend's edition of the local paper. It was bland enough, and the reporter had been conscientious enough to follow fairly closely what Stephen had told him. Stephen himself was very pleased to find, when Tom showed them the copy of the paper he had saved for them, that almost as much of its space was given over to the cricket week, and in particular to his century and a half. "Well, there's no harm in that, is there?" he said to Richard, reading it again in their room. "I hope not," muttered Richard, meaning it, but not yet convinced.

Stephen looked up from the paper and studied his friend closely. What he saw was enough to make him forget his absorption in the account of his epic innings, get up and lope over to Richard where he sat miserably tracing patterns with a forefinger on the counterpane of other bed. "What's up?" he asked.

For a long time Richard did not answer, sitting unhappily with his head hung low, staring at the carpet a yard in front of his feet. When he did finally reply it was in a low, hesitant voice. "I... I don't know," he faltered. "It's just that... oh, I don't know. It's just that there's something... something seems dishonest about it, that's all."

Stephen stared at him. Then he moved a little closer, and put an arm round Richard's shoulders. "I'm sorry, love," he said gently, "but I don't get. Who's been dishonest, and how? What about? It's all true, isn't it? He talks about my becoming the owner of the pub, and about the cricket match. Well, what in the world's wrong with that?"

Richard raised a troubled face to him, and Stephen was astonished to see that it was streaked with tears, and that his eyes were wet. "Richard," he said urgently. "Richard," he repeated, shaking him gently. "For Christ's sake, tell me what's biting you?"

Richard sat for a further long pause, collecting his thoughts, and Stephen had the sense to let him do so in silence. "I said it was dishonest," said Richard at length. "Not untrue. Dishonest. It doesn't say how you came to inherit the place from Graham, does it, for starters? There's no mention of Graham at all, not by name, anyway. That reporter took it on himself to assume that you wouldn't want publicity for the fact that you inherited it from a lover — a gay lover — and you let him go on assuming it. He assumed that you — or rather we — wouldn't want it talked about that we're gay, and you let him go right on assuming that, too, didn't you?"

Stephen gazed at him in mingled irritation and surprise. "Well, bugger me, we didn't want that publicised, did we?" he said.

"Why not?" snapped Richard. "It's the most newsworthy part of the whole story, isn't it? He's a professional newspaperman, and he's fallen down on his job, and he must know he has. You encouraged him to do so."

"But... but... Christ, Rich, you said yourself, you didn't want the bloody story to appear at all," said Stephen. His voice rose to a squawk of baffled frustration at his inability to follow his friend's argument.

"No," said Richard, "I didn't. I don't want publicity from newspapers, ever. Not about anything. If I went over Niagara Falls on a tea-tray I wouldn't want the newspapers prying into it. If I won the fucking Nobel Peace Prize I wouldn't. But if they did, I wouldn't want them leaving half the bloody story out of it, just in case it upset a few reactionaries in a piddling Sussex village who still think it's the middle of the seventeenth century, and that people like us are some kind of perverts, or 'unnatural', or something." He flung Stephen's arm off his shoulders and threw himself facedown onto the pillow.

Stephen sat staring at him for a long time, with a mixture of bewilderment, confusion, hurt feelings and plain incomprehension making changing patterns in his eyes. When he spoke his voice was very gentle. "I'm sorry, old chap," he murmured. "I'd never realised you, er, felt so strongly about things. I mean, I'd never thought of you as a... as being militant like this. About being gay, I mean. Can you try and be a bit more specific? About what you really wanted, I mean?"

Richard sat up, glaring at him angrily. "I didn't want anything in particular," he said snappishly. "I didn't want that shit-mongering reporter poking his long nose into our affairs at all. But if he had to have his pound of flesh out of us, I'd have rather he had it blood and all. He's gay himself, he told us so. Yet he was the one who suggested that we should carefully suppress any mention of our being gay, and he did that to avoid adverse criticism of us from the people here. In other words, he was willing to go along with the hypocrisy and deceit that this report amounts to. Well, that's his affair. If he chooses to go uncle tomming to heterosexist, reactionary bastards, that's his problem, and I hope he chokes on it. But I'm damned if I see why we should be trapped into the same miserable hole-and-corner attitudes. Jesus," he spat, his face creased in distaste, "he did every bloody thing bar inventing girlfriends for us!"

Stephen sat and thought about it. "Hmmm. Yes," he mused. "I suppose I see what you mean. But surely," he went on, rallying, "surely it's not that important, is it? Aren't you making a bit of song and a dance about it? I mean, this" — he picked up the folded newspaper and brandished it under Richard's nose — "this'll all be forgotten in two days from now. Anyway, it's more about the cricket than about us — or rather, me." A thought occurred to him. Initially he thrust it from him in revulsion, like something unclean, loathing himself for being able to conceive of something so unworthy. But it kept on creeping round his defences, insidiously demanding to be made flesh by articulation, and at length he couldn't help himself. "You're not... I suppose this is nothing to do with the fact that you don't get a mention, is it, Richard? I mean, I would have liked him to have given us equal coverage, treat us as joint-owners, cos that's what we are. But..."

Richard sat up rigidly, staring at him in astonishment. A steely gleam came into his eyes, and he flushed angrily. "You can bloody well take that back, Stephen Hill," he snapped furiously, "or I'll walk out of here and not come back."

"Richard, Richard," gasped Stephen, deeply distressed. "For Jesus Christ's sake, be reasonable. Come down off that fiery pillar. I only meant..." He stopped, wondering exactly what he had meant. "I'm sorry, Rich," he said softly after an interval. "I do take it back. It was wrong, and I knew it even before I said it. Only... only, I couldn't work out what it was that you were so angry about..."

Richard scrutinised his face long and hard, looking for evasion. He saw nothing but anguished, puzzled concern, and after a moment his face softened. "Well, I'm sorry too," he said eventually. "I didn't mean to get so steamed up. You're right, I suppose. It will all be forgotten in a day or so. I just don't like seeing someone I love, and respect, and... and admire, sailing under false colours. That's you — but it's me too, by implication. I... I suppose I felt... oh, I don't know what I felt. I suppose I just felt that you'd let yourself get manoeuvred into a false position by that bloody man, and drawn me into it with you." The angry gleam died down in his eyes, and the bright red flush ebbed out of his face gradually. "Anyway," he conceded, "it's probably all a storm in a teacup. I'm just making a fuss about nothing. Must be my period coming or something," he added, and sketched a rather fragile, damp edition of his usual brilliant smile. Stephen's mind performed small somersaults of relief; but a calm, remote part of it still continued to worry away at the problem. He still had no real idea of what his friend had been so upset about. For the present, however, he was glad enough to see that the storm had blown itself out, and to accept the fact at face value. He gave Richard his brightest grin, swung his legs up onto the bed and pulled Richard gently down beside him.

10

It was a quiet Wednesday evening. Stephen and Richard had turned up to play for the village against one of the many touring sides who made up more than half the club's fixture list. The game had hardly got under way when it had been washed out beyond hope of salvation by a summer downpour which appeared from nowhere and left the entire ground first submerged and then, as the water soaked into the parched turf, blanketed with enormous hailstones the size of marbles. The players had waited about for an hour in the hope of salvaging something from the wreckage of their game, but the first cloudburst was followed by a series of short, torrential showers, and they had given up. By three o'clock they had had a miserable tea and trooped dismally down to the Crown, where they were dotted about in groups making the subdued, grimly cheerful conversation common to people trying to make believe that beer-drinking is an adequate substitute for a ruined cricket match.

Richard was ensconced with the Elderton Park scorebook and a calculator, behind an almost palpable barrier of solitary concentration, wrestling to get the seasonal batting and bowling averages up to date. Stephen was chatting in a corner to Major Sealey, a small, soft-spoken man with an upright bearing, a fine head of white hair and a military moustache, and keen, intelligent eyes undimmed by his seventy-odd years. Rather to the boys' surprise he had been one of the older regulars at the inn who had been notably unworried when their relationship had become known; indeed, as Tom had mentioned, he had from time to time made counter-balancing comments, soothing or acid as the mood took him, when Gibson the dentist and his cronies had been particularly unpleasant on the subject. In marked contrast, the Major had formed rather a soft spot for Stephen. Richard, whose eyes were very sharp, had more than once observed him watching Stephen with a measuring eye, and had speculated whether he was seeing him as the son he had never had — the Major was a widower, Tom had informed them, and childless — or as a bright young officer in his regiment. At all events, he was often to be seen, standing ramrod-straight, chatting to Stephen; and Stephen, who with all his faults was a naturally well-mannered and gracious boy, and responded very quickly to kindness, treated the old man with conspicuous and unaffected respect, like a favourite and indulgent grandfather.

"Would you mind if I asked you something, Major?" Stephen said on this occasion.

"Not at all, my boy," said the Major, who never abbreviated names whether their owners liked it or not and tended to an old-fashioned "my boy" with anyone under the age of forty-five.

"Well," said Stephen, "I hope it isn't rude of me to ask, but why do some people keep their military ranks and others not? I mean, why are you still Major Sealey? I know sev... well, a couple of other people who were in the army, and they're just plain Misters. I'm only asking because I'm curious," he added disarmingly, realising a little belatedly how it might have sounded. "I mean, I wasn't being..."

"Sarcastic," supplied the Major for him, putting him out of his misery. "No, I know you weren't. As to the answer, well, I don't really know. I think it's mostly a matter of habit. And of personal preference, I imagine. The army was my life, you know, for a very long time. When I retired I was so used to being Major Sealey that it seemed natural to carry on. People seemed happy to call me 'Major', and... there you have it. I imagine others, perhaps less happy than I was in the service, dropped their ranks and were glad to.

"Reminds me of a story I heard," he went on. "Supposed to be true. Witty, in any case. Some retired Colonel had a birthday, seventy-five or something of the sort, you know. Can't think why. Too dashed old for birthdays myself, my boy, but there it is. Anyway, his local rag decided to honour the old boy with a write-up — war-time exploits, that sort of rot. They duly sent a photographer round, and some kind of cub reporter, and he was very pleased with his picture, but a bit less pleased to see a misprint describing him as 'the battle-scared warrior'. He wrote to the editor to complain, and of course, they printed an apology in the next week's edition; trouble was, this time they still got it wrong. Said, 'This should, of course, have read *the bottle-scarred warrior*'. Haw-haw-haw! Damned funny, don't you think?"

He signalled to Tom, then turned back and gestured at Stephen's glass, still haw-hawing to himself at his little tale. "Let me get you a..." He stopped speaking, and gazed past Stephen in the direction of the door, his jaw dropping slightly. "Good gad!" he murmured. Stephen smiled involuntarily, as he always did when the Major produced one of his old-fashioned expressions. Then he turned to see what had brought the startled expression to the old man's face, and his own eyebrows rose in surprise.

The door had burst open, and Stephen was in time to see two new arrivals come in, huddling together under what looked like an old-fashioned policeman's cape, and hurrying to get out of yet another torrential shower of rain. They entered in a flurry of giggles and cries of how soaked they had managed to get in the short dash from the car park. There followed an uninhibited shedding of the cape, with an accompanying spray of drips, to the considerable outrage of those of the customers nearest the door, who happened to include the dentist Gibson and some of his friends.

"Sorry, sorry, sorry," trilled one of the newcomers, laughing merrily. He gaily tossed the soaking cape over the coat-stand behind the door. The cape was bright powder-blue. The one who had spoken was the smaller of the two, a bright, athletic-looking youth in his twenties. The other was taller, slim to the point of emaciation, and ten years older. The younger one had long brown hair tied in a pony tail, the older one very short blond curls, moulded and rigid in a heavy application of hair gel. And then there were the clothes. A dozen conversations were arrested. Glasses halted in mid-hoist all over the bar, and mouths opened to receive draughts of beer remained open in dumbfounded surprise. Stephen turned away, unable to suppress an involuntary grin. Gibson the dentist curled an eloquent lip, and sought out first Richard, then Stephen, and finally the Major, with a bright, sarcastic gaze.

The younger of the new arrivals was wearing a deep pink tee-shirt, stencilled with the words "I'm getting mine..." on the front and "...how about you?" on the back. Beneath it he was wearing a pair of very short and well-packed shorts. They were made of shiny scarlet satin, and tight enough, as Gibson was instantly heard to remark in a stage whisper audible across the bar, to show if he was Jewish or not. His friend had a pair of worn jeans, mottled light blue and white, cut off above the knees to convert them into Bermuda shorts, and a tee-shirt like the other one. His bore the legend "Muffin the Mule is not an offence..." on the front, and "It's just freedom of choice" on the back.

"Good gad!" repeated the Major. He saw Stephen's grin, and a faint smile dawned on his own features. Tom hovered. The Major collected himself and got his brandy and Stephen's lager. Tom took his money, brought his change, and then remained, looking at Stephen with an interrogative expression. Stephen, suddenly bubbling internally with mischief, affected not to see him, and turned back to the Major to resume conversation. Tom hovered uncertainly for a moment, then went towards the newcomers, who were waiting politely at the bar beside Gibson and his crowd near the door. On the way he sought out Richard and caught his eye, raising his eyebrows in a direct question. Richard hesitated, then shrugged and made a barely perceptible gesture in Stephen's direction. Tom glanced back, saw that Stephen was still busily not looking his way. He shrugged himself, and went to serve the two young men. The eloquent silence held for a second or two more, wavered, and ended as people got over their surprise. A moment later there was a buzz as conversations got under way again, everyone busily creating a frightfully British atmosphere of 'nothing out of the ordinary'.

"It's true, then," said the Major in his usual soft tones. Stephen raised his eyebrows interrogatively.

"There have been a few rumours about the place recently," elaborated the Major, seeing that he was waiting for an explanation.

"Rumours?" said Stephen. "What kind of rumours?"

"Rumours that this pub's beginning to become used as a... as a kind of meeting-place, I suppose you'd say," went on the Major, flicking a glance in the direction of the two newcomers. "For... people of that kind." He said it in a carefully neutral tone.

"People of my kind," said Stephen gently, smiling affectionately at the Major to make it clear that the remark was not meant as any kind of reproof.

"No, dammit," said the Major, managing to make it a snap

without raising his voice above a murmur. "I know about you and your young friend, but that's not the same thing at all. I won't have you making comparisons between decent lads like yourselves and... people like that. Good God! Look at their clothes, man. Walking around in satin bathing costumes and wearing indecent legends. I'm as broad-minded as the next man, Stephen. A good deal more so than a good many, I dare say. But I draw the line above displays like that." He clicked his tongue in annoyance. "This will play straight into the hands of Pat Gibson, don't you realise? I've never liked that bounder, and I've been having to defend you and your young friend in the face of his offensive remarks. This'll keep him in sneers for the rest of the summer." Stephen stood considering, the smile fading from his face. "What are these rumours you spoke of, Major?" he asked eventually. "I haven't seen anybody like that in here. Surely they were probably just passing and came in for a drink."

There had been little enough to go on to begin with, it seemed. Beginning a week or two ago, an unusual influx of new faces at the pub had been enough to cause comment. The village was a mile or so inland, far enough to keep it off the route of most of the holiday-making herds. The pub itself was tucked away off the only approach to a main road the village possessed, and passing trade was fairly uncommon even in the summer. Gradually it had been remarked that the newcomers were invariably male, usually in pairs. On one occasion someone had seen a couple of strangers leaving the pub late at night, and had the suspicion that he had observed them to exchange a quick embrace in their car. But it had been dark, and he hadn't wanted to appear inquisitive, so he couldn't be sure. But people had started to keep their eyes open. It had become noticeable that the unfamiliar arrivals tended to start to look faintly puzzled after they had been in the bar for a short while. Then they tended to drift away, still looking vaguely puzzled. And few, if any of them, it seemed, had been back for a second visit.

All this Stephen retailed to Richard in their usual room later that evening.

"But that's nothing for them to get paranoiac about, even here, surely," said Richard, with the beginnings of an angry glint in his eyes.

"Well, no," said Stephen. "And that's just what I said to the Major, too. He agreed. Or at least, he didn't. No, he didn't, really. He thought it was gays. But he didn't think there was anything wrong with these people coming in for a drink. Until this evening. And I mean to say... well, you saw those two, didn't you? He said he drew the line at people like them, and I must say... they were a bit much, weren't they?" he said, grinning at the memory.

"They're entitled to a drink," said Richard, "the same as anyone else. Aren't they?" he added, with an ominous set of his mouth.

"Yes, of course they are," said Stephen mildly, observing the change in Richard's expression and voice, and being careful not to tread heavily on sensitive areas. "But it was bloody funny, wasn't it?" He chuckled, not noticing the further setting of Richard's brows. "I mean, old Tom dithering about wondering whether to serve them or tell em to sod off. And the poor old Major practically had apoplexy for a minute there. Till he saw me grinning. Then he saw the funny side of it himself. And that prick of a dentist — well, I thought he was going to have a heart attack. Then I thought maybe he was going to come and have a go at me, but I think he's a bit frightened of the Major. And everything going quiet like that. The funniest thing of all was that they didn't seem to have the slightest idea of the stir they were causing." He chuckled again.

"They knew, all right," said Richard quietly, after a long pause in which he let Stephen's chuckle die slowly for want of support. "Oh?" queried Stephen, alerted to something in Richard's tone and sitting up and taking notice, so to speak. "How d'you know that?"

"Because I went out after them when they cleared off, though you may not have noticed," said Richard, still speaking ominously quietly.

Stephen stared at him in surprise. "Oh?" he said. "No, I didn't notice. What did you do that for?"

"To apologise, first of all," said Richard. "And secondly, to see if I could find out what was at the bottom of it. I did, too."

Stephen stared at him. "To apologise?" he repeated stupidly. "What did you want to apologise for? What was there to apologise for? And what do you mean about finding out what's at the bottom of it? At the bottom of what? I'm getting confused."

"You've got your reporter friend to thank for all this, I think," said Richard, looking at Stephen in some annoyance. Stephen stared at him, and said nothing.

"I went out," said Richard, "to tell those two how sorry I was that they'd got the kind of reception they did — you know, the electric silence, the cold shoulder, being frozen out, Tom not knowing whether to serve them or not, as you said. All that. I saw how puzzled they looked as they left, and I thought they were owed that much courtesy. It was the only bit they got, wasn't it? They were very glad to be able to ask someone what the score was. They had realised what kind of a stir they'd caused, and it had worried them — a lot. They'd thought, you see, that they were visiting a new gay pub in the area. They'd been looking forward to it. When they saw your precious Major and all the others like him, and heard that smug, vicious bastard Gibson making his clever remarks, they realised they'd dropped something of a bollock, and it came as a bit of a shock, I can tell you."

"New gay pub?" repeated Stephen. "Good God. But why in Christ's name did they think that?"

"That's what I asked them," said Richard. "Somebody has very kindly instructed the very large gay community in Brighton that the Crown Hotel is a pleasant country pub where gay people can be assured of a friendly welcome, owing to the fact that it's now in the hands of a young gay couple. Namely, viz and to wit, us. It'll probably be in the directory in the back of *Gay Times* next month," he added, giving Stephen an oddly quizzical look. "Who else can you think of who might have A, known we're gay, B, known that we — sorry, I should have said you — own this pub, and C, known the gay community in Brighton to talk to about it?"

Stephen sat thinking about it in some perplexity for a while. "Well," he said at length, "I don't really see what harm it can do. I don't mind if a few gay people start using the pub. Do you? Come to that," he went on, "you've been in a funny sort of mood since we came up. Are you uptight about this? And if you are, why? What harm can it do?"

"I'm not uptight," retorted Richard. "But I'm none too happy about the way things are going here. I didn't want to get involved with that bloody newspaperman at all in the first place, simply because I don't trust a reporter — any reporter. But there wasn't a lot we could do about it, once that bloody Tom had talked. As it is, what he's done, in one way at least, is to turn this place into a gay pub. Well, that's all very well in its own way. But it's going to cause all sorts of grief and aggravation, isn't it?

"Well, okay. I can put up with that. But I'd much rather it had stayed relaxed as it was. Since it isn't, I say gay people have got as much right as anyone to come here. And to wear what they like, as well. And I've got the strong feeling that it's precisely that part of it that you don't like. I saw you grinning like a cat with the Major when those two came in, and I wasn't very impressed."

"I don't like that sort — camp ones, I mean," protested Stephen. "But in any case, Rich, I don't understand the point you're trying to make. I mean," he elucidated, seeing that Richard was waiting for further enlightenment, "surely, if you think gays have got the right to come here, if you feel so strongly about it, well, why that reporter's done just what you'd have wanted, hasn't he?"

"No," said Richard in a hard, sharp voice. "He's got the gays coming here. And he's got me a lot of explanation to do, too. That's what I resent: the strong likelihood of my having to fight on their behalf — even if I don't particularly want to."

"I don't understand you lately," said Stephen mildly. "I don't see why you've got to fight on anybody's behalf."

Richard breathed hard, fighting a losing battle with the impatience that sometimes overtook him when Stephen seemed to be wilfully misunderstanding things. "Listen," he said in concentrated tones. "If nothing whatever had been said, I wouldn't have gone on a crusade demanding the right of gay people, including high-camp ones who look like Quentin Crisp, to come drinking in this outpost of the British Raj. I'm not like some people, wanting to take on all the problems of the entire gay community, or the entire world, for that matter. But since something has been said, I'm not going to stand by and see my own kind — people like us, Stevie — insulted and jeered at. Not in my presence, anyway."

"But Rich," said Stephen, in a meek voice containing only the mildest undertone of protest. "Rich, my lovely, there's no earthly reason why you should have to fight any battles, over gays visiting the place or anything else."

"Oh yes, there is. Good God, man, you saw what happened when those two came in this evening."

"I know that, love," said Stephen with a faint sigh. "But I can squelch that kind of demonstration if I want to, can't I? Without the need for you to get involved in fights and rows about it."

"How?" challenged Richard.

"I own the place," said Stephen flatly. Richard stared at him. "If I decide I want to allow people in this pub," continued Stephen, speaking very calmly and deliberately, "I'll do so. I'll inform Tom, and he can inform the customers. Or not, as he thinks fit. If I want to restrict entry to this pub," he went on, warming to his theme, "to one-legged limbo dancers below the height of four feet seven inches, I can do that. If I decide that to gain admittance you have to come wearing a yellow suit with black polka dots and carrying a big red flag, I can fucking well do that, too. With one brief word in Tom's ear, or a notice on a scrap of paper pinned to the door. And if all the inhabitants of this village decide they don't like it, they can do the other thing. It's known as private enterprise. I own the place, so I can be as enterprising as I like. Or as unenterprising.

"I don't particularly want to upset the village. I like it here, and I like the people — most of them, anyway. I like the cricketers, and the old Major, and Tom, though I wish he'd kept his gob shut about us. But I'll upset the whole bloody lot of them, rather than see you upset, sweet Richard. Because the last thing I want — the very last thing in the whole wide world — is to see you upset. So all right, if you want the whole gay set in Brighton to come drinking here and feel welcome, I'll ordain it. If the regulars don't like it, it's too bad. It's about time they joined the twentieth century round these parts, anyway. And it'll be a great way of pissing on Gibson from a great height, won't it?

"The only thing I'm sorry about," he mused, "is that I can't say I fancy people like that twat that was here tonight. Red satin pants," he growled.

"There's nothing wrong with camping it up," observed Richard, mollified by Stephen's declaration — and a little surprised, too, by the hard-edged, gratingly adult way in which he had come out with it.

"I don't go in for that kind," said Stephen, wrinkling his nose in distaste. "I mean, Christ, you don't have to go mincing around with limp wrists and a fucking handbag just cos you're gay, do you? I don't," he added as an afterthought, as if that clinched the matter.

"Most don't," said Richard mildly. "But some do. If it makes them happy, what's wrong with that? You of all people ought to feel sympathetic towards a minority."

"Eh?" said Stephen. "Why should I? I'm not a minority group, am I?"

Richard stared at him for a moment, then burst into a laugh. "You really do take my breath away sometimes, Stevie," he said, looking fondly at Stephen through tears of laughter. "You're gay, aren't you?"

For a moment an odd little smile of puzzlement lurked round the corners of Stephen's mouth while he considered this. Then he laughed also. "Well, d'you know, I never really thought of it like that," he confessed. "I s'pose I am, come to think of it. But I've never felt very different from anybody else. Never felt different at all, actually. And I've always wondered why those camp types had to go round trying to look like women. I mean, why can't they just be men, like they are?"

"It's always been easy for you, hasn't it, Steve, love?" said Richard, a little sadly, though he was still chuckling softly to himself.

"Dunno what you mean," said Stephen.

"No," murmured Richard. "I don't suppose you do. But you've never minded a little camping up when I've done it, have you?"

"Ah, but that's different," objected Stephen. "I love you. So when you do it, it's just play, isn't it?"

Richard stared at him, and all the irritation and impatience dropped away from him. He gave Stephen a slow, sweet smile of invitation. "Come and show me you still love me," he said in a small voice. "I'm feeling a little bit vulnerable right this minute, and I could do with some comfort. Some strength, too. Even if it is feeling over-butch tonight. Come and love me, Stevie, my lovely." And Stephen, who could be melted out of even his hardest frame of mind by Richard when he chose to be cajoling, went across the room to the other bed, and set about comforting him.

* * *

In the bar at midday the following day Stephen took Tom aside, bought him a drink and left Richard serving the half a dozen early customers. "Got a problem," he opened. "And I want to hear your views before I decide how to approach it."

"Go on," said Tom, suspecting what the problem was.

"Apparently a lot of gay people have started coming here," Stephen said evenly, betraying nothing of his own feelings.

"There've been a few," admitted Tom. "Nothing very noticeable, though — till that pair last night."

"You got any idea why they should have suddenly started using the place?"

"Nope," said Tom. "Unless..." He made a small gesture with his hands. It said that he didn't really want to say what he had to say, and didn't think he needed to, either.

"Somehow they've heard about Rich and me, and thought they'd get a welcome here on our account?" supplied Stephen, raising his eyebrows. Tom nodded confirmation.

"What are your own feelings?"

Tom pursed his lips and thought about it. Stephen, watching closely, saw him wondering briefly whether to be diplomatic, and saw the notion rejected. "I've got nothing against them," Tom said eventually in a carefully neutral tone. "You know that, I think. I'm not particularly on their side, but I'm not against em either. I'm on my own side, which means on the pub's side. I want whatever's best for the pub, because that's what's best for me, in the long run. Is that helpful?" Stephen sat in thought for a moment. "Suppose I issue an instruction," he said slowly, considering as he spoke, "to the effect that they're to be served unless you have any other reason to kick em out — if they're pissed, or using dope, or anything like that? How would you feel about that?"

"I'd accept that, of course," said Tom. "I don't want to see the local people upset, particularly. But I don't believe in prohibiting people, whatever they are, unless they misbehave somehow. I can't say I found that... er, exhibition last night very edifying, shall we say. But they did nothing against the law, and they did nothing to damage the pub. No, I wouldn't have anything to say against that."

"Well, then," said Stephen, "I don't see that there's anything to issue instructions about, is there? I mean, if I leave the matter in your hands — you're in operational charge of the pub — and you use your own discretion, that seems to cover the situation, doesn't it? You'll eject anyone breaking the law, but you won't refuse to serve anyone because of his dress, or appearance, that right?"

Tom thought about it for a moment. "Up to now," he said, "before you and Richard appeared on the scene, that is, I'd always run an unofficial dress code of my own in here anyway. I won't serve anyone who's dirty, and I won't serve anyone not wearing a shirt. The customers don't want sweaty armpits beside em at the bar, and I don't want to have to clean motor-bikies' oil or clods of mud off people's boots off the carpets. Other than that, I've tended to live and let live. I'd carry on with those rules if you gave me a free hand."

"Fair enough," said Stephen. "What would you have done if two punks had come in with pink and green Mohican haircuts and safety pins through their noses?"

"Well, we've never had any," said Tom, laughing as he imagined the effect of such an apparition on the locals. "But if they were clean punks, and had shirts on, I'd've served em, and hoped they didn't stay too long."

"Okay," said Stephen, getting up and picking up the glasses. "Carry on as you were, then. If gay people come in and they meet your own criteria, serve em, and treat em like any other customers. If Pat Gibson or any of the others make trouble about it, treat them as you'd treat anybody else making trouble in the bar, and let me know about it next time you see me, okay?"

"Okay," said Tom, and Stephen went to refill their glasses feeling pleased with the ease with which he had resolved a potentially thorny problem.

They had a chance to test the effectiveness of their policy only a few evenings later. Elderton Park by chance had a blank date in their fixture list the following Saturday. Stephen, unwilling to go without his game if he could find one, had gratefully accepted the local captain's offer of a place in the village side instead, and he and Richard were having a quiet drink before heading for the ground. There was a sprinkling of local drinkers ranged along the long bar, including Gibson, in his usual place near the door. Just after noon two strangers came in and stood next to Gibson at the bar. One of them, a slender boy with fine sandy hair, was clearly wearing eye-liner and lipstick. His movements were extravagant and uninhibited. Tom served them and took their money without changing his expression. Stephen and Richard halted their chat and watched covertly, with great interest, wondering what would happen next.

For some time nothing happened at all. The two newcomers stared round the bar, their eyes lingering on the two boys for a moment. But they made no move, and for a while Stephen and Richard turned away, listening to the scraps of conversation audible from the other end of the bar. It was clearly to do with the misdeeds of some former boyfriend of the made-up youth, and was illustrated by a series of snatches of dialogue and accompanying flamboyant gestures.

Predictably enough, after a while it became too much for Gibson's endurance. There was a series of rumbled sneers and loud comments about fairies, pansies and the like. The boys turned and took notice, in time to see the made-up one flutter his long, almost white eyelashes winningly at Gibson and offer him a bright, mocking smile. At the same time he advanced a short pace towards Gibson, who, though short, was a stocky, powerfully built man, who looked as if he could have broken his slight tormentor in two with his bare hands.

"Get away from me, you disgusting painted little tart," growled Gibson, enraged. "Piss off to one of your own places and give em AIDS there, and keep out of decent people's pubs, why don't you?" And he took a step towards the slight youth, raising a hand threateningly.

Tom glanced briefly at Stephen, who gave him a slight nod.

"Knock that off, Pat," said Tom in a matter-of-fact tone.

Gibson swung round on him in surprise. "What?" he roared, staring at Tom in surprise. "Are you telling me to knock it off. Me? This... this... lipsticked little freak of a whore's handbag comes in fluttering its eyelashes at me, and you're telling me to knock it off. Why, I'll..."

"You'll calm down and behave yourself," observed Tom, still speaking conversationally, "or I'll throw you out. And bar you, if you give me cause." He put down the towel and the glass he was wiping and stepped towards the hatch in the bar, watching Gibson with an expression of polite enquiry on his face.

Gibson goggled at him for a moment, so astonished that he forgot all about the two young men, who were watching the scene with undisguised delight all over their faces. Then he remembered them, and swung round on them again. "Good God, Tom, look at him," he spluttered angrily. "I ask you, man. Look at him."

"You're not the arbiter of public taste, Pat," said Tom mildly. "Or the resident fashion correspondent."

Gibson did some more spluttering. "Do you think I want that standing next to me at the bar?" he demanded, gesturing at the decorated young man with a hand as if exhibiting him at an auction. "There's plenty of room," murmured Tom, making an identical gesture to indicate the long expanse of polished and vacant bar. "You don't have to stand beside anyone you don't want to. Just as long as you don't start threatening or insulting the customers. I don't want any trouble in my bar. Or rather, I should say, I won't have any trouble in my bar. Now simmer down and have a drink."

Gibson stood for a moment, and there was silence as everyone waited to see if he would calm down and accept his discomfiture quietly. For one moment he tensed himself, and it looked as if he would hurl himself on Tom or the two young men. Then he picked up his glass, almost hurling it to his lips, drained it, and stamped out of the bar with an inarticulate snarl of mingled outrage and disgust.

The young man thanked Tom shyly, peeking up at him from under his light lashes. Tom, however, was on his way up the bar to Stephen and Richard, who were wearing identical grins. "You did everything bar saying 'There's a good boy', chuckled Richard approvingly.

"I'm not too happy about it, Steve," muttered Tom.

"Why?" demanded Stephen bluntly. "It's only Pat Gibson. If you have to kick him out, kick him — hard. I've got no sympathy to waste on him."

Tom looked at him for a long moment. "Okay," he said. "If that's the way you want it. But he'll try to make trouble for us."

"What can he do?" scoffed Stephen. "You were dead right," said Richard encouragingly. Tom gave him a long, straight look. "I hope so," he said. He shrugged, and left it at that.

* * *

Over the next week or so unfamiliar faces continued to appear in the hotel in slowly growing numbers. Many of them still went away looking a little puzzled or disappointed, but a fair number of them seemed to take a liking to the place, and returned. There were subdued rumblings from a few predictable voices among the locals, but Gibson had talked among his circle of mates, and when they found they received no support from Tom they remained subdued, and there was no trouble, until the event that made Stephen's discussion with Tom, and their ready solution of the question, meaningless.

It wasn't until towards the end of the following week that they discovered that the reporter's interest in them had taken other, more practical directions; and that was when the trouble started.

11

For a moment Janet Knight thought she had seen nothing but a sheet of old newspaper stuck in the bushes beside the road. Then she saw clearly what it was that had caught her eye, and uttered a small, half-frightened gasp of surprise. "What's up?" her husband said, shooting a quick glance in her direction. It was just after three o'clock on a wet, windy Saturday morning, and Geoffrey Knight was driving fast. They had been to a dinner party with friends in Arundel, and the conversation had run on far into the night. It had been very pleasant, but he was anxious now to get home to Bognor and bed. His wife had been dozing, almost asleep, up to the moment when she had seen whatever it was and become suddenly very wide awake indeed. Then he saw the thing himself, and jammed his brakes on so hard that their safety belts locked, slamming them back into their seats.

Knight slipped his belt and opened his door in a single movement. As he did so he observed his wife doing the same. "You stay here," he said roughly. Fear gave his voice a brusque tone that he had never used with her before. "Keep the doors locked, and if it's trouble, drive off." He slid swiftly out of the car into the intense darkness before she could think of anything to say in reply.

His heart beating unpleasantly fast and sounding so loud in his temples that he felt it must be audible, he had enough presence of mind to open the boot and grab the heavy jack-handle before padding circumspectly back along the narrow, unlit country road. He did not know that he had raised the jack-handle above his head like a club, or that he looked utterly terrifying, a black, menacing shadow of deeper darkness against the night sky.

Fifteen yards back from the comforting twin red glow-worms of his tail-lights, he saw something white that moved. He edged still more gingerly off the metalled surface of the road, across a narrow strip of verge, and into the thin bushes beyond — and suddenly drew in a gulp of breath, with a thin hiss of horrified surprise. It was almost a shriek.

The boy was naked, soaked, spattered with mud and leaves, and in a state of utter, inarticulate terror that was close to catatonia. His eyes gleamed in the faint light from the few stars visible through the scudding clouds, huge with his fear. He was incapable of uttering a sound, but he raised a thin arm in front of his face to ward off Knight's raised arm and the jack-handle. Knight suddenly became aware of the weapon, and realised how he must appear. He lowered the handle and stooped swiftly to take the child by the arm. "What in God's name are you doing out like this?" he said. It wasn't, he said, discussing it shakily with his wife much later, the most intelligent thing to have said, but he was too paralysed by the shock and horror of what he saw to think very sensibly about what to say.

In any case, it didn't matter much what he said, because the child was unable to say anything at all in reply. "Jesus!" muttered Knight. "You must be perished. Come on." He scooped the boy's slight body into his arms, dropping the jack-handle, and ran awkwardly back to the car. The boy was quite well-made for his age, which Knight thought was about ten or eleven, and he was glad to regain the comforting security of the car. He kicked the door, and his wife's face glimmered whitely, her features drawn and tight with fear. She recognised her husband, and opened the door.

"It's a little boy," he gasped. "He's... I don't know... he's been out in the weather, he's got nothing on, he's filthy. Get in the back and look after him, will you? Get him to hospital."

He reached round and unlocked the rear door while his wife was scrambling out of her seat and into the back of the car on the other side. In the dim, sickly glow of the interior light they saw that as well as the splashes of mud, grass and leaves stuck to the child's wet body, he was also liberally covered with ugly dark bruises. Janet Knight drew in her breath in horrified astonishment. "Great God!" she exclaimed, her voice low and appalled. "What in the world's happened to him? It's all right now," she whispered, taking the boy into her arms and hurriedly wrapping him in her coat. He stared up at her from the same huge, terrified eyes. His mouth worked, but no sound came out. Her own eyes filled, suddenly and infuriatingly, with tears. She cradled his head on her lap and rocked him gently, murmuring to him, and acting throughout more from instinct than from any coherent thought. "There, there," she said softly as her husband almost hurled himself into the driver's seat and roared off. The jack-handle lay, a blunt instrument devoid of all the menace it had briefly held, in the wet grass beside the road, and neither of them remembered it until many hours later, when they would return for it in the company of the Sussex Constabulary.

In the back Janet Knight was hardly aware that her husband

was driving like a maniac for the last few miles back into Bognor Regis. She blinked the tears out of her eyes and wondered vaguely, with the small part of her mind that was not concentrated on comforting and soothing the child, what could possibly have reduced him to such a state of such primordial terror and hurt, like a small animal, unable to remember speech.

An hour later the Knights stood talking to a young night-duty houseman in the hospital where they had screeched to a halt fifteen minutes after discovering the child. The doctor was bone-achingly tired, but his almost ill-looking expression of shock showed clearly through the tiredness and the normal doctor's mask of impassive, seen-it-all-before worldliness. "It's a police matter, that's certain," he was saying to the Knights. "He's been deeply trauma-tised, and he's in very deep shock. I don't know exactly what's happened to him, that'll have to wait for full examination. At the moment he's under heavy sedation. But it's sexual, for certain. He's certainly been... Well, I won't go into details. But I'm calling the police in, and I think they'll want to talk to you. If you wouldn't mind hanging about for a bit... I'll ask one of the nurses to give you some tea, or coffee. Do with some myself, come to that. Lucky we're not busy." He gestured into a small room, and they went in and sat down, looking at each other and, for the first time since they had stopped the car in the dark, tree-shadowed lane, beginning to feel a little afraid.

* * *

A quarter of an hour later two uniformed policemen arrived. The same doctor sat and described the boy's condition in general terms, offered a fairly precise surmise of what had been done to him, and agreed to go to the police station the following day to make a full statement when the boy had been examined more thoroughly. Then he led them through corridors to the small private room where the boy, heavily sedated, was sleeping, watched over by a tired nurse. He allowed them to peep at the child briefly, but would not allow them to examine him at all. "S'all right, doc," said the senior officer. "No point in disturbing him now. Poor little devil," he muttered feelingly. "We'll come back tomorrow, with women officers. Time enough for questions when he's recovered a bit. For now we'll just have a word with the people who found him." The doctor nodded, and led them through more corridors.

They found Geoffrey Knight sprawled out in a wheelchair. His wife was reclining on a medical gurney, her back propped against a pile of pillows. They were both asleep.

"Seems a shame to wake em," said the PC, a grizzled giant in his early fifties.

"Have to all the same," muttered the other man. He wore the two pips denoting an Inspector, though he was twenty years younger than the PC. "If this is anything like as nasty as the doc says we're gonna need all the help we can get. Be nice to get these two eliminated as quick as poss, save a bit a time. CID'll be takin it over in the morning."

"Nah!" said the giant PC grimly. "This ain't CID work. Legwork, guv, for us, that's what this little number'll turn out to be, for sure. Knockin on doors, mass fingerprintin job, maybe even takin DNA samples from every man who can get it up, like they did with those murders in Leicestershire, member?"

The Inspector nodded gloomily. "Christ, I fuckin hate this," he muttered dismally. The PC nodded in sympathy, knowing what he meant. "Same with me, guv," he said softly. "I been in this miserable job twenny-nine years, I've seen most a the things people can do to each other, an it still puts the fear a Christ right up my spine when kids are involved. I can stand most things, but this..." He left the sentence unfinished. "The guys'll all wanna help on this one," he went on a little less glumly. "They'll be offerin to work overtime without pay till we take this bastard down." The Inspector nodded. "Okay," he muttered, and bent to shake Geoffrey Knight by the shoulder.

"Urrgh! Whassamarrer?" grunted Knight, waking with a jerk.

"Police," said the Inspector. "Just like a few words with you, sir, please. Shan't keep you long, then you can get home to get some proper sleep. If you'll just come with me..."

"Yes, of course," muttered Knight groggily. "Sorry. Didn't mean to drop off like that. Must've gone out like a light. Funny. You wouldn't think you could sleep after..." He stopped speaking abruptly as he remembered. Then he heaved himself out of the wheelchair with some difficulty and followed the Inspector out of the room, down the corridor and into another small room much like the first. They seated themselves uncomfortably, Knight in a canvas and tubular steel chair and the Inspector perched on the edge of a table. "Right, sir," began the Inspector, "if you'll just tell me exactly what happened, in your own words, that'll be all we'll

need for tonight. Start with your name and address, if you will."
He drew a notebook and ballpoint from the breast pocket of his
jacket, and looked expectantly at Knight. In the room where they
had been dozing, the PC was saying almost exactly the same words
to Janet Knight.

Shortly afterwards the Inspector agreed an appointment for
the Knights to visit the police station later that day, thanked them
seriously, and, having from unconscious routine asked Geoffrey
Knight if he had been drinking at the party and been assured that
he hadn't, let them go. They went out into the first dim grey light
of dawn, while the two officers accepted mugs of coffee and com-
pared notes. "They're clean," said the Inspector, glancing at his
companion for confirmation.

"As a whistle, I'd say," agreed the PC. "Fortunate for the kid
they happened to be so late. He mighta spent the rest a the night
out there, poor little sod. Coulda died of exposure, easy. Lucky
they were decent citizens, too. Public-spirited. Lotta people'da shot
straight past. We'll have to go out there an recover his jack-handle,
guv. That'll be some confirmation."

"Yeah," nodded the Inspector. "Just ring the people at this
party, I think, be on the safe side."

"They'll be pleased," murmured the PC, glancing at his watch.

"Toss you for it, Tom?" offered the Inspector.

"All yours, guv," said the PC, grinning. "You get paid more
than I do. This is where you earn it."

"All right, all right," said the Inspector. He sighed, and picked
up the telephone. It was a long time before someone answered at
the other end. "Yes, yes, I know what time it is," the PC heard his
colleague saying as he went off to look for another mug of coffee.

* * *

By four o'clock that afternoon the boy had emerged from his deep,
drugged sleep at the hospital, and had spoken at some length and
in some detail to a friendly woman in her thirties, who treated him
like a playful but very gentle older sister. She was actually a vastly
experienced Detective Sergeant, extensively trained in the subtle
arts of examining and questioning sexually violated women and
children. What the boy told her left her filled with pity, but also
deeply outraged, and at the same time consumed with admiration
for the philosophical and phlegmatic way the boy had accepted

138

the frightful ordeal to which he had been subjected.

"He's toughing it out," she told appalled male colleagues waiting for her when she emerged after a long session with the boy, "because that's the way he is. Tough. Tougher than most grown men'd be, by a long chalk. Jesus, I've never heard anything quite like this one. There were three of them, and they gave him the full treatment. Descriptions," she added brusquely, thrusting some sheets of paper into their hands. She gave them a hard-eyed glare. "Get em," she said, and went back to resume her ministrations to the boy. By five o'clock the Knights, less than refreshed by six hours of sleep, were in separate rooms at Worthing police station, making detailed statements of the incident to grim-faced detectives. The police thanked them, sincerely enough, and Janet Knight ventured to ask how the boy was faring. Everyone glanced towards the bald, broken-nosed Detective Chief Inspector in charge of the enquiry for the moment.

He thought about it for a moment. "Well, I suppose there's no harm in your knowing that much," he murmured, suppressing his normal professional reticence. "You've got as much right as anyone to know, I guess. He's as comfortable as can be expected. He's been the victim of a... a savage sexual assault, by three men. Last night. They weren't content with gang-raping him. They did that, sure. Then they inflicted every sexual humiliation on him that you can imagine — no, I'll correct that, you wouldn't be capable of imagining half of them, I should think, Ma'am. Finally they beat him up, apparently partly for pleasure and partly as a deterrent to talking to us or telling his parents, and then left him naked and bleeding on the side of the road. They drove him ten miles further away from his home first, though, just to make it that little bit more difficult for him to make it back. It's by the grace of God almighty and you being late getting away from your party that this isn't a murder enquiry.

"But I'll tell you a little bit more. He's tough. Apparently he's decided that it's happened, and he's not going to let it bury itself deep down and fester. And mostly, according to our very capable female investigator, who knows more about this kind of victim than the rest of this force put together, his main feeling is that he's angry. Very, very, bloody angry. He's a good kid, by the sound of him." And to the utter, embarrassed astonishment of the horrified, white-faced Knights, two tears appeared sparkling in the corners of the elderly, grey-haired detective's hard brown eyes. He plucked a handkerchief from the breast pocket of his suit, dabbed them with surprising delicacy off his face, and gave them a very thin smile. "Surprises you? Look at them," he said, jerking a thumb at the other detectives in the room. "They're not embarrassed for me. There'll be a lot of tears shed over this boy, until we catch the bastards that did it. I've got boys of my own not much older than he is. Now then, I've told you far more than I should have done. I thought you were more entitled to know something than most — seein you most likely saved the kid's life. But I've got to ask you to keep everything I've said — every word of it — to yourselves. Seriously. You won't see anything in the papers about it tonight, because we're asking the press to suppress it for a bit. That okay?" They nodded in unison. "Okay, then," he resumed. "If you'll go with these officers here, they'll drive you out to the spot where you found the boy, and rescue your jack-handle for you."

By the evening, virtually every detective in the Sussex CID had called in, returned from leave, in some cases risen from sickbeds, and volunteered to work overtime until the case was cleared. Men in suits began to move quietly, though it could not be said inconspicuously, among the customers of every known gay pub, club, bar and meeting place within a radius of twenty-five miles from the recreation ground where the boy had been attacked. "It isn't a gay witch-hunt," they murmured hundreds of times to appalled gay barmen, drinkers and club-owners, who without a single exception promised to do everything they could to help. Because the Crown Hotel had only very recently begun to acquire a name as a place sympathetic to gay people, it was Tuesday evening before two quiet, saturnine young men slipped into the bar and asked to speak to the landlord.

* * *

Tom listened carefully to what they murmured, having to lean towards them over the bar to hear their low voices. When they finished speaking he was looking a little sick. "Just a minute," he said. "I'll get the owner. He's, er, gay himself. He'll want to talk to you." They nodded and waited in silence while he went over to Stephen and Richard, who were chatting to Major Sealey and Alfie Brett from the cricket club in a far corner.

"Steve," Tom said quietly. "You're wanted." Stephen raised his eyebrows, and glanced towards the two men he indicated.

"What's it about?" he asked. "Police," muttered Tom, and led him quickly back to the two detectives.

"Can I help you?" asked Stephen politely, coming up to them at the bar. They looked him up and down suspiciously. "You're the owner?" one of them said, disbelief clearly visible in his face.

"Yes," said Stephen, with a faint smile. "It's all right," he added. "I know I look like a schoolboy. I was one until last year. But I am the owner."

"And you're gay?" asked the younger of the two. He said it in such a matter-of-fact tone that there was no innuendo or impertinence in it. Stephen gazed at him steadily, realising that it must be something serious. "Yes, I am," he said evenly. "What about it?"

They told him. His eyes widened. "Jesus Christ," he breathed softly. "Is he... is he all right?"

The two officers looked at each other for a moment. "He's as well as can be expected," the older one said. "If I believed in God, I'd say 'by the grace of God'. As it is, yes, he's making out. What we'd like to know is, have you, or has anyone here, seen anyone looking like these men in this bar? Especially in the last few days, but at any time? Think carefully, please." They produced three "WANTED" posters, reduced to A4 size, each showing a photofit-style impression of a man's face. Stephen stared hard at them, racking his memory for any recollection of the three men. Eventually he said "No. I'd love to say I'd seen them, but... No. I'm sorry. But I'll ask some of the others. Have you asked Tom?" He gestured at Tom behind the bar.

"Just about to," said the senior man.

"Okay," said Stephen gravely. "I'll go and fetch the others." He went quickly back to Richard and the other two, who were the only early drinkers in the bar as yet. The detectives watched closely as he spoke in a low voice, with many gestures in their direction. Then the whole party came back to them in a body, all looking grim.

Nobody recognised the three men, and the detectives prepared to leave. "Can we keep copies of those posters?" asked Stephen. "I'd like to put them up in the bar, if you've got copies."

"Good," said one of the officers, with the first beginnings of a smile. "I was going to ask you to do just that." He handed Stephen the three bills.

"Would you like a quick drink?" asked Stephen a little tentatively.

"No, thanks," said the older man. "We've got several more places to visit on the rounds tonight. Thanks all the same. And thanks for your help."

Stephen looked crestfallen. "We haven't been much help, have we?"

"You've volunteered to do what you can," said the detective seriously. "And you're on our side, I can see that plainly enough."

"Anybody would be, surely," said Stephen in surprise.

"The gay community have been, certainly," said the man. "They're taking this very much to heart. I suppose they know something like this can do them a lot of harm as a whole, but I don't think that's been the reason. I think they're genuinely desperately anxious to have these animals nailed. There are collections going on already in some of the bars in Brighton. Reward money." There was no suggestion of a hint in his voice, but Stephen was already reaching for the back pocket of his jeans. "Will you take a cheque and pass it to them?" he asked, producing his chequebook.

The police officers looked at each other. "We shouldn't," the senior one said. "But I'll take it if you ask me to, and pass it to someone." In answer to Stephen's query he gave him the name of an account. "I happen to know they've set up a bank account for it," he said in explanation. "I contributed to it when we were on the rounds there last night." He glanced at the cheque Stephen handed to him and his eyebrows rose. "That's generous," he said expressionlessly. "Thank you."

"Well worth it, if it helps bring those... brings them down," muttered Stephen, gesturing at the handbills on the bar.

"Could I ask something?" put in Richard, who had said very little, and was leaning on the bar, looking a little sick.

"Of course," said the detective, turning back.

"Couldn't you do one of these DNA fingerprint tests?" Richard said earnestly. "You know, on everyone locally. They did it with a murder case, didn't they?"

The two men looked quickly at one another. "It's being considered," one of them said eventually, a little reluctantly. "It may come to that. It takes forever, and it's a hell of an operation to organise. But it may come to that. Would you agree to such a test?" he added, watching Richard curiously.

"Of course I would," said Richard. "Me too," added Stephen.

"Well I don't suppose it'll be necessary for you two," said the man. "You're too remote from the descriptions we've been given. But I'm glad to hear you say it. You're about the two hundredth to suggest it, incidentally." They thanked everyone present again and went out as quietly as they had arrived, leaving a very subdued company discussing the affair.

"Bloody hell," muttered Stephen. "This is a nasty business." A thought struck him. "Can you imagine what Pat Gibson'll say when he hears about it?" The others nodded glumly.

The following morning the story broke in the national newspapers.

* * *

Over the next few days everyone who visited the Crown saw the handbills; and though no one had any recollection of ever having seen the three men in the photofits, most made a point of commenting favourably on Stephen's readiness to display the posters, and his anxiety that no one should fail to look closely at them. One or two of the anti-gay faction among the regular clientele began to tone down their hostility. Unfortunately, for every one thus muted, another was lost to the sympathetic camp because of the continuing, and increasing, number of new arrivals believing they were coming to an established gay pub — which rapidly became the true position, with the newcomers gradually starting to outnumber the regular local patrons. Pat Gibson and his cronies remained hostile, although, recognising that Stephen's ownership of the pub gave him an overwhelming advantage if he decided to use it, they tended to keep their sarcastic remarks to themselves. Even so, Major Sealey, who had become very fond of Stephen, demanded one day, in his peppery way, to know "why you keep putting up with that insufferable bounder. I really don't understand why you allow him to continue making these frightfully offensive remarks. After all, my boy, you own the place. You might at least demand that he tone it down a bit, what?"

"It's all to do with a promise I made, Major," said Stephen, smiling to himself as he imagined the pleasure of ejecting Gibson and his friends from the bar. "A promise to Tom, to begin with, but more to myself — and most of all to someone who's dead. I promised that I wouldn't come sweeping in here making changes right, left and centre. I know Gibson's a monumental pain in the arse, but he's local, he was here before I was, and he belongs here. I'll do my utmost not to throw him out. Besides, there's another reason. I won't let him goad me into losing my temper. I've got one, as anybody who knows me'll tell you. Ask Rich. But I don't want to have to go around knowing I let that crass ass ride me into losing it. And really, Major, when you think about it, he's more idiot than menace, isn't he?"

"Hmph!" snorted the Major, but bestowing an indulgent smile on the back of Stephen's head as he turned to pick up his glass, "you're taking a very grown-up attitude, I must say."

"Well, Major," said Stephen, turning back and grinning affectionately at the old man, "I am grown-up, really, aren't I? Well, very nearly, anyway?" And he changed the subject, for the time being.

While the news was all centred on the attack on the boy, however, Gibson's party appeared to feel that they were specially licensed to say what they liked, until one day Stephen's patience gave out at last.

Stephen and Richard were at one end of the bar, talking quietly about Graham, as they often did in quiet moments together. The pub was quite full and noisy, and Gibson's crowd were grouped at the other end of the bar in their usual place near the door. As the drinks went down and the voices became louder the boys became gradually aware of a series of offensive remarks, and, having once noticed them, they then became rather more rapidly aware that the remarks were directed at themselves. Eventually Gibson himself happened to turn and caught Stephen's eye. "Wonder if... molested any... small boys lately," he said loudly, and followed it with a guffaw.

The pub suddenly became very quiet. The Major and some of the cricketers turned and watched, intensely curious to see what Stephen would do in the face of so obvious a personal challenge. It was an insinuation — indeed, an accusation — so vile, and so deadly, that it could not go unchallenged. The Major set his glass down quietly on a table and drew himself up. Stephen, glancing in his direction, saw plainly that if he himself did nothing, the old man intended to go into battle himself. Stephen turned momentarily back to Richard, who was white in the face, with intense pain and even greater rage in his eyes. Leaning close, Stephen murmured something soothing in his ear. Richard nodded, and walked quietly over to the Major and his group. Gibson, seeing the small movement of affection between the two boys, mistook it for withdrawal, and let loose a low chuckle. In the now silent bar it sounded obscene, as, indeed, it was.

Stephen, pale with anger, took one long stride towards Gibson's party and stood watching until Gibson, alerted by the expressions on his friends' faces, turned back to face him. There was a murmur from one of his group of "Come on, Pat. Fair do's."

"Fair do's?" jeered Gibson, openly derisive.

"You're on your own, Pat," said the man who had found the remark a little too much to stomach. "I'm not going along with that kind of thing." And he emptied his glass and went quietly out of the door. Another of the group looked uncomfortably at Stephen, round at the other groups of drinkers, all of whom had suspended operations to watch the long-awaited confrontation, and finally back at Gibson. "There's a limit," he said quietly. "And you're over it. I'm dissociating myself from what you just heard," he said in a louder voice, looking along the bar at Stephen. Stephen nodded. The man followed the other one out.

"I think I heard you making accusations against me, Gibson," said Stephen in a soft, dead voice.

"I made a remark to my friends," said Gibson cheerily. "I don't expect to have my personal conversations eavesdropped on. We've always imagined we were among gentlemen here. Still..." — he let the pause draw out for the maximum effect — "if the cap fits, no doubt you'll wear it." Stephen hesitated briefly, fighting the rage that threatened to boil over. He was aware that if he lost his temper he was doomed. "I take it you're aware," he said at length, speaking still in a soft, deadly tone, "that what you said was a slander, of the vilest kind I can imagine. There are enough witnesses here to make it stick in court, as I'm sure you can see for yourself. Even two of your own mates are too squeamish to stand by while you accuse me of that kind of thing." He waited, staring levelly at Gibson, hoping that the pounding of his heart wasn't visible through his shirt. It felt as if it was trying to beat its way out of his body altogether.

Gibson, temporarily disconcerted by the unexpected defection of two of his own spear-carriers, and a little impressed despite himself by Stephen's icy bearing, debated with himself what to do. Pride won. "You know what I think about your kind of freak," he said, speaking as if he had a mouthful of lemon. "As far as I'm concerned any one of you's quite capable of that assault. You're diseased, and you oughtn't to be allowed to circulate among decent people. And looking at your little fancy piece there, you seem to have a taste for fifteen-year-old schoolboys. Maybe you like em younger than that as well. I don't know. All I know is that this used to be a pub where gentlemen could meet for a civilised drink, and now you can hardly move for shit-stabbers and arsehole bandits." He stared at Stephen for a moment longer, with utter contempt all over his face, then turned back and started talking to his cronies. Some of them were grinning broadly, pleased by his outspokenness. Others, however, were looking increasingly uncomfortable.

Stephen stood in thought for a moment. His mind worked overtime, running faster and faster, like a plane on a war film, hit, burning and careering out of control with an ever-intensifying scream of engines as it plunged to its fiery end. Finally, his anger became unbearable. It flared and boiled until his mind could no longer contain it. Whole systems of fuses blew in his mind. Then the whole lot went up in a single blast.

He walked very slowly, a pace at a time, along the bar towards Gibson. He, for his part, was carried away by his access of self-righteous outrage. By the time he realised that he was in physical danger, he was a very long way too late.

Stephen came to a halt a pace from the older man. He towered over him by several inches, and although Gibson was considerably the bulkier and heavier, for the first time a fleeting hint of fear flickered in his eyes. But he had been a loud-mouth for a very long time, too used to dominating his party of cronies, and the brief flicker vanished. He glared exophthalmically up at Stephen's face and resumed his normal weapon of bluster. "Go away, my little man," he sneered. "Haven't you got it into your head yet that I feel unclean with someone like you within ten yards?"

Stephen breathed deeply, and felt the blood draining from his face. "Has it ever crossed your mind," he said at last, speaking very softly, between teeth that he was clenching so hard that they made a faint grating sound inside his own head, "that I'm a fair bit bigger than you?" He waited, watching the man's face like a cat. When he saw no reaction he went on. "I expect you have. Most of the people who get a kick out of being unpleasant to other people are little short-arses, aren't they? Probably why so many dictators have been little bastards, like you, wouldn't you think? Little fuckers getting a hard-on from shoving bigger blokes around, right? Is that what's underneath all this, little man? You get a nice big

146

boner on when you have a normal-sized man in front of you and kick some arse, eh? Well, it's backfired this time and no mistake."

Gibson gazed at him, seeing clearly now the dangerous frame of mind he had created. But he was conscious of being a fully-grown man, while his youthful oppponent was still only a lithe, willowy boy. He bridled visibly, and balled a heavy fist.

"Don't," said Stephen, speaking even more softly, almost whispering, in a voice that was dark and reeking of menace. "Don't do that. Don't even think it." This time Gibson obeyed, unclenching his fist, without even realising that was what it amounted to. The almost palpable aura of menace that now surrounded Stephen like a miasma, and even more the subtle undertones of madness in his voice and face, were enough to compel his instant compliance. It had dawned on him at last that he might come to owe a great deal to the most rigid restraint.

"If you lay a finger-nail on me," went on Stephen, whispering coldly into the man's face, "I'll drop you in your tracks. Right where you stand. And then..." He stopped and waited, watching the deep flush ebbing from Gibson's face. He watched while he turned from purple to red to pinkish to a boiled, fish-belly white, still himself wearing the same ghastly, vampirish travesty of a smile. He felt a bolt of pure power flush through him. In that moment he felt capable of anything. His lips drew back still further from his gums, leaving him with a feral snarl on his face that was pure evil, and wholly mindless. Gibson flinched. Stephen smiled, and he flinched again. "The door's behind you. Use it. Don't trouble to return," Stephen said, and then, realising that this was as fine an exit point as he would get, turned silently and went back to where he had been standing with Richard.

Gibson, to Stephen's chagrin, lost his appearance of paralysis immediately the spell was broken. "I don't mind being barred," he said reflectively. "I've been wondering when you'd manage to scrounge up the pluck. And of course it'll be a pleasure to be able to drink in a normal place again. There's just one thing to be said. I'm not going to be thrown out by one of your kind and take it lying down. I'll leave you with something to remember me by, at least." He took a short and leisurely stroll along the bar to Stephen, raised his glass slowly over his head, and slowly and deliberately emptied the three-quarters of a pint of bitter remaining in it over Stephen's head. "Try that to begin with," he said in easy, matey tones. He then reached out, took Stephen's own pint of lager off the bar and repeated the performance. He was still standing poised with the empty glass above Stephen's head when Richard, the Major and half a dozen others arrived, caught him by the arms and whisked him to the door.

12

"That's that," said Stephen. He pulled a handkerchief from his jeans and dabbed at the beer streaming down his face, then walked across to where the Major, Alfie Brett and one or two others were comforting Richard. He found a dry area of his shirt, used it to wipe beer from his hand, and ruffled Richard's hair, grinning at him affectionately. "I reckon I could do with a shower," he said softly. "Want to come up and talk, or would you rather stay here, Rich? I'll only be a few minutes."

Richard hesitated for a moment. Then he gave the Major and the others a damp smile and went quickly through the door into the residential part of the hotel, followed more slowly by Stephen. A buzz of conversation broke out in the bar the moment he shut the door behind them.

Stephen sat in the tub and used the hand shower to clean himself off, while Richard perched on the lavatory seat watching him in silence. Neither spoke until Stephen had finished operations with the shampoo to wash the sticky mess of beer out of his shaggy mop of hair. It was only when he got out and began towelling himself vigorously that Richard broke the silence.

"Something like that was bound to happen," he said.

"Course it was," said Stephen. "I've been wondering for weeks when that cunt would find it all too much of a strain. The only thing that surprises me is that it took so long for him to burst his boiler. I s'pose he didn't like the idea of having to go seven or eight miles every time he wanted a pint, but even so, knowing what a bigoted prat he is, I was surprised. Still..." he mused, "it's out of the way now, and the air's cleared. We shan't have any more trouble, I don't reckon."

Richard still looked unhappy. "I think you're wrong about that," he said. "I think there's going to be more, not less."

Stephen swivelled round and looked at Richard. "Why d'you think that, love?" he asked carefully, propping his bottom against the side of the bathtub and towelling his hair absently.

"I dunno," muttered Richard. "I've just got a feeling, that's all... that this affair's not over yet. That Gibson deserved all he got, no doubt about that. But he's a vicious bastard, as well as an idiot. I reckon he'll try to make trouble for you — and me, as an incidental. Actually," he continued, suddenly struck by an afterthought, "I've got a feeling he disliked me more than you. Think what he said about me just now."

"If you ask me," said Stephen thoughtfully, "asking Pat Gibson which of us two he disliked most would be like asking him if he'd rather be drowned in pond water or ditch water, don't you think?" He said it so gravely that Richard promptly dissolved into peals of laughter, washing his wretched expression and his gloomy forbodings away in their healthy passage. Stephen caught it, and jumped naked on his friend. They fell onto the bed and dismissed Pat Gibson and all his works from their minds, romping like the children they almost were.

* * *

Before long, though, it was Richard's gloomier apprehensions that turned out to be justified rather than Stephen's cheery optimism. The national newspapers and the television companies lost interest in the attack on the boy; but the local paper and radio station kept up heavy pressure on the police, whose vast and laborious efforts produced not a single lead in over a month.

From time to time a detective would slip quietly into the bar, talk softly to Tom, or to Stephen or Richard, and slip out as unobtrusively as he had arrived. But occasionally also they began to receive unscheduled visits from organised groups of uniformed officers, usually made up of an inspector or a sergeant with two to four PCs. "Isn't it strange," murmured Major Sealey to Richard on one such visit, "how the words 'burst through the door' always come to mind? They never seem just to come through the door, or walk through it, or enter the room. They always 'burst in', somehow, haven't you noticed? I suppose that's why the newspapers never fail to use the cliché." Richard nodded glumly.

So in they would clump. They would stare round, then disperse among the groups of drinkers, eyeballing for the most part, occasionally asking a few questions about nothing in particular. The leader would summon Tom or Stephen with an imperious crooking of a gloved finger, and a civil but ostentatiously official little chat would be held across the bar. "Just making routine checks on licensing law observation," the inspector or sergeant would say, in a tone which clearly indicated that he didn't have to make any kind of explanation if he didn't want to, and was only doing so out of the goodness of his heart, as Stephen observed sourly after one such visit. "Yeah," said someone else. "Routine checks on gay pubs, I'd bet all the money I wish I'd got." Richard directed a swift glance at the speaker and observed that it was one of the local customers, who had never hitherto been heard to say anything hostile.

Sometimes it lasted two minutes, sometimes ten, and then they would go out again. There was never any trouble as such, but the visitations always had an unsettling effect on the drinkers, many of whom would suddenly decide they'd had enough, drain their glasses and disappear the moment the unwelcome visitors had driven noisily off. On a couple of occasions the move backfired on the departing drinkers, who found themselves pulled over by the waiting raiding party just down the lane. They then found out, too late, that they had in fact had a shade more than enough.

Mutterings began to be heard, even among those parts of the clientele who had never been overtly hostile to Stephen and Richard themselves, to the effect that if it hadn't been for the sudden new-found popularity of the pub among the gay community from Worthing and Brighton, old so-and-so wouldn't be about to lose his licence, and so on.

And still the new faces came, often now in parties, sometimes noisy and frolicsome, sometimes slightly tipsy, and very occasionally quarrelsome and seeming to be looking for an argument with the locals. After one such evening Stephen spoke urgently with Tom when the last patrons had been half-urged, half-pushed out into the car park. The result was that from that night onwards anyone arriving less than stone-cold sober, by however microscopic a degree, was refused drinks, which in turn provoked raised voices, protest meetings half-way in and half-way out of the doors, and further mutterings of complaint from the regular clientele, less subdued now, and beginning to get a little pointed.

One evening there happened to be more than usual of their new customers from Brighton, celebrating someone's birthday. Things were beginning to get a little rowdy, a lot of drink was being sloshed onto Tom's carpets, and he, the boys and the few of the regulars who had resolutely stayed on were becoming very anxious, when there was a sudden thunder of engines outside. The merrymakers heard, and the pub suddenly became very quiet. A few moments later a group of about fifteen leathered bikers came stamping through the doors, making a noise like a panzer division in their cleated boots, ranged themselves along the fully-occupied bar by the simple expedient of elbowing aside anyone who hadn't had the sense to vacate it anyway. Tom took one look at the row of brawny, tattooed forearms resting on elbows along the bar, suspended his dress code on the spot, and began serving pints of Guinness and quad rum and coke chasers. Within minutes armwrestling contests were going on along the mirror-like bar surface. Stephen, Richard and the handful of locals looked first at each other, then at the suddenly sober birthday party, in dismay. At the same moment the bikies started looking about them with interest.

"Well, well, well," chuckled one of the the largest, hairiest, oiliest and most terrifying of them suddenly. He hadn't spoken very loud; but in the silence that had gradually settled over everyone present except the bikies, the remark had the effect of a bomb going off, or a sudden, explosive fart at the most intense moment of a memorial service. "How d'you fancy scrumming down with Two Para's rugby team?" murmured Stephen, sotto voce, in Richard's ear. Richard, his nerves strung out to breaking point, emitted a slightly hysterical giggle. He suppressed it instantly, but he wasn't quite quick enough.

"Well," said another gruff voice cheerfully, "nice to hear someone's got a sense of humour, an ain't lost his voice." The speaker, another enormous fellow with a huge black lumberjack's beard and long hair tied in a greasy pony-tail half-way down his back, stared round, as if trying to identify the source of the giggle. On the way his eyes lit on numerous gaudily attired young men, most of them trying to look inconspicuous. The bearded giant grinned and nudged his neighbour. They held a brief whispered conference, then the henchman detached himself, elbowed his way through the press, and returned after a moment with the biggest man he could find among the birthday-partying crowd. The hapless man — who was, though well over six feet tall and heavily built, in reality little more than a boy, about Stephen's age, looked greenish and terrified as the lieutenant thrust him up to the bar beside the giant.

"Hi, hi, hi there, brother," said the bikie cheerfully. "You and me're gonna have us a little game, righty-right? How you feel about that?"

"I... I... wh...what k-kind of game?" stammered the boy.

"You choose, why doncha?" murmured the biker. He leaned easily on the bar, his pint mug almost engulfed in his huge, grimy paw. His square, yellow fingernails were the size of postage stamps, ridged, split and blue-black with grimed-in oil and dirt. He took a gargantuan pull at his glass, emptying three-quarters of a pint down his thick, corded throat. He banged it down and summoned Tom with a jerk of his head, meanwhile picking up his rum chaser and tipping that down after the beer. He never took his eyes off the frightened boy, grinning at him in an apparently friendly fashion. He had laughter lines etched deeply round the corners of his eyes. When the boy had remained silent for a very long half a minute the bikie laughed. "Nothin to say, my man?" he said conversationally. "Well, say I choose the game, eh? How's that?"

"Look," said the boy. He was trying very hard to keep his voice level, but it still hovered perilously close to cracking.

"He can talk," marvelled the giant. "Carry on, my man."

"I... we... I don't want any trouble with you..."

"Oh, really?" said the giant. "Well, ain't life full a surprises? But what makes you think I want any trouble with you, man?"

The youth looked nonplussed for a moment. Then, deciding he'd got nothing to lose, he went on, in a rush, "Look, if you're trying to get me to play any kind of fighting game, or trials of strength with you, or anything like that, you can see for yourself, you'd tear me in half one-handed. I wouldn't be any competition for you at all, would I?"

The giant stared at him for a moment. Then the grin was in evidence again. "Well said, my man," he murmured. "You got guts, son. So what I'm gonna propose to you is, why don't we just have a little arm-wrestle, you an me, just for fun? Ain't gonna be no lighted matches under the loser's hand or anythin a that kind. Jest let's do it, an see if I'm as good as you reckon I am. What you say, my man?"

There was nothing the young man could say. He rolled up the sleeve of his shirt, set his elbow as firmly on the bar as he could, and proffered his open hand. "Nah, nah, son," said the giant patiently. "Like this." He lifted the boy's arm, slid a folded bar towel underneath his elbow, then engaged him. The other youth was big, and his hand and arm were meaty and well-muscled; but the giant had to slew his arm towards himself to lower his fist sufficiently to take hold, and the young man's entire hand and

152

wrist disappeared in his huge fist.

The bout was over in less than a second, announced by the slap of the young man's arm and the back of his hand on the bar. "Once more," rumbled the bikie. The second bout lasted a second or two longer, as the youth did his best to work out the trick of it. "You ain't tryin, man," said the bikie. "Better have one last go." The third attempt was no more successful than the last. But then, to everyone's surprise, he let the boy go. "You ain't no arm wrestler, kid," he said. "But you got some pluck down there. What you drink?"

The youth was caught on the hop between vast, overwhelming relief at the unexpected promise of escape and fear that it was nothing more than the play of cat with mouse, that he failed to take in what the giant had said. "Your wits not workin too brill tonight, son," rumbled the giant. "I said, I'm buyin you a drink. What is it?"

"Oh! I... er... well, if you're... a half of lager," spluttered the boy. "Thanks."

"Ain't no one drunk a half a anything with me for fifteen years," said the giant reflectively. "Not when I been buyin, any road." He called Tom, bought a pint of lager, and stuck it in the young man's hand. "What's your name, my man?" he said.

"Er... M-mike. Mike T..."

"Mike'll do," chuckled the giant. "Ain't interested in last names no way. There's your drink. Cheers."

"Ch-cheers," said the boy.

"Down the hatch," said the bikie genially. The boy stared at him. "Off you go, kid," he said. The boy raised his glass slowly, and drank it steadily down. He was a long time about it, but the pale amber lager disappeared in one long, slow draught. When he set the empty mug down there was a roar of applause from the bikers. "Not bad, m'man," said the giant admiringly. "Have another."

"N-n-nunno, th-thanks," pleaded the youth. "I... I've got to... to drive tonight..."

"So've I, son," said the bikie gravely, and poured most of a pint of Guinness down his throat in no time at all. "Come on, son, have another. Ain't often anybody says no to me. You're one a this gay crowd, ain't you?" he added without the slightest warning of the change of subject. Now it's coming, thought Stephen to himself in dread. The boy at the bar stared at his tormentor, his eyes growing large in fear. "Like bikies?" asked the giant pleasantly.

The boy stared at him still longer, feeling an irrepressible urge to assert himself rising in his spirit. He fought it, in vain, and then gave in to it, rather as some people have sudden, irrepressible urges to jump off when they look over cliff-tops or the parapets of high buildings. At last, unable to help himself, he eyed the giant's lips in the midst of his huge expanse of black beard and moustache, emitted a faint, expiring giggle, and said "Well I don't know, but I think if you took your teeth out I could fancy you."

There was a moment's dead silence. Then there was a simultaneous hiss of indrawn breath from all round the bar, followed by another silence more profound than the first one. Then, finally, there was a roar of applause from the bikers, mingled with catcalls and whoops, all directed at the arm-wrestling champion. He leaned backwards in his comfortable stance at the bar, then straightened up to come a little closer to his full height, and surveyed the young man appreciatively. The boy quaked, hoping only that the end would be relatively quick and painless. "Well, m'man," the bikie said eventually. "You brought your balls with you tonight, din'tcha? I like that. I like it," he roared. "You better have a drink on me, kid," he said, signalling to Tom. He gave the boy the new pint of lager. Then, after looking down at him for a moment, he stood up straight, so that he was now looking down on the boy from a height of about six feet seven. "Like I said, boy, you brought your equipment with you tonight. Jist thank your good fairy" — he glanced across at the birthday party pointedly — "that I'm in a good mood myself tonight. Cheers." And he lowered another half-pint in a draught.

"Ch-cheers," said the boy for the second time that evening, and began to swill his lager.

"Ain't no need to hurry, kid," said the giant. He turned to speak to the biker on the other side of him. The boy felt the others behind him part to let him through, and realised that he had been dismissed. He edged backwards through the bikers, hardly able to believe his good fortune, and escaped.

"Better find someone a bit bigger," said the giant biker. "Ain't gonna find us much sport here, though, I don't think, on second thoughts. Shall we take our valued custom elsewhere, friends and neighbours?" And as if by some pre-arranged signal the bikers all moved off in a single movement, almost like a single organism, flowing in a stream to the doors. They vanished in seconds, and, astonishingly, almost in silence. The last to leave drew the door softly closed and latched it without a sound. There was a roar of engines, and, inside the bar, a rush to the windows. After a moment they roared off in an orderly single file, hogs, choppers and an occasional classic English machine, led by the arm-wrestling giant astride a vast black Harley Davidson.

Two minutes after the last biker's tail light had disappeared round the bend in the lane, one of the uniformed police raiding parties arrived. There were four of them. They made ten times the noise coming in as the bikers had made going out, and spent the entire time they remained there wondering why everyone seemed so pleased to see them, and why apparently all present seemed to want to buy them a drink. They went out after a quarter of an hour, very puzzled and suspicious policemen indeed.

"Well," said Stephen to Tom, Richard, the Major and the couple of members of the cricket club who were there, when the initial round of exaggerated sighs of relief had subsided. "Were we lucky, or were we lucky? Or what?"

"I dunno," said Tom, "but I was beginning to get a bit worried, I can tell you. Did they have some kind of look-out out there, d'you think? They seemed to know when the law were coming."

"I know that gang," volunteered a slightly-built, scantily-dressed boy in the birthday crowd, who were now beginning to recover their nerve and eddying about once more with the return of normality.

"You do?" said everyone in earshot.

"Yes," the boy said, looking round shyly as he saw that everyone was craning necks to see who had spoken. "They use some of the places in Brighton. They're one of the local bikers' chapters. Only they're all gay. I think that's why they didn't... you know, why there wasn't any trouble..."

His further remarks were drowned in the uproar that this revelation evoked.

"Great God! Are we going to have them coming in here now..."

"...got to be done about this..."

"...put a stop to this..."

"... couldn't care less if they're as gay as my hairdresser's underpants. I'm bloody glad they were if it meant..."

"...doesn't go to a hairdresser... only got to look at him to see that..."

"...coppers were as suspicious as hell, you could see that a mile off. That means more trouble to come from them..."

"...mark my words..."

The reluctant arm-wrestler was widely feted as a hero, including by the Major, who sought him out, gave him a grandfatherly pat on the arm, bought him a drink, and insisted on introducing him to Stephen and Richard.

"You're the same sort as these two," he said, twitching his moustache approvingly. "Friends of mine, both of them. If you're as you are, and you've got the pluck to face that great oaf like that, you're the right material, make no mistake about that. And don't let any of this silly hostility upset you, my boy. These two don't."

* * *

But the Major was wrong. When the party eventually broke up, the last few late-stayers were got rid of and they had had their customary nightcap with Tom in the silent bar, made cosy by turning off all the lights except the one above their own corner of the bar, the boys lay on their separate beds, staring at the patterns of shadow and light on the ceiling above and talking things over in low voices, far into the night.

"I wish we'd never heard of this place," said Richard. "I certainly wish old Reggie had never left it to Graham, or that you'd sold it or something."

Stephen lay in silence for some time, thinking about this. Eventually he said, taking care to keep his voice neutral and free from accusation, "Look, Rich, love, I'm sorry, but that just doesn't make sense. I mean it doesn't match up to everything you've said before." Richard said nothing, waiting for him to elaborate. "You see, sweetheart, it was you who first got upset and aerated about that reporter bringing the pub any publicity at all. But when the publicity caused problems with the gay crowd starting to come in from Brighton and places, it was you who insisted that we had to serve everybody equally, without fear or favour, you might say. Yeah, well I agreed with you about that — or rather, you convinced me. But now that we've made that the policy of the pub, you're upset again, because that policy's brought a bit of trouble. You can't have it both ways, Rich, surely?"

Richard thought about it. "I don't want it both ways, Stevie," he said. "Where this pub's concerned, I think I've come to the conclusion that I don't want it either way. I'm just thinking back to the old days, when we were living happily at my place, going about together... we used to go down to the cricket club for a drink, and to the old Golden Harp... where we met old Terry, remember? I'd like to have a talk to Terry about this situation, see how he'd deal with it, wouldn't you?"

"Well I don't know what Terry would think," said Stephen mildly, "but surely it's no good always looking for somebody like Terry Garrard to solve problems for us, is it? I mean surely, the only way people like us will ever learn how to deal with situations for ourselves — like this one — is by dealing with them and learning by experience? Isn't it?"

"I don't know, Stevie," said Richard miserably. "I don't know how to solve problems like these, and I don't know if I want to know. All I know is that I'm unhappy here, and I don't want to have to keep on facing things like policemen, and terrible attacks on little kids, and eleven-foot motor-bike maniacs. I don't see why we need to have problems to solve at all. Why can't we just go back to how we were, happy and enjoying life?"

There was no answer; but after a few moments he heard the sound of Stephen getting up off his bed and padding across the room. Next moment Stephen came down beside him and cradled him in his arms. He held him tenderly, carefully, as if handling eggs, rocking him gently in his arms, running his fingers through Richard's abundant blond hair and covering his face with little kisses. "Do you really want us to get out of here, Rich?" he asked gently. He heard Richard draw in his breath sharply, but there was no answer for some time, so he went back to caressing and soothing him. "If you really want to get out, Rich, my lovely, I'm willing to. I'll leave it to the lawyers to go on managing the place like they were before. Or I'll sell it, if you like. Trouble is, the problems won't go away just because you and I go away, will they? If we clear out, someone else'll have to cope with the problems that have cropped up because of us, won't they? Still, I'm ready to sell. I'd sell it tomorrow if it would stop you from being unhappy. I'd give it away, come to that. It's up to you."

"Up to me?" said Richard, sounding very surprised in the darkness. "It's nothing to do with me, Stevie. It's your pub, and I don't want to influence you over something as big as this."

Stephen stiffened, and rolled away from Richard in order to stare at him in the darkness. The faint light of the moon coming through the windows lit up his hair like a heavy white-gold halo, and his eyes shone dimly from the shadow of his face. "Richard," he said eventually, and there was great pain and hurt as well as surprise in his voice. "You can't duck out of issues like that. You really can't, love. No, don't get upset. I'm only saying you can't have things both ways. You can't get upset about the problems here on the one hand, and then say it's nothing to do with you on the other hand when I suggest bailing out. It's not up to me, as you put it, Rich. It's not nothing to do with you. And you can't simply wash your hands of it and say you don't want to influence me. What the hell do you think you've being doing for the last eighteen months, or whatever it is? Since we first met? Christ, Rich, practically everything I've done since then has been done because of you, on advice from you or for you. You've influenced me every single day. Christ, Rich, are we married, or aren't we?"

There was a suppressed chuckle from somewhere half beside and half underneath him, and Stephen took a moment off from the debate to reflect how he loved Richard's chuckle. It was the same soft, sexy gurgling laugh that had been one of the things that had endeared him to Stephen from the earliest days of their acquaintance, and right through the gathering process of their love. He lay savouring the thought for a while, then sighed, switched off the lazy mood and returned to the argument.

"What I'm trying to say, Rich, my dearest," he said, a little wearily, "is that I can't just take all the responsibility for everything on myself. Like for instance, I can't just announce tomorrow morning to Tom and everybody that I've decided to withdraw and let them go back to running the pub as they did before — you know, let Pat Gibson back in, ban gay people — you wouldn't like that, would you, but you know bloody well that's the first thing they'd do. I can't leave them in a position where they've got to hire forty-eight bouncers on permanent stand-by in case the bikers come back so they can tell em to fuck off. Or at least, I s'pose I could, but I don't think that would be a very responsible way of going about the thing. We've had an influence on this place, Rich. You've had an influence — a big one. It'll never be the same as before we appeared on the scene, whatever we decide to do right now. So okay, sure I'll sell the fucking place, if that's what you want. But I want you to at least acknowledge that it's in part your decision. Christ, after all, it's half yours, anyway, isn't it?"

There was a silence. Then Richard said very quietly, "Is it? I don't know what you mean, Stevie."

"For Christ's sake, Rich, are you trying to be thick?" demanded Stephen, his voice rising to a squeak of frustration — rather as Richard's sometimes did when he was feeling the same kind of thing with Stephen. "Look," he said patiently. "You are my best friend. You are my lover, my sexual partner, but that's not the half of it. You are my trusted, adored, worshipped, whatever you like, you are my most beloved other half. If I went in for people of the female persuasion I'd've married you and you'd be my wife. If I could marry you, or if we were Danish or wherever the hell it is, I'd've married you anyway, and you'd be... whatever it would be called." They both sniggered as two minds turned simultaneously to a consideration of possible forms of words. Once again Stephen lay for a moment, savouring and enjoying themoment. It reminded him poignantly, almost painfully, of something that he struggled briefly to identify. Then he saw, in a moment of intuition, that it had reminded him of precisely the former state of innocent, untroubled happiness of their first few months as lovers, when everything was simple. Once again, he lay grasping the moment for a while, reluctant to let it go, before returning to the fray.

"Look," he said again. "You are all the things I just spoke of. If that's so, it follows that you are the half-owner of everything I own. I don't want all that money, this place, all the rest of it, without you. In a straight choice between having you and having everything else I've got I'd give the lot to the poor, or put it on a horse. Meanwhile, I've got it and I've got you, and it can make life very cushy and easy for us — provided you're still part of the package. But you're half-owner, and that's flat. Which means that you've got all the responsibilities that go with ownership, as well as the opportunities it offers. Fuck me, Rich, I sound like a pamphlet. But you see what I mean?"

Richard lay silent for a long time, allowing Stephen to stroke and caress him softly. "You're too good for me, Stevie. You needed someone like Graham, you know. I always told you you frightened the life out of me. But yes, love, I see what you mean. I'd just... I suppose I'd just not wanted to think about it much. But yes. I understand. But I'm still not happy about us being here. Let's talk about it some more later. Just hold me now, please, Stevie. Please hold me."

"All right, love," said Stephen. "I'll tell you what we'll do. Tomorrow we'll talk to Tom. We'll say we're going off somewhere for a while — going on a cricket holiday or something — and won't be around for a bit. We'll leave the pub in his hands, but we'll tell him not to alter things too much. Then we'll give ourselves a break — maybe we will have a holiday, come to that. We'll take your parents out somewhere slap-up. Spend a bit more time with Bill and the gang at the club. Praps we could go and have a look at some of those places in Brighton that they're always on about. I've never been to a gay pub, have you?"

"Frequently," murmured Richard, arousing Stephen expertly with his fingers and slipping his tongue into his mouth.

"Wait, Rich," said Stephen urgently, fighting down his rapidly rising passion. "Lemme finish... mmm." He struggled free from Richard for a moment, wanting to say what he had to say. "We'll take a holiday, Rich. I wonder why I didn't think of it before. We need a holiday. We owe ourselves one, and we can sure as hell bloody well afford one, so fuck it, let's go and spend some of our ill-gotten gains. Meanwhile we'll leave the boozer to its own devices. Now you can do whatever you like to... ooooh, Richard... oh, Christ..."

13

They woke late the next morning, and got under Tom's feet swiping a breakfast of hastily jammed-together ham sandwiches, lager shandy and pork scratchings from behind the bar.

Then they decided to go off for a stroll. It was a dreary day, overcast and autumnal, not yet raining but with a heavy damp in the air. They wandered without any special aim, and by some instinct their feet led them to the cricket ground, a place they both found restful, and looking particularly peaceful and attractive now that all the surrounding trees were turning copper and gold.

They were on their third leisurely circuit of the boundary, mooching companionably together and saying very little, when a soft voice behind them made them both jump.

They spun round in unison, and found Alfie Brett, the elderly groundsman, striding noiselessly behind them in ancient black wellingtons. One of them, they both noticed simultaneously, had a red and black bicycle-tyre patch on it. They grinned at it involuntarily, and halted to wait for him. He smiled at the boys and caught them up.

"It's a restful place to come, all right," he murmured as the three of them ambled on round the boundary. "They all come up here when there's problems to chew over."

The boys looked at each other. "How in the world did you know we were talking over problems?" asked Richard.

Alfie laughed softly. "Because I've seen the problems, my dear boy," he said. "Plus your demeanour as you strolled round. It's where they all come, as I said. At a guess, I'd say you were discussing how to extricate yourselves from the small spot of difficulty you've got yourselves into with the pub."

They exchanged surprised glances once again. "We were, at that," Stephen grunted, stooping to pick a long stem of grass and chewing it meditatively. "Though how you could possibly know that beats me." The old man laughed softly, but said nothing. "We... we're in something of a disagreement about it," Richard volunteered.

"I thought so," said Alfie at last. "Would you care to talk about it to someone else? An outsider — a sympathetically disposed outsider, of course — can sometimes throw additional light on a problem. Sometimes he sees something the people involved are too close to the problem to see."

"I certainly would," muttered Stephen, spitting out the remains of his grass and picking another one. "Me too," contributed Richard.

"Well, let's see," said Alfie, halting at the rear of the pavilion and lugging a heavy bunch of keys from the pocket of his battered, old-fashioned grey flannel trousers. As he unlocked the rear door it began to rain, heavily and steadily. A vast bank of black cloud rolled nearer from the direction of the sea. "Let's sit in the clubhouse," said Alfie, looking up unconcernedly into the rain. "This won't stop today. Come on, get inside, both of you, or you'll catch your deaths. We'll have a brew."

Then he shuffled the keys again and let them through a further door, into the main room of the pavilion. Inside he set them to opening a couple of the heavy shutters on the windows looking out across the veranda. Then he found yet another key, let himself into the small kitchen where the players' wives made the teas on match-days, found three huge mugs — the club had no use for cups — and busied himself making the tea.

They shifted a table so they could look out of the windows across the pretty ground, and a few minutes later the fragrance of tea filled the neat little room. "I hope you like lapsang souchong," said Alfie. "I never drink anything else."

"Fine," said Richard.

"Never heard of it," said Stephen, taking an experimental sip. "Smoky," he said a second later. "Nice though." Alfie chuckled.

They sat for a while sipping the tea, and Alfie ambled over to the kettle to make more. When they all had fresh mugs he had folded his lanky frame down onto his seat once more, plunked his elbows on the table, and looked steadily at the boys.

"Well," he said after a pause. "At a guess, I'd say you were worrying about how to ease yourselves out of the pub, without abdicating the responsibilities you feel you have for the... not so much the problems as the... changes that have taken place recently. Changes you feel that you yourselves are to some extent responsible for. Or that you, perhaps caused to happen.

"Or rather," he went on, not giving them a chance to speak, "I'd guess that one of you feels that, and that's the cause of the discussion."

They looked at him in some amazement at this apparent feat of mind-reading. He saw their expressions, and chuckled again. "Elementary, my dear Watsons," he said gently. "No," he corrected them, "old Alfie's not a mind-reader or a magician. Just a very great deal older than you two children. Don't take offence," he said, seeing Stephen's brows contract slightly; and he gave them a sudden smile, of peculiar sweetness, grandfatherly but utterly free from patronising, fond and — '... serene, that was the word', Richard said when they talked about it later.

"Don't forget," went on Alfie, speaking to them with great gentleness, almost tenderness, "that from where I'm looking most people under thirty-five look like children. I've seen it all before. People tend to forget that, partly because the habit of reverence for the old is fast dying — and a good thing too, considering what the old have done over the last few decades — but also because I make a point of never coming the old soldier." He took a short, blackened pipe from the pocket of his old green fatigue jacket, filled and lit it unhurriedly before going on. "But I think you two could perhaps use a little impartial counsel. It's available if you want it." He sat silent, watching them. The fragrance of the tobacco mingled with that of the tea.

"Yes, please," said Stephen simply. "Tell me," said Alfie, replying in kind. So they tried to explain, hesitantly, uncertainly, in a series of beginnings without endings, the deeply-buried unease and discontent that was troubling them. After a while Alfie raised a hand, stopping them gently.

"So you, then," he said, gesturing with the stem of his pipe in Richard's direction, "are unhappy, because you feel that life has become too complicated of late, and you want to go back to how it was, with just the two of you, comfortable, wanting nothing that you haven't already got. You have what you really want, and need: each other. And so, sufficient unto the day the joy thereof.

"You, on the other hand," he said, aiming the pipe at Stephen, "are unhappy because you feel that the changes that have taken place at the Crown have been largely your doing, and you feel responsible for the fact. You feel that whatever you do now, whether you bail out and run for cover, or whether you stay here and... tough it out, I think the expression is, you have some responsibility to leave the pub in as good order as you found it. Not necessarily the same as you found it, but running and in good order. You don't feel inclined simply to wash your hands of the place and leave it to other people to sort out problems that you feel you yourselves at least partially created."

They stared at him, wide-eyed. "That's absolutely it," cried Stephen after a moment's pause. "That was exactly how we were arguing it out last night. "But Alfie, which of us is right?"

"Why, both of you," murmured Alfie gently, puffing contentedly on his ancient, half-burnt-away pipe.

"Both of us?" queried Richard. "How can we both be right?" Alfie unfolded himself and ambled off to the kitchen to make fresh tea. He came back with it, set it down and got himself and his pipe comfortable once more. Outside the rain came down harder, drumming on the roof and lashing itself from time to time against the windows. "Good for my vegetables," Alfie murmured. Then he turned back to the two boys, staring at him anxiously across the table as they sipped the scalding, aromatic tea.

"You're both right," he said eventually, "because neither of you is wrong. Both points of view are equally tenable, or legitimate, if you like the word better. You" — he gestured at Richard — "are quite right to feel that your first duty is to each other. You" — with a wave at Stephen — "are equally right to feel some responsibility for the waves you have set up in a lot of other people's lives here. People who didn't know of your existence until a few months ago. You appeared in their midst, and you suddenly changed them, and things that were familiar to them. People like familiar things. The most elementary form of security is stability. You rocked a lot of people's boats — not deliberately. In fact I'd guess you did your very utmost to avoid rocking any boats if you could help it. Well, in the end you couldn't help it, and the boats got rocked in any case.

"What you have to realise is that you can help very few things that happen in this life. Change happens, all the time. To try to resist it is as futile an occupation as trying to resist the tide." He fell silent for a while, and sat gazing out of the window, puffing clouds of blue smoke from the little pipe, an old man at peace with himself and his small world, watching the rain saturating the cricket field that was his own particular love and pride. Neither of them would have dreamed of interrupting.

At length he resumed. "There's an expression you'll have heard," he said. "It's become a cliché of our time. 'You can't turn the clock back' — that or some variant on it. The fact that it's usually uttered by consummately silly asses — journalists and so forth — doesn't make it a scrap less true. That's the point about clichés, isn't it? That though they may be parrotted by fools, they're still only clichés because they're true? Well, this one is as true as any. You can't turn back the clock, or the roll of events that have happened. So what else can you do but accept them? You can't alter the fact that the village pub here, which used to be a fairly typical Sussex pub, is now identified as a gay pub. You can't alter the fact that it may become a staging post for motorbike lads. What you can do is to accept that if you hadn't started these balls rolling, someone else very probably would have done so, this year, next year, sometime, never. So, accept that it was, in fact, yourselves, and then bail out if you wish. It won't make any difference, to anything. I can tell you what will happen, if you like; or I can leave you in the dark, if that's what you'd rather. But in either case, your knowing won't make the slightest difference."

"What'll happen, Alfie?" asked Stephen in the end. "If we clear out and leave this place in peace?"

The old man sat smoking and gazing placidly out at the rain, now steady and torrential, for some time. "It'll be a compromise," he said. "It always is, in the end. In real life, that is. Some people, politicians for instance, whose sense of their own importance is so overweening that they actually believe in their own ability to change

164

things, affect to despise compromise. But they're wrong, and their foolish ideas are always buried deep under layers of compromise within a snap of the fingers of their departure.

"So, if you boys leave us here, within a few days things will have gone back some way towards how they were before you had ever been seen in this village. But they won't be all the way back to how they were before, because that would be contrary to the laws of the real world, and therefore impossible. And a good thing, too. It was high time someone began the process of dragging this village into the twentieth century. You were appointed to that task.

"I'm a fatalist. I believe everything that happens happens for a reason, according to some ordained plan. I think that's what believing in God means. So I think it was your appointed task to jolt this village out of its complacency, its comfortable, right-wing self-righteousness, with all the nasty little faces of racialism, homophobia and the rest of it. It hasn't been at all easy to be gay in a place like this all these years, believe me."

He stared out of the windows for another interval, then turned in his seat and gave them the same affectionate smile. The boys, for their part, sat goggling at him as if the lean, stringy old man had suddenly become radioactive and started glowing in the dim light.

"You mean... you're... like us?" asked Stephen cautiously.

The old man gave him a slow, sad smile. "Yes, indeed," he said.

"But what did you do?" asked Richard, trying to imagine living in a community as small and as tight as the village.

"As I said, it was never easy," said Alfie. "Not that I've been celibate. Don't get me wrong. But it was always difficult. It was illegal to attempt to put my sexuality into effect, remember, until I was old enough to be your father. I was on the edge of middle age before they even found a comparatively neutral word for us." He saw the incomprehension on their faces, and chuckled. "You boys bandy the word 'gay' about," he said, "and think nothing of it. Try to imagine, if you will — if you can — a time when there was no such word. 'Gay' came over from America in the nineteen-fifties. Before that they used to have all kinds of words for us, but none of them was pleasant, almost all were downright insulting. Gussies, they used to call us, and nancies, nancy-boys, fairies, lilies. Then poof and poofter came on the scene, and I'm not sure I didn't find those the most offensive of the lot.

"All the same, we managed. I used to catch a train to London. Or, very often I used to ride my bike into Brighton, and we used to hold clandestine meetings — in pubs, occasionally, but they were nothing at all like gay pubs nowadays, open dancing, kissing and camping it up. It was all dreadfully hole and corner, with everyone in constant dread of the police. Sometimes we used to meet at someone's home. Sometimes it would be outdoors: in a bus station, the library, anywhere. It really was very unpleasant and difficult. But it was all we had. And in some ways it was more fun, I think. There was the constant sense of being in a battle — a battle for one's very survival as a person. But I think we'd have exchanged our circumstances for yours, given an offer." He chuckled again. "The irony is that now everything's happened as it has in this village, I'm a good way past the age when I might have wanted to do anything about it. All the same, I can derive a certain perverse pleasure from seeing the village shaken up and forced to face such things. It never wanted to, and it doesn't want to now. But you've forced the issue, and I'm enjoying the spectacle. No one has ever known about me here."

The boys stared at each other, wondering what to say. Richard, with his natural grace, found the right words. "I think, Alfie," he said diffidently, "you've just made it all worth while. For me, at least. I'm glad now that things have turned out as they have."

Alfie turned to look at him, and once again the slow, serene smile illuminated his face. It made him look much younger, and both boys saw a glimpse of the handsome, clean-chiselled face he must have had when he was a young man. Then he laughed. "There was another thing we used to do back in the days when I was not much older than you are now," he said, chuckling and gazing into space as he remembered.

And then he told them. They looked at each other, seeing the identical reaction in each other's face. "Oh, yes!" crowed Richard. "It's a great idea."

"That we've got to do," said Stephen at the same moment. "How do we go about it, Alfie?" he asked. Alfie, laughing, made a few suggestions. "I rather thought you might see it like that," he said. "As a challenge, I mean." They fell to excited discussion of the possibilities, and Alfie made more tea.

It was a good deal later in the afternoon when the rain eased off sufficiently for them to make their way back to the pub at a brisk trot. The sky was already almost black with heavy banks of rain-clouds, and evening was drawing in. When they got there

Stephen went straight to the telephone and rang the Elderton Park clubhouse. In answer to his enquiry the steward told him that Bill had been in and left, so Stephen rang him at home.

"Weather's all right there," he reported to Richard when he finished talking to Bill. They got drinks, and settled in their usual corner of the bar, chatting inconsequentially to Tom. There was no one else in the bar yet. After a while Stephen got up. "Just got another call to make," he said off-handedly, and left the other two chatting.

When he returned to the others he was bubbling over with ill-suppressed excitement. "Got a little something fixed up for to-morrow," he said. "Liven this place up a bit." Richard looked at him in surprise. "Tomorrow?" he said. "We'll be back home to-morrow, won't we? For the match," he added.

Stephen stared blankly at him for a moment. "We'll go to-morrow morning," he said, still quivering with internal excitement. "This is one of my best ideas yet." He refused to go into details, saying in answer to all Richard's efforts to prise it out of him, "You'll just have to wait and see." Then he turned to Tom. "We'll be away for a while, Tom. There's no cricket here this week, and we're going off on a bit of a holiday."

"Oh," said Tom neutrally. "Righto." He thought about it for a moment. "Might not be a bad thing," he said eventually. "Let things calm down a bit, get back to normal, if you see what I mean..." He tailed off as it occurred to him how his words must have sounded. But the boys grinned at him, understanding. They both liked Tom, and were sympathetic to his awkward, and sometimes very difficult, position between the two factions in the pub.

"There's one other thing, Tom," said Stephen casually. "Something you could do for us, if you will." Tom raised his eyebrows. "Yes," said Stephen. "I could do it myself, but it would be a lot easier for you, if you'd be willing to do it as a favour for me."

"Go on," said Tom, mystified.

"I want to get Pat Gibson back in here," said Stephen. This time Tom's eyebrows climbed still further, and remained aloft, so great was his surprise.

"Really?" he said. "I'm amazed. Can I ask why?"

"Er, well, I'd rather you didn't," said Stephen. "Just say that I'm trying to put right anything I think we — or rather, that is, I — may have done to upset people here. I didn't want to rock any boats, and I don't even want someone like Gibson permanently put out because of our getting involved here. Will he come back, d'you think?" he finished boyishly.

Tom laughed. "Not half, he will," he said. "He's already wishing he'd kept his views to himself. He has to drive eight miles every time he wants a pint, and with all this police activity he can only drink a couple, then he has to go onto non-alcoholic lager, and you know how Pat likes his beer." He chuckled again at the thought of it.

"So you think he'd accept an olive branch?" asked Stephen, grinning. "You think he'd come back in here if you told him I'd suggested it?"

"Hmmm," mused Tom. "I don't think he's any fonder of you than he ever was, if you want to know the truth. But I think he'll swallow any number of principles if it gets him back in here. But can I suggest what I tell him?"

"Go ahead."

"I'd say I tell him you and Richard are away for a while, and that you've put the running of the pub in my hands while you're away. I'll say I'm not barring the gay folk, but I've been given authority to run the pub how I like, and that I've decided to lift the bar on him. That way he can come back in here without feeling beholden to you. He'd rather have it that way, I'm sure."

Stephen thought about it for a moment. "Yeah. I like it," he said. "Great idea, Tom. Good thinking." Richard nodded his agreement. Tom looked closely at them. "There's something underneath this," he said shrewdly. "You're not telling me all of it, are you?"

"It's on the secret list just now," said Stephen, a little apologetically. "Not that we don't trust you, Tom," he went on hurriedly. "But it's something strictly between Rich and me and one other person at the moment, and I can't let anyone else in on it yet. You'll be the first to know the moment I've got it all fixed up, I promise." And Tom had to be content with that.

* * *

The following morning Stephen ostentatiously awarded himself a lie-in. Richard was up fairly early, and when Stephen was still dozing at after ten o'clock he began to badger him to get up, worried about being late for their match at Elderton Park, "Come on, Steve," he hissed urgently at him, stripping the quilt off and tugging at him. "Wake up!"

Stephen rolled over and made a grab for him, grinning. "Never mind that," said Richard, evading his clutch. "Come on, Stevie, get up. We'll be late for the match. You do remember you're playing today, I suppose. I've got a long drive beforehand, too. Come on, for Christ's sake."

"You haven't," said Stephen, giving up his pretence of sleep and hugging his knees to his chest. "No drive for you today, old love." He laughed at Richard's puzzled expression and went on "I've laid on a bit of a treat for us, my lovely." He refused, maddeningly, to say a word more. But at least he did get up.

When they had scrounged a breakfast he made Richard lock his mother's car in the private garage behind the hotel. Richard, still mystified, obeyed. Stephen lolled about lazily in the bar, drinking shandy slowly and chattering to Tom and a couple of early drinkers.

At a couple of minutes to twelve Stephen passed his glass to Tom and collared Richard. "Come on," he said. "Mustn't be late." Richard stared at him, speechless, then followed him as he picked up his bag and headed for the door, calling out a bright "Cheerio!" to Tom as he went. Richard followed him through the paved area outside the pub, across the narrow road in front of it, and onto the little triangular green opposite. By chance Pat Gibson was just driving past from his home facing the far side of the green. "On his way to whichever pub he uses," grinned Stephen. He waved gaily to Gibson as he drove past, receiving a glare in return.

"Hear anything?" he asked Richard a few moments later, cocking his head. Richard did likewise, and a moment later said "Yes. Helicopter, isn't it? Why?" Stephen said nothing, but listened attentively as the thudding sound of the helicopter came closer and closer.

"Crikey," said Richard when the sound of the rotor had become deafening. "He's low, wherever he is." A moment later he gasped in astonishment as the helicopter roared into sight, drumming over the pub barely thirty feet above the chimney tops. "He's off his head," said Richard. "Unless he's..." He turned to gaze at Stephen as the penny finally dropped. "Stevie," he said, his eyes alight. The small craft was meanwhile dropping down in the centre of the neatly kept green. Stephen promptly started towards it, and he followed, coming up behind him as Stephen began to talk to the pilot, a burly young man with a shaggy blond beard and a long ponytail. He was wearing scuffed brown cowboy boots with run-down stack heels, clean jeans and a lumberjack shirt, and the ponytail was tied with a ribbon in Brigade of Guards colours. When Richard managed to hear a few syllables over the deafening thump of the rotor, he turned out to be Australian.

"Our transport for the day," beamed Stephen, gesturing expansively behind him as if the machine belonged to him personally. He slung his bag into the luggage compartment behind the seats for pilot and co-pilot, and gestured above the noise for Richard to do the same. Stephen was already climbing into the craft. Tom and the early drinkers came hurrying out of the pub to see what was happening, in time to see Richard disappearing into the machine and taking the third seat, behind Stephen in the co-pilot's seat. Less than a minute after it descended onto the green it was airborne again and thumping off in the direction of Elderton Park Cricket Club.

* * *

"Well, mate," said Bill as the helicopter soared away from the outfield and disappeared fast into the patchwork blue and grey sky, "you keep on comin up with surprises for us, don't you? Last year you were a burglar, in a small way a business. This year you turn up for matches in a chopper. What a you got planned for next season? Wouldn't like to jump out of a cake at the annual dinner an dance, would you?" Stephen grinned, still bubbling at the success of his stunt.

"What beats me," said Richard, feeling much the same wild elation, "is how he got permission to land on the green down there — and here for that matter."

"He didn't," chortled Stephen. "He's a freelance operator. One of the companies I rang suggested him. They all said they couldn't do it, but one chap said I might try him. They said he was mad enough to do anything once. I rang him straightaway, and he said he'd do it."

Led by Bill the crowd of cricketers who had come streaming across the ground from the pavilion when they had seen that the helicopter was really going to make a landing on the outfield went back to continue getting ready for the match, chattering among themselves about their pre-match surprise. Stephen saw himself being pointed out to various members of the opposition, and suddenly laughed aloud, for the simple pleasure of being alive. "We'll have that holiday anyway, shall we, Rich?" he said, peeling off from the main bunch to go with his friend to the scorebox.

"I could do with one, I think," murmured Richard, still a little wild-eyed from the excitement of the trip, his first in a helicopter. He found himself feeling strangely old. He also had a sudden, and disagreeable moment of premonition that maybe he would not be with Stephen for very much longer. He shivered, once, violently.

"What's up?" asked Stephen, sensitive to his friend's state of mind as usual, and instantly anxious.

"N-nothing," said Richard. "Just somebody walking over my grave."

Stephen stood watching him for a moment. Then he nodded and smiled. "Okay, love," he said. "I'd better go and change."

"Do you want to know how many you need for fifteen hundred runs this season?" asked Richard in a small voice.

"No, thanks," said Stephen. "If I knew how many I'd dither about and not get them. Tell me afterwards." He ruffled Richard's hair, then headed for the dressing room. On the way he encountered Bill, looking for him. "We're batting," he said with a rueful grin. "Put in. You're number three as usual, Stevie, okay?"

"Okay," said Stephen. "And Bill..."

Bill looked at him, raising his eyebrows.

"If you get a chance, will you sit and have a chat with Rich?"

"Yeah, course," said Bill, a little puzzled by his serious tone and expression. "Why? What's the matter?"

"I don't know," said Stephen seriously. "He seems to be a bit depressed, or... I don't know, really. All I know is that he doesn't seem his usual self lately. You might be able to get something out of him — something about what's upsetting him. He likes you, and... and... he doesn't seem to want to talk to me much right now. Will you have a sit with him, see if you can worm anything out of him?"

"Course I will," said Bill. He left Stephen to go on his way to the dressing room, and himself went across to the scorebox where Richard was setting up for the day. He found him sitting at the desk inside the open flap, staring into vacancy, with his chin in his hands.

"You all right, our kid?" Bill asked him, seeing immediately what Stephen had meant. "Or is there summin the matter?"

Richard came out of his trance and gave him a watery smile.

"N-nothing much, Bill," he murmured, a little sadly.

Bill stared hard at him. "Don't give me that," he said kindly.

"Oh, it's nothing very much," said Richard, making way for Bill to squeeze his bulky frame past him and take the other seat at the desk. "Just Stevie."

"What's the matter with him?" asked Bill. "He seems all right to me. Never seen him in higher spirits."

"He's growing up," said Richard. "Fast. I used to be older than he was, quite a lot older. Now... I... sometimes I feel as if I'm nothing more than a retarded kid, while he... he seems to have grown up, all of a sudden. And he's growing away. Away from me. And I... I... I need him, Bill. Only I don't know what to do to keep him."

"Well, I'll tell you a good way to start," said Bill, ruffling his blond curls gently for a moment with a huge red paw. Richard blinked at him hopefully.

"You can start by getting it all off your chest," said Bill. "I'll go and sort out the order, then I'll be back. They haven't got a scorer, so I'll volunteer for first shift with their book. Then you can tell your Uncle Bill all about it." And gradually, between balls and overs, at first in fits and starts, then gradually getting into his stride, Richard did.

* * *

When he had finished pouring out his half-formed worries and fears, Bill sat pensively for a couple of overs, mechanically recording the progress of the match in bold, firm strokes of his pen, while Richard maintained his usual immaculate pencilled sheet. At last he delivered his verdict.

"You're worryin too much, our kid," he said. "Mostly about nothin. Up to now you been a bouncy, easy-goin kid with nothin to worry about. Now you've gone from one extreme to the other, an you're tryin to take all the problems a the entire gay community on your own shoulders. Well, no one can do that, an no one, no community, is worth the trouble. I seen enough a you an Stevie to know people like you're just ordinary people. They don't need you to take their worries on board. They'd rather sort out their own troubles, an in the long run there's no one else who can in any case. So your cue is, let em sort em out for emselves, an stop worryin.

"Also, you're worryin too much about upsettin this boozer a yours. They can take care a their problems, too, and they don't need you or Steve to worry about em, either. Sure you've made changes down there — much-needed, some of em, by the sound of it. Okay, so what? You wanna make changes to somethin you own, so make em. But if you're gonna make em, have the courage a your own convictions: make your changes, an then sleep easy. You've said you're gonna take a holiday. Right. I think that's very sensible. Have your holiday, an make it a long one. You can afford it now, can't you? So what the hell's standin in your way? Nothin. When you go back to the pub, go back an breeze in as if nothin's happened, an start runnin the show how you wanna run it again. Anyone doesn't like it, well, fuck em, son. It's your show, not theirs. They don't like it, they can go somewhere else. Your friends'll stay with you. Anyone who doesn't ain't a friend, an any friends you lose by tryin to make things better ain't worth keepin.

"I like this idea for takin a rise outa this dentist, what's his name? Gibson. Yeah. Do that. I'd like to be in on that meself, as it happens. Will you keep me posted about it? Good. Other than that, leave the runnin a the place to your man Tom. He struck me as a good sort when we were down there. Let him run it within your guidelines, an you an Stevie concentrate on enjoyin life. That way you go some way back to bein how you used to be, an at the same time you shoulder whatever of your new responsibilities you wanna shoulder. That's the only one's you need to shoulder. You can sell the boozer any time you like, remember. An really, son, that's about it. Ain't much else to say."

Richard sat absorbing Bill's homily, thinking about it. When he looked up at Bill's craggy face Bill had his reward. Richard's face was alight, and he looked more sure of himself than he had for weeks. "Thanks, Bill," he said earnestly. "You're a good sort. And you're right, of course. I'll do as you say."

Bill grinned down at him. "Champagne for your real friends, our kid," he said. "An real pain for your sham friends. Never forget that. Ah. End a the over. I'm gonna find a relief."

He squeezed past Richard and left the scorebox. Richard called him as he passed in front of the hatch. "Steve needs six for fifteen hundred runs this season," he said, "and eleven for his fifty."

"I'll tell em," said Bill reassuringly, and hurried across to the enclosure to find a substitute scorer.

A couple of overs later there was a roar as Stephen flicked a fast leg-cutter through mid-wicket for four. "Fifteen hundred, Stevie," came a bellow in Bill's stentorian voice. "Jugsville!" Stephen was out next ball. He trailed in, managing to look sheepish and delighted at the same time, and was engulfed in a tidal wave of white-clad figures and half-dragged, half-carried headlong to the bar. A few minutes later he emerged from the pavilion with his hair tousled and wearing his sweater rucked up round his waist, and came over to the scorebox with two pint glasses. He slipped into the box, put the glasses on the desk and stroked Richard's thigh gently underneath it, out of sight of anyone passing or pausing to lean in and pass the time of day. "Bill says you had a bit of a heart-to-heart," he said at length.

Richard nodded. "Yes," he said, happily. "We did. He talked a lot of sense into me. It was high time somebody did, I think."

Stephen grinned at him, and drank a lot of lager. "Good old Bill," he said reflectively. "I sometimes think he's got more common sense in his head than most of the rest of the people we know put together."

"I'm going to enjoy this holiday," said Richard.

"So am I," said Stephen. "Cheers."

14

They played out a frustrating, rain-sodden draw the next day. On the Monday morning Stephen settled down to make a series of telephone calls. The last to be ticked off the list was to a local taxi firm, and there he drew a blank. The receptionist was perfectly civil and willing to send a cab to her youthful-sounding caller until he told her where he wanted to go. That, she informed him, was over a hundred miles away. "I don't think your pocket money'd quite run to that, sonny," she said, laughing openly at him. To his intense irritation she refused to take his angry protestations seriously, and eventually got a little irate herself, telling him she'd got better things to do than play silly buggers with little boys, before smacking the phone down on him with an angry click. He glared at the receiver in his hand as if it was personally to blame, then banged it down quite as hard as the girl at the other end had banged hers. "Bloody cheek!" he snapped. "Cheeky cow!" He looked up to see Richard laughing at him as well. For a moment his brows creased. Then his face relaxed into a grin. "I'll box a bit cleverer than that with the next one," he said, flicking through the yellow pages and preparing to go into battle once more.

When the next firm answered he was meekness itself, asking humbly for a cab to take him a mile to the town centre. It was promised without question.

They were waiting outside Richard's house when the car arrived, and Stephen enjoyed himself greatly watching the rapidly changing expressions on the driver's face. "There's been a slight change of plan," he announced, slipping into the front seat, while Richard clambered into the back.

"Oh, yeah," yawned the driver. "Where to now, then?"

Stephen told him, and he promptly switched off the engine and shot a suspicious look sideways at his passenger. "You know how far that is, son?" he demanded. "I ain't got time for schoolboy pranks," he added before Stephen had had time to open his mouth to answer.

"Why," said Stephen, meditatively, "does everybody who works for taxi firms call you 'son', or 'sonny'? Is it part of the training? Do you have to go to taxi college, where they teach you to call anybody my age that? And why can't I get any taxi driver to take me seriously when I tell them I want to go somewhere a long way away?"

"Because it'll cost you about seventy quid," said the driver sharply. "An there ain't many schoolboys got that kinda money to blow on cab fares, that's why."

Stephen watched until he saw the man preparing to resign his assignment and throw them angrily out of the car. "Cash in advance?" he said sweetly. The driver halted half-way through his sideways turn in readiness for reaching across Stephen, opening the passenger door and shoving him out of it, and eyed Stephen suspiciously. "Eh?" he grunted.

"I said, if you're worried about whether I'm good for the fare or not, would it ease your mind if I offered you it in advance?" said Stephen negligently, affecting not to have seen what had gone before.

"I... oh," said the man, nonplussed. "Well, if you've got the fare... I s'pose I can take you, if you like. You see my point aview, though? It's not usual for young lads to have that kinda money... Let's see it," he added, with a return to the suspicious edge in his voice of a minute before.

"It's quite usual for me, I assure you," Stephen murmured,

and he pulled out a thick wad of notes. The driver's eyes widened. They widened still further when Stephen casually peeled off a fifty pound note from one end of the wad and a twenty from the middle and held them out to him.

Eventually they explained briefly, and after a momentary contracting of his brows the man joined in the laugh against himself. He also pocketed the seventy pounds, radioed a message with the change of desination, and set off. After the first awkwardness they got on very pleasantly.

Tom was opening the Crown when they got there, so they strolled in and bought the still somewhat disbelieving cab driver a drink. When he'd gone, wondering what kind of a world it was coming to when schoolboys could own large and fancy pubs, they talked briefly to Tom, then got Richard's mother's car out and made their getaway before anyone had arrived for an early drink. They were back at Richard's home shortly after mid-day.

"I've got to pop into town for a few minutes," announced Stephen when they got there. "Can you be ready to come in and meet me in about an hour, say?"

Richard looked at him in surprise. "Can't I come with you, then?" he asked.

"Nope," said Stephen. "Got something to do first. Just be ready for my phone call, okay?" He persisted in being mysterious about it, and eventually he escaped, leaving Richard consumed with curiosity, and put another of his telephone calls into effect.

* * *

Richard picked up the telephone before the first ring had stopped echoing in the room, and twenty minutes later he walked through the doors of a large pub near the town centre. Stephen was waiting with a drink set up for him on the bar. "Drink it quick," he said, and Richard, his curiosity intensifying, obeyed readily.

When they had finished their drinks Stephen led the way from the pub to a large and flashy car showroom, containing a lot of plump and gleaming BMWs. "Ta-raa!" he yelled cheerfully, gesturing to a Series 3 in smart dark blue. "Help yourself."

When Richard had got over it, he went into raptures, barely managing to restrain himself from falling on Stephen there and then. "But can we just take it away?" he said in wonder.

"Course we can," said Stephen. "I paid for it with a banker's draft. That's what I phoned the bank about this morning. I just went down there to pick it up. It looks like a cheque," he added, "only it can't bounce, cos it's the bank themselves writing the cheque. And I got the garage to put number plates on it. All you've got to do is get yourself insured. The chap here says you can do that in five minutes at the AA. You'll also want a green card, for abroad. Shall we go?"

Richard hadn't got his driving licence with him, which was not surprising since Stephen had given him no idea of what he was up to. So they had to waste a few agonising minutes finding a taxi to take them home and wait while Richard dashed in and grabbed his licence. "Bring your chequebook, too," murmured Stephen as Richard was getting out of the cab. Richard paused to glance at him in some surprise; but he was too excited and in too much of a hurry to waste any time wondering why Stephen should have said what he had.

A minute later the taxi was whizzing them back into the town centre again, this time to the local AA office. When they had got rid of it Stephen explained. "I didn't like the idea of you having to look as if you were getting the money for the insurance off me," he said, a little bashfully. "And in any case," he went on, more sure of himself, "I didn't want you to have to keep on looking to me for money. It's not right. So I... er... I paid something into your account. You know, so you don't have to worry about... things..." He blushed, and tailed off.

Richard stopped in mid-stride. "How much?" he asked bluntly.

"I... er... well... Five thousand," said Stephen. It sounded like a confession.

Richard stood, half-way across the pavement towards the steps up to the AA office doors, staring at him, speechless. He forgot his excitement and his hurry. For the moment he even forgot the beautiful dark blue BMW waiting for him. He, too, blushed scarlet for a moment. The look he gave Stephen in that moment repaid the money many times over. Stephen's doubts dissolved into nothing on the spot. "I... I didn't quite know how to ask you to take some," he said, gently nudging Richard out of the way of hurrying shoppers. "So I thought the easiest way would be to just... well, you know... sort of, pay it in. You don't mind?"

Richard gave him a long stare, half of it a kind of exasperation, as if to say 'Whatever am I going to do about you?', and the other half an affection too deep to be expressed. Touched beyond his power of speech for the moment, he simply slipped a hand under Stephen's elbow and squeezed it hard. "I'll try to find some way of saying thank you in a bit, love," he murmured. "Right now, I can't think of anything to say at all."

"Never mind that," said Stephen uncomfortably. Unaccountably, he remembered a pulp western he had read once, in which the chief character, who would rather have faced a man with a gun than be thanked for anything, simply said 'shucks' and changed the subject whenever anyone tried to thank him for his heroic services. He decided to try it himself. "Shucks," he said. "Let's get your insurance."

Richard stared at him, his expression changing rapidly. "Shucks?" he repeated, unable to believe his ears. "Shucks?" he cried again, and the word dissolved into a yell of laughter. Which was all to the good, because it made Stephen grin, too, and broke the tension of the moment. They laughed at each other for a long, magical moment, enjoying it. Then they remembered their business, and scampered up the steps into the office.

They spent a few minutes there, and returned to the showroom at a canter. There they had to pass a further few minutes with the very surprised and even more delighted salesman, with Richard hopping up and down impatiently, until at last the salesman, grinning broadly at their excitement and at the thought of his own commission, took them back into the showroom. He rumbled the heavy glass street doors open while the boys bounced up and down in the car, intoxicated by the leathery smell of the upholstery and the gleaming, impressive instrument panel. Then he strolled over and leaned in the side window to give Richard a quick run through the controls. Richard listened carefully, suppressing his eagerness, and at last they were ready to go.

* * *

When Richard had got used to the controls of his new car, and spent a couple of days driving it about in the hope of seeing people he knew, they set off on their holiday. For the first leg they drove gently across France. Although they had made no particular plan, and though they zig-zagged erratically hither and thither, stopping at wayside inns that took their fancy, their path continually led them roughly in the direction of Alsace, and neither of them even pretended it was a coincidence when, on the fifth afternoon, they pulled up beside the auberge in Saint-Hippolyte where Stephen had worked, and Richard had come to put him back together again. It seemed to have happened a lifetime ago.

There was a series of rapturous reunions in the auberge, where they took a room on an open-ended let. The owner of the auberge offered Stephen his old job back, declaring that he had been the best *serveur* he had ever employed, and Stephen did open the bar up one morning, and served behind it for a couple of hours, to the noisy delight of all his old regulars. At one point he happened to catch Richard's eye while this was going on. Both faces became grim and set for a moment, as the identical thought crossed their minds. Everyone at the auberge knew they were sharing their room there, just as everyone there had known how Stephen and Graham had stood.

But the moment passed, and the clouds passed from both their faces as they realised simultaneously that there was no reason why they should go back to the Crown until it suited them, or ever if they didn't want to. It was as if a monstrous black cloud had moved on and uncovered the sun again.

They spent almost a fortnight in Saint-Hippolyte in the end, blissfully happy. Autumn was well advanced by now, and they spent several bright, chill mornings with the landlord, tramping in the dense forests in the nearby Vosges, prospecting for wild mushrooms, and later enjoyed vast platefuls of their treasures, fried with garlic. Richard made a vast fuss of Nicole, taking her dancing, which Stephen detested and he rather liked, and, in the end, breaking her heart for a while. When the time came for them to move on he went to the same florist's shop as he had visited once before and for the second time presented her and the landlady with vast bouquets of flowers; and when they drove off, with the entire crowd of staff and regulars coming out into the street to wave them off, she stood sadly beside the matronly landlady and for second time muttered moodily, "Jesus, what a pity."

After that they ambled, insofar as the BMW was capable of ambling and Richard was capable of letting it, through a large corner of the Black Forest, then down through Basel and on a winding trail through rural Switzerland and into Austria. They listened to Mozart at Salzburg and to Schubert and Strauss in Vienna. They wandered down through the great Italian lakes, then across into the Aosta valley and through the Mont Blanc tunnel, then wandered back through Geneva into France, roared down the Autoroute du Soleil, where Richard at last let his already beloved car have its head, and ended up meandering down through Spain.

* * *

"Christ, this beer's cold," said Stephen, sitting in shorts, shirt and sunglasses beneath an umbrella in Malaga. "I could have a tooth out and not feel a thing." Richard nodded happily, and smiled for a reply. There was a silence while they sipped the liquid nitrogen beer, and they both knew that they were both thinking the same thing. Eventually it was Stephen who put it into words. "Time to go home?" he said, looking at Richard and raising his eyebrows.

"I think so," said Richard.

They left the same afternoon.

* * *

When they got back to England they spent a further few days pottering. They took Richard's parents out for a lavish dinner. The cricket season had ended while they were away, but they went to the pavilion most nights for a drink, and one night ended up going with half the club for a drunken late-night supper at a local Indian restaurant, where Stephen had his first vindaloo and burnt the roof of his mouth off. "Be the other end tomorrow mornin, our kid," said Bill comfortingly. "Gandhi's revenge, mate. Put a bog roll in the fridge tonight, if I were you."

But throughout these first few days they both knew that they must sooner or later go down to Sussex and see how things had developed in the pub. When they did, it seemed that things had managed, if anything, to get worse.

Tom gave them a grin when they strolled in, brown and cheerful. But it didn't stay on his face long, and he lost no time in drawing them into a corner of the bar and confiding his anxieties.

"It's not looking very good, lads," he said.

"You'd better tell us the lot," said Stephen gravely. "We've been thinking about the situation here, and what we ought to do about it. What's been happening?"

Boiled down to essentials, Pat Gibson had been allowed back as Stephen had asked, and had immediately begun fomenting open revolt among those of the local regulars who were sympathetic to his views. These now included a very substantial majority of the entire local clientele. His trouble-making had received boosts of various kinds. There had been another of the "routine" police visits. On one occasion half a dozen members of the gang of bikers had trooped in, terrifying Gibson and his supporters, though they did nothing more than line up along the bar, drink several huge drinks very quickly and troop out again. "Did they push Gibson about, by any stroke of good fortune?" asked Stephen, glowering darkly. "Or make him arm-wrestle?" added Richard, bringing an explosive guffaw simultaneously from all three of them.

"No, they didn't," said Tom, laughing regretfully as he imagined the scene. "Pity."

But the biggest cause of resentment was the increasing influx of gay people, most of them in pairs but, increasingly also, in groups and parties, from along the coast and, in a new development, from elsewhere as well. "We're getting a lot of enquiries about holidays," said Tom. "Firm bookings, too. A hell of a lot."

"Well, bloody hell," said Stephen, raising his eyebrows. "There's nothing wrong with that, surely?"

"From gay groups," said Tom. "Most of them quite open about it. Gay travel agencies, gay counselling groups, a couple of university gay societies — I even had an enquiry from Gay Mensa, asking if we could accommodate their annual convention and dinner. Honestly, Steve, it's been gay this and gay that, the phone's hardly stopped ringing with em."

"I take it you've been taking the bookings," said Stephen, assailed by a sudden spasm of doubt.

"Oh, yes," said Tom. "Course I have. You've made a mint out of em while you've been away. But it's all adding to the anti faction's case. That's the trouble. They can say quite categorically, now, that you've turned this place into an acknowledged gay pub, and nobody could dispute it. They could produce enough evidence any night of the week."

The boys looked glumly at each other. "We should've stayed in Spain," said Richard.

"Yes," agreed Stephen. "But what I don't understand," he went on, turning back to Tom, "is, what does all this actually amount to? I mean, you say it's all adding fuel to their flames, or whatever it was you said, but what can they actually do? Christ, I own the place, don't I? It's not as if I'm a tenant of the brewery, to be patted on the head or kicked out on my arse at the whim of the local area manager, is it? I actually own the place outright. Lock, stock and barrel. I mean, surely, if I wanted to keep man-eating crocodiles in the bar and piranha fish in the fucking swimming pool, I could, couldn't I? I can do what I like. Can't I?" he ended, a note of doubt suddenly creeping into his voice as he saw Tom's face darkening.

"In theory, yes, you can," said Tom. "Unfortunately, in practice there's one thing they can do. They can object to your licence. That's not dependent on what type of pub it is at all. All they've got to do is claim that you're allowing all kinds of undesirables, even encouraging them, to come into the village, and ask the local licensing justices not to renew your licence when it comes up for renewal at the next Brewster Sessions next February."

"Undesirables?" queried Richard and Stephen at the same time.

"What's desirable and what's undesirable is a subjective thing," said Tom neutrally. "Use your imagination. Can you imagine what kind of people the local justices are. Right, well you rate your chances of telling them that gay people in large numbers are perfectly acceptable, ordinary citizens. And even if they were close enough to the twentieth century to accept that little powder keg of an idea, well imagine it now when Gibson and co mention our friendly local team of bikers."

The boys' faces had been growing grimmer and grimmer through this recital; but Tom still had further ammunition to discharge. "And, just to round it off, you may get a still better idea of your chances when I tell you that the last time the local law decided to spring one of their little routine visits to see if I still know how to run a pub professionally after only seventeen years in the trade," he went on bitterly, "they decided to lie in wait down the lane, according to their amiable little Spanish custom. They caught somebody in their little net, too."

"Oh, Christ," groaned Stephen. "Not..."

"Oh, Christ indeed," said Tom. "One of the local bench of justices. None other. So very soon, Steve, the Lord Chancellor, in person, is going to don his full-bottomed wig and his gold-brocaded robes of office and his knickerbockers and his genuine seventeenth-century button boots, and come down to the village here in a ceremonial motorcade, complete with a fleet of motorcycle outriders with blue lights flashing and klaxons playing the national anthem, and in a public ceremony here, on the green, he will request and require that unfortunate local justice of the peace to bend over before him and drop his trousers. And then the Lord Chancellor is going to take the justice's official parchment scroll of appointment, stuff it formally up his arse and fucking set light to it, to an accompaniment of a fanfare of trumpets, or maybe Handel's Firework Music, played by the band of the Royal Marines. And, Steve, among the merry-making hordes of local peasants and yeomanry disporting themselves on the margent green while this quaint old English ceremony is taking place, there will be all that justice's colleagues — his former colleagues, I should say — and his replacement, all looking on, and all thinking to themselves 'There but for the grace of God...'

"Those, then, Steve, my friend, are the local justices to whom you — or, as things are arranged at the moment, I — shall have to go in February to plead the cause of why we should continue to have our licence. Work it out for yourself, son," he finished wearily. "Speaking for myself, I'm making my own arrangements. Fortunately for me, I'm a bloody good publican, and I know a hell of a lot of people in this game, so I'll find myself a boozer all right. You'll be all right, because when the licence is gone you'll have a prime site and a beautiful Grade One listed building to sell to an Arab for his English country retreat. Everyone else will be the losers. But Pat's not thinking that far ahead. He thinks you'll have your licence taken away, there will be a suitable interval for the fuss to die down, and then someone respectable will take over and run the pub as it was run before your sudden comet-like appearance on the scene. He'll be back in his corner with his mates, and everything will be tickety-boo, just like it was before.

"I'm very sorry, Steve. I think you know I'm on your side. I'm only telling you how things are. But that's what I reckon they're cooking up for you, and you might as well know it as far in advance as possible."

They looked at each other. "Okay," said Stephen decisively. "I've been thinking about this a lot. Now, here's what I want you to do, Tom. First of all, you tell Gibson and all the others that I'm giving up the ghost. I'm admitting defeat, I'm pulling out. Tell them that I've asked you to keep on as manager, running the pub my way until I've made all the necessary arrangements with the lawyers in London to unload it, but that after that, naturally I shall have no further say in the place whatever. Okay so far?"

Tom nodded, watching him very closely.

"Right," continued Stephen. "You tell Gibson also that I shan't be here much at all between now and when I sell up. But say that I'm going to have one farewell occasion here, and ask him to bear with me as far as that goes. Okay?"

"Okay," said Tom slowly. "But... this doesn't... it doesn't sound quite your style, if I may say so, Steve. About the last thing in the whole world I could imagine you doing was capitulating — especially to someone like Gibson. Is there anything else you'd, er, like to tell me?"

"Oh, yes," said Stephen. He looked up, and they saw that his eyes were shining merrily. "Oh, yes. You'll know in time, Tom, don't worry. For the moment I've got a lot of arrangements to make. But I'll let you know exactly what's going on well in advance. For the moment, I'll just tell you this much. I want you to pass this all on to the opposition, especially Pat Gibson and his gang. Okay?" Tom nodded once more. "Right then," said Stephen. "The plan's this..."

* * *

"D'you think Tom'll be all right?" asked Richard as they pulled away from the pub.

"Yeah, I'm sure he will," said Stephen absently, his mind already working on the arrangements for their farewell performance at the Crown. "I'd back him to know how to take care of himself." He looked up abruptly at Richard. "You do think I'm doing the right thing, don't you?" he said.

Richard, concentrating on negotiating the narrow lanes, didn't answer until they hit the open coast road. Then he said briskly, "I don't think there's any doubt about that. This place has been bad news for us since the moment we first set foot in it." "Except my hundred and fifty," said Stephen, smiling fondly to himself at the memory.

"Yes. Except that," said Richard, with an answering smile. "But the pub itself's been nothing but grief and misery. For me, anyway. I'm glad you're getting rid of it, and I don't see that it's any worry of ours who you get rid of it to."

"Good," said Stephen. "We'll do it, then." Richard put his foot down and drove fast towards Brighton.

* * *

They spent a while wandering from pub to pub together in

Brighton, sightseeing. Though the new clientele at the Crown had to some extent prepared them for the gay scene, and although Richard had occasionally been to such places before ("out of curiosity," he had said in answer to Stephen's question), they were a little taken aback by some of the things they saw. However, they had specific objectives, and after a while they ceased to notice things that had initially caused their eyes to widen and, at times, their mouths to drop open.

Eventually they agreed to separate. Stephen copied out a list of the places they could try, marked those that he planned to call on, and handed it to Richard. They gave each other a friendly kiss, neither passionate nor a mere peck, and felt a sudden warm douche of pleasure and relief at being able to express their feelings and themselves so freely in a rather densely filled public place. Then Stephen strolled out, unaware of the numerous pairs of eyes that watched him admiringly as he did so. Richard, meanwhile, went to the bar, where he got himself a drink and had no difficulty in getting into conversation with the landlord.

It took them a week, in all, to find both the people they were seeking.

15

"You'll do it?" exclaimed Stephen excitedly to the man sitting with him in a discreet alcove in a Brighton pub. The other man nodded, grinning. "Yeah," he said. "I think it's a great idea. I like it."

"And you're sure you can find the others?"

"No problem," said the man. He had already taken a pen from his pocket, and was scribbling names rapidly on the back of an envelope.

"Great!" said Stephen. "I'll cover all costs and expenses, don't forget. I don't care what you have to do — if you have to fly someone down from Edinburgh or something, do it, I'll pay, gladly."

"Won't be necessary," said the man, still chuckling. "I can get as many as I need without ever going farther than London. They'll be fighting each other for the privilege of being in on this. All I need from you is a number where I can ring you, to tell you I'm all ready to go."

Stephen laughed delightedly to himself, and wrote Richard's parents' number carefully in the diary the big man proffered. "You won't forget me in all this, will you?" he said.

"What!" cried the man, cowering and peering from behind his hands in mock horror. "Perish the thought!"

"Good," said Stephen, satisfied at last. "Well, be sure to mark me down. This may all be great fun for you and the others you're going to get hold of; but it's my show — well, mine and Richard's — and I want it to be a roaring success."

"I shan't forget," the man assured him.

"Great," said Stephen once again, and left him to go on to his second meeting.

* * *

"You really are interested in buying it, then?" he said, hardly able to believe that such a transaction, so vast, as it seemed to him, could be agreed so easily, almost casually, with such an absence of fuss.

The entrepreneur nodded. "Yes," he said. His voice was firm but unemphatic, his decision made with no haste but without delay. "I'll buy it, if the price you ask is right."

"How do we know if we're asking the right price?" asked Richard, who was sitting in on the second, and much the most important, of Stephen's three meetings that day.

"Have your own advisers present, of course," said the tycoon easily. "They'll know when I'm offering you good money, when you ought to accept. If I don't offer you a fair price, they'll tell you so. Then it'll be up to you whether you accept their advice or whether you're so anxious to get rid of the place that you're willing to disregard their advice and unload anyway. But I shan't try to cheat you, or beat you down to a give-away price. That's not how I've ever done business. Contrary to popular legend, most people like me aren't double-dyed crooks, who only think we've done a day's work if we've diddled some little old lady out of her life savings, or bought somebody out for the price of a lunch when we should have set him up for life. We're just businessmen like any others, only a bit richer, and with a shrewder eye than most for the really good offer."

"You don't seem very worried about the problem with the licence," said Stephen doubtfully.

The man laughed. "No need for you to worry about that, is there?" he said. "If I buy the property from you now, it will have been my problem for months before the Brewster Sessions come up. Why worry yourself about my future headaches?

"Still," he went on, "it's nice of you to concern yourself. You don't need to, though. I've been dealing with little local difficulties like this one for far too many years to be worried by it; I employ people, specialists in this kind of field, to get round just this kind of problem; and, if you really want to know, I've got far too many people... on my side, to feel anxious on that account. No, you stop worrying yourself about things you don't need to worry about, and concentrate on the ones you do."

He got up to leave, thrusting out a hand to Stephen, then to Richard, and giving each a hard, brisk handshake. Then he swung round and marched out of the pub without looking back.

"Well," said Stephen, "That's that."

"Just our hairy friends to go now," said Richard, giving him a friendly cuddle and getting up to fetch fresh drinks.

* * *

Pat Gibson came into the Crown in his customary noisy fashion and found his usual corner occupied. One of the two men leaning casually on the bar and chatting was big. The other was enormous. Gibson went and took up position as near to his usual spot as he could, and called out to Tom, who was serving at the far end. Tom nodded and went on serving. When he was finished he came down and said loudly, "Pat Gibson, none other. What's it to be, Pat?" Gibson stared at him for a moment in surprise. "Well, the usual, Tom, of course. What else?" He did not observe the bigger of the two strangers give him a rapid but close look up and down, and then unobtusively nudge his companion.

He took a long pull at his pint and sighed appreciatively. Then, with none of his usual cronies yet in to talk to, he propped the bar up and listened, without any great interest at first, to the conversation going on behind him. Very shortly, however, he pricked up his ears, as he realised that the two newcomers were talking about rugby, which was his own great passion in life.

After a while one of the men smiled at Tom and signalled for new pints. When Tom delivered them the man said casually, "Any interest in rugby in these parts?" "Oh, yes," said Tom. "Lots." He hesitated. "Any special reason for asking?"

"Yes, there is, as it happens," said the big man. "My friend here" — he indicated the still larger man with a jerk of his thumb — "and I are looking round for a base for a short tour. We want to get in a bit of serious pre-season practice. We thought some proper match practice would be very useful, alongside the usual training. Then we thought maybe we might combine business with pleasure, and maybe set up a short tour. I do a lot of business down this way, so I thought immediately of this as a good area to look round in."

"Pat's your man," said Tom, gesturing behind the two men to Gibson, who was by this time openly listening in to the conversation. "Pat Gibson," said Tom, "and..."

"Nick Lister," said the spokesman, turning and offering Gibson a huge paw. "And Alan Bridges," he added, waving the paw at the still bigger man. Bridges straightened up to his full height as Lister introduced him, and Gibson, who had had to look upwards to offer a smile of greeting to Lister, had to take a pace back to do so for Bridges, who stood somewhere about six feet nine. Hands were shaken and greetings exchanged all round, and Gibson called for an immmediate round of fresh pints.

"Rugby man?" asked Lister.

"Fanatic," said Gibson enthusiastically. "Frustrated fanatic, unfortunately. We don't get too many rugby men in here, more's the pity. It's damned good to see you two. Makes a welcome change," he went on, with a meaning glance at Tom behind the bar.

The two strangers gave the neutral, polite smile that people give when something is referred to that the company clearly understand but to which they are not privy.

"Sorry," said Gibson, interpreting the smile. "Of course, you wouldn't know. This pub's become infested with a lot of unwelcome visitors just lately." The two raised their eyebrows. "Yes," went on Gibson. "We've been having the pleasure of a lot of very weird characters just lately."

"Weird?" said Lister, raising his eyebrows in polite enquiry.

"Yes," said Gibson bitterly. "Bloody queers — mostly from Brighton."

"Oh," murmured Lister and Bridges together.

Yes, fraid so," said Gibson easily. "Coming in by the busload. New owner's one himself, Christ help us, and the news got around, I suppose. Birds of a feather, you know."

"Yes, of course," murmured Lister.

"He's leaving, though, thank Christ," said Gibson dismissively. "Anyway, let's get back to your tour."

They fell to talking rugby shop, and in a very short time the idea had been suggested of a challenge match between the newcomers' team and a team of local star players, to be got together by Gibson. "I think it's a great idea," he enthused. "I don't play myself any more — anno domini, you know. But I can promise you a good side. I don't know how good you are, but I'm confident I can raise a side that would give any of the big London outfits a good game. Would you be willing to leave it with me, gents? I'll have the side ready in a week. How does that sound?"

"Sounds fine to me," said Lister, and Bridges nodded, grinning his support for the idea.

They talked rugby for a further twenty-five minutes, then the two strangers excused themselves and went out, leaving a jubilant Gibson chuckling to himself and talking excitedly about the match to Tom, who kept his own counsel, but accepted a drink.

"Ha-ha!" crowed Gibson as the door closed on them. "This is a bit more bloody like it! Christ, Tom, what a pleasure it is to get some real men in the bar for a change. Bet your life we'll get these rugby men back here before the end of this year. And if these two are about, the rugby should be damn good, too. Makes a change from these bloody queers, doesn't it?"

* * *

The nearest rugby ground available for hire was ten miles away, and despite the fact that it was a filthy day, with bone-chilling sheets of rain lashing hard on a biting, gusty wind, practically every soul in the village had managed to get there somehow. Boys had ridden there on bikes despite the weather, or crammed into fathers' impossibly, and illegally, over-loaded cars. The aged and the carless were offered lifts, the unpopular cadged them, and no one had the heart to refuse.

Alfie Brett stood under a tree chatting with Major Sealey, with whom he had entered into a tacit alliance on the boys' side as the dispute in the pub and the village had rumbled on. The Major was also one of only two other people to have been let in on the secret of the match by Stephen, whom he had virtually adopted, for the time when he was in the village, as a kind of surrogate grandson. The other was Tom, who was also in their small but select group, sharing a huge golfing umbrella borrowed from Richard's father for the occasion. Tom had been grieving earlier that he would have to keep the pub open and thus be the only man in the village not to be allowed to see the epic match. "Balls!" Stephen had scoffed. "I haven't sold the pub yet. Close the bloody pub and be damned." Tom had not argued, and had spent the next few minutes yip-yipping quietly to himself as he went through his chores in the bar.

Pat Gibson stood on the steps up to the little stone grand-stand surveying the scene in mingled satisfaction and perplexity. The almost total turn-out of the villagers was a source of immense satisfaction; but he couldn't help noticing that the crowd was swelled to well over double the number that the villagers could provide. A lot of the strangers were quite obviously friends, sup-porters and non-playing members of the opposition. Rugby men, quite clearly, he thought to himself, looking over the racing caps, hulking frames and beer guts prominently on display all round the ground. Former rugby players all, and very good news for the pub. But he couldn't help thinking he recognised a number of other faces, too, among a large and prominent section of the crowd. "You know what," he said suddenly, turning to one of his cronies on the steps beside him. "I think some of the queers have turned up as well."

The crony, by chance, was one of the two who had defected on the occasion when he had offered his deadly insult to Stephen in the bar. The two of them had come to a rapprochement since Gibson's brief exile and return, but the man had been forced to do a certain amount of thinking by the earlier incident. Now he turned to Gibson and observed mildly, "Well, they can like rugger as well as anyone else, can't they?"

Gibson stared at him for a moment. "Well, I suppose they might," he conceded grudgingly. "But you'd think they'd prefer embroidery or something, wouldn't you? Or at least something poncy, like show-jumping."

The other man looked at him impatiently. "Be your age, Pat," he said in more or less good-natured contempt. "You don't have to be a cunt if you don't want to be, you know." And he swung round and tramped down the steps and off round the ground in search of more sensible company for the game. Gibson stood star-ing after him in astonishment. Then he pulled a puzzled face, shrugged and made his way to his seat of honour in the little box at the front of the stand, overlooking the half-way line.

A few minutes later the teams ran out on opposite sides of the stand from the dressing rooms underneath it, and he had some further surprises. The first thing that leaped to the eye was the visiting team's brilliant, brand-new kit. Their shirts were black, covered with an intricate pattern of interlocking triangle shapes in a glaring, shocking pink. Their shorts were the same pattern in reverse coloration. Their socks were the same violent pink, with black bands at the tops.

The second thing Gibson saw within the first few seconds, while the teams were still streaming onto the pitch, was that the leader of the visiting fifteen, wearing number 1 for loose-head prop, and also, more significantly to the goggling Gibson, the captain's black armband, was Stephen Hill. By the time he had got over the impact of these twin, and unwelcome surprises, the teams had whipped through a pre-match chuck-about made exceptionally brief by the vile weather, and were lining up for the kick-off.

Gibson, fighting down a feeling that his day had been spoiled before it had properly started, but troubled by a nagging suspicion that his leg had somehow been pulled, settled in his seat, took a silver hip flask from the pocket of his heavy overcoat, and prepared to enjoy the match as best he could. He made a mental promise to himself, however, that he would make some pretty vigorous enquiries afterwards; and if his leg had been pulled, he told himself, it would all go on the score to be settled later on.

Considering that within minutes of the kick-off the ground bore a strong resemblance, in both appearance and consistency, to Passchendaele Ridge, the game was a remarkably good one. Gibson's invitation team had a sixteenth player in the first half, in the fierce, gusting wind, which was behind them and swept them again and again into Stephen's team's half of the field. Stephen's team had the heavier pack, with a superlative engine room in the mighty Bridges and his fellow second-row, who, though he stood a mere six feet five, was built on the lines of the Sydney Opera House. But even this advantage was cancelled out, partly by the wind and partly because Stephen himself was not the best choice for loose-head. Accordingly, after twenty minutes, during which he found himself being popped up out of the pack as easily as if he had been a child, he called a hasty conference with Turner, Lister and one or two other notables. The result was that for the next scrum he and the heavier of the two flankers changed places.

All the same, Gibson's team scored first — and second. After a very few minutes' play they made a swift break down the left flank and after a dazzling, open piece of play their left winger squeezed himself through a gap too small to let a large rabbit through, slipped a couple of desperate tackles, and scrambled the ball over five yards to one side of the posts. Their former Wasps full-back converted it. Ten minutes later their ex-Harlequins fly-half, who was left-footed, put a penalty right in the middle from the left touchline, and, for good measure, almost from the half-way line as well. The score at the interval was thus nine points to nil, though it should have been 9–3, had not Stephen's full-back missed a sitter of a penalty, blown wildly off course by the gale. All things considered, Stephen's side reckoned as they sucked oranges at half-time, they had done very well to restrict the score to that; and they would have the wind with them from now on.

As it turned out, they had taken the lead within five minutes of the restart. They won a scrum, against the head, just inside Gibson's team's 22, and for the first time in the match their considerable superiority in pack-weight took effect. They pushed their lighter opponents almost to their own line before the scrum half plucked it out, feinted, went the other way and fell on it just over the line, a fraction ahead of the defending pack's falling on him. A minute later their right centre intercepted a pass near his own corner flag, ran eighty yards without being touched, passed the ball backwards over his own head as he fell to a perfect tackle from the defending full-back, and was able to sit up just in time to see Stephen Hill patting it down between the posts with no one near him. Both were converted without difficulty.

After that it was even, deadlocked in the middle of the field, with neither pack getting dominance and the line-outs and scrums going as expected and every move being broken up within a few yards.

Then, with seven or eight minutes to go, Gibson's team scored a sudden, unexpected breakaway try which left their opponents standing thirty yards from the scorer; and although their full-back missed the conversion because of the same kind of freak sideways gust from the treacherous wind that had caused his counterpart to miss an identical kick in the first half, things were immediately made worse by a penalty which he did score, this time being helped by the same wind, which sent a clearly misdirected effort swerving late and deadly between the posts. Stephen's team drooped a little, the stuffing knocked out of them. It was temporary, but there was very little time left for them to pull themselves together.

And then, when all seemed lost, with the referee looking closely at his watch — though he later told them that there had been three minutes left — the pack again set up a move. Awarded a scrum far over to the right ten yards into the opposition's half, they set up a fine rolling maul that took them to within ten yards of the line. The scrum-half picked it up, dummied to the left and darted off round the right side of the heaving pack, and flicked it in the direction of his waiting fly-half, who fluffed it and knocked it on. The referee had his whistle in his mouth when he saw Gibson's full-back gather it perfectly and set off like a hare. He had covered ten yards when he mysteriously lost his footing and squirted the ball forward, straight into the arms of the opposing fly-half, who, scarcely able to believe what he saw, nevertheless did see a neat straight line for him to run down, and went for it. He shot through the opening like a rat up a drainpipe, and was finally helped over the line by a crashing tackle from behind by one of the enormous opposition props that lifted him clear off his feet and thrust him the final three yards to where he crashed to earth, a foot over and only ten yards from the right-hand post.

As the full-back prepared to attempt the conversion the whole team stood with their eyes anywhere but on his slender, mud-covered form. They had forgotten the icy wind, forgotten the freezing, drenching rain, and forgotten everything else. They were not even aware that the entire crowd watching had gone silent until the thud of his boot hitting the ball sounded like a thunderclap round the ground. Then they all jumped, and became aware of the hush, and all looked up to follow the ball... which soared high, higher, carried on the treacherous, swirling wind towards the uprights. Not one of them could have said truthfully whether it had gone between them or not; but the two flags went up unhesitatingly, and fourteen hearts returned to their normal stations from the throats they had been climbing, while about them the crowd gave vent to a single, full-throated howl, of relief from tension as much as of applause for a truly magnificent kick.

As for the full-back himself, asked about it afterwards he claimed to have felt no tension at all; but when his nonchalant answer had been drowned in hoots of derision, he added the postscript that he had been so terrified that his entire body had been numb, and his entire mind blank. That part of it they believed.

A minute or so later the referee blew a long, long blast on his whistle, and the game was over.

The players streamed off the field, their hair and kit plastered to them in the torrential, sheeting rain, chilled by the razor-edge on the wind off the sea, and smothered, to a man, in mud. They were wearing mud like a garment. Their eyes peered from white, mud-surrounded circles that made them look like the negative of a photograph of thirty giant pandas. Their legs, hands and faces were caked with it and their colours were all reduced to a uniform dun-brown drab.

It so happened that the visitors ran in on Gibson's side of the stand; and just occasionally, as they came sprinting off the field, eager to get to the baths, he saw a bright pink triangle, shining through the cloaking, caking mud like a small, triumphant beacon to commemorate their triumph.

* * *

The Crown was fuller than Stephen and Richard had ever seen it. They stood in their usual corner of the bar, with the Major, Alfie and Tom, who had given himself the evening off, and a number of huge men from their team, listening to the roar of several dozen different conversations. All were on the same subject: the match was the only topic. Many were on the same lines: was a replay a possibility, and how soon?

Pat Gibson stood miserably with a crowd of his usual mates, most of whom were too busy enthusing about the match to offer much in the way of consolation. A latecomer pushed through the door and forced his way through the scrum to his party. It chanced to be the man who had left him on the steps just before the start. "Nice change to see a few real men round these parts," he said, grinning maliciously at Gibson. Gibson gave him a sickly smile in return. Finally, however, he remembered his position as the man who had personally initiated the match, indeed suggested it. And slowly, reluctantly, and with a hatred of Stephen Hill, who he felt sure was at the bottom of his humiliation, that could have been expressed in no known language, he had to accept the false position in which he had been placed.

Mentally squaring his shoulders, steeling himself, he rapped loudly on the bar for silence.

"Ladies and...," he began. Then he stopped, looked theatrically round, and started again. "Sorry," he said. "Gentlemen — and one or two friends..." There was a chuckle. "He's doing it well," murmured Major Sealey, and his party nodded.

"I'm not going to keep you from the urgent matters in hand for long," went on Gibson. "I'd only like to say two things. First of all, my sincere, personal thanks to everyone here. To the players, of both sides, for putting on such a tremendous game in conditions that could hardly have been worse. It really was a tremendous show. And to everyone from the village and elsewhere, for turning out and standing in those same diabolical conditions to watch the match. Thank you, all of you. And second, I'd like to add my own congratulations to all the plaudits they've had already to the winning side. I'm sorry my own side couldn't quite pull it off, but I'm delighted to have seen how very nearly they managed it, and how superbly they played.

"So, congratulations to the gallant victors — I'm sure the celebrations will be the gayest of affairs..." — this time his sally was greeted with a roar of laughter — "...and that they'll be in the pink before they escape from here tonight..." — another roar — "...congratulations next to the equally gallant losers..." — more thunderous applause — "...and finally, congratulations to everyone else, for the simple gallantry of having stood out in weather like that for an hour and a half to watch." The applause for this was louder still. Gibson beat on the bar again, and there were roars of "Order, order".

"I've nearly finished," he went on when quiet was restored. There were cries of 'boo!' and some of 'hooray!'

"As most of you know, I'm a dentist, and of course everyone knows, we dentists haven't got much money — we live hand to mouth..." — this got the best roar so far, but it was dwarfed by the next one, that greeted the end of his short address. "But I've scratched about down among the moths and spiders, and I find I can just about manage to set em up for the house. So that's it, gentlemen. Thanks for playing, for making it such a magnificent match in the most impossible conditions, thanks for watching, thanks for listening, and now, the drinks are on me. Thank you."

The last couple of words were lost in the tumult of cheering and clapping that engulfed the pub. Gibson himself was acclaimed, clapped on the back and congratulated till he was giddy. And all the time at the bottom of his mind was the burning, scorching realisation that he had been duped, manipulated like a marionette.

The moments of his apparent triumph were some of the bitterest moments of his life.

"That was pretty handsomely spoken," said Alan Bridges softly to Stephen. It was Bridges to whom Stephen had been directed when he had begun making enquiries in Brighton for rugby enthusiasts among the gay community, and Bridges with whom he had arranged the entire affair, from the careful baiting of the hook, the playing and eventual landing of Gibson, the design of the strip, and the match itself. "Are you sure he's the ogre you make him out to be?" Bridges went on.

"Oh, yes," said Stephen. "It was a very good speech, I'll grant him that. Very convincing. But don't kid yourself."

"No, don't," put in Lister, the hulking prop who had assisted in the hooking of Gibson. "Don't forget what he said when we met him here before. And don't forget what a mean eye he's got."

"He did it very well," commented Major Sealey. "But the man's a bounder for all that. Always said it, and I'm not changing my mind on the strength of a pretty speech. Should have been a politician. Mealy-mouthed enough. Man's missed his vocation." The rest of their little group chuckled. It so happened that it fell into a brief, unaccountable pool of quiet, and several of them happened to glance in Gibson's direction. They thus chanced to see his face as he turned to glance across in the direction of the chuckle. "I see what you mean," murmured Bridges as the hubbub resumed its normal level and Gibson's red, glaring face was hidden behind the shifting mass of people once more.

At that moment the doors opened and the bikers came in. This was the result of Stephen's third meeting in Brighton. They immediately began mingling with the rugby crowd, and in minutes arm-wrestling contests and other bar sports were going on all round the bar.

Time passed. Bikers, rugby players — Gibson's invitation team as well as the victorious gay fifteen — spectators and villagers gradually attained their own chosen degrees of uproarious behaviour and of drunkenness, and the atmosphere became one of general drunken friendliness. People who had never met before that day swore drunken oaths of allegiance and friendship in perpetuity. A number of liaisons were made on the spot, and several couples slipped off into the residential part of the hotel to make use of the empty rooms. Tom, observing this at one point, glanced interrogatively at Stephen, who grinned, a little vacantly, at him and shook his head. When Gibson, after staring round and seeing that everyone but himself was enjoying life hugely, slipped off to go across the triangular green to his home to nurse his bitter meal of gall and wormwood, no one even noticed that he had gone.

* * *

"Well, that's it," said Stephen quietly as they got fragilely into their clothes the following afternoon. They had had Tom be sure to secure their own room before the match, and when they had finally crawled to bed at four in the morning they had fallen straight into bed, in their clothes, and slept the sleep of the very drunk indeed. It was after one in the afternoon when they surfaced, and neither of them felt very well. They lay there, talking quietly, until they were able to reel off to the lavatory to be sick. Stephen won by a short head, with Richard following a couple of minutes later. Then they both felt much better, and also began to notice how hungry they were. "How d'you think it all went?" he went on.

"It was fine, Stevie," said Richard. "I haven't enjoyed a day as much for yonks. If only... if only I hadn't had quite as much to drink last night, I'd have enjoyed it even more..."

Stephen sketched a pale, shaky version of his usual robust grin as he looked at his beloved friend. "Well, love," he said, "we'll get some grub down you and you'll soon be okay again. I don't feel so hot myself, actually..." He stopped speaking to make a sudden precipitate dash for the bathroom once more. Richard stood trying to suppress the heaving of his stomach by sheer will-power alone, but after a few moments the sounds of woe issuing from the lavatory were too much for him, and he, too, had to make a run for it. Then they went down to see what they could find in the way of breakfast.

They found Tom, reliable and capable as always, still methodically clearing and cleaning the aftermath of the night before. There were quite sizable damages, mostly cigarette burns on carpets, his beloved highly-polished bar and even, mysteriously, one on the ceiling. "Must've been a second row man," said Stephen, looking up at the unmistakable burn mark. "Nobody else could reach up that far."

"Get away with you, Steve," said Tom, not sounding as if he

cared very much who had done the damage. "It coulda been a midget on stilts and nobody woulda noticed last night, would they?"

"No, I s'pose they wouldn't," said Stephen with a grin. "How are you feeling, Tom?"

Tom awarded himself a break from his labours, went and got them all a drink, and sat down heavily on a bench seat. The boys sat down on chairs, sipping their lager uneasily. "I feel flat, I suppose is the word," said Tom, after a long pull at his drink. "I mean apart from feeling pretty bloody wrecked after last night — though nowhere near as wrecked as you two look," he added with a faint smile. "Just lookin at you two makes me feel a good deal better." They gave him twin shaky, rather sheepish smiles. "But I'm also feeling a bit upset about what's been going on, and even more about what's going to happen. I know what you're going to do tonight, don't forget, and I don't like it much. Not that I blame you for what you're doing. I don't think you had a great deal of choice in the end, as things were going. But I don't like change much, and now I'm going to have to face a bigger change than I've ever faced in my life."

"It keeps you young, so they say, Tom," suggested Stephen.

"That's just it, Steve," he said wearily. "I'm not young. Not any more. A lot less than a year ago I was drifting happily through middle age, getting older, a bit fatter and a lot lazier, and thoroughly enjoying the process. Then you arrived, and it's been hurly-burly and hustle and hassle all the way. Now I've got to make a bigger adjustment than any before. Not that I'm not grateful to you for securing my position, don't think it. I am, very grateful indeed. There's a lot wouldn't have even thought of it. But I don't know if I can cope with this sort of upheaval at my age."

"Course you can," scoffed Stephen. "I think you can, too, Tom," said Richard quietly. "I see how you feel, and I can quite see that it must feel a bit... intimidating to you. But I've got a great respect for your qualities, Tom, and adaptability's one of them. I think you'll be all right. The new man's a decent type, too. Fair, and pleasant. You'll be okay, I'm certain."

Tom looked gratefully at him. "I'm glad you think so, Richard," he said sincerely. "Because I've got a great respect for your judgment, too. Anyway, there's not much help in worrying about it, because it's going to happen whatever I say or think." He sighed.

"It's not definite, you know," said Stephen thoughtfully. "I haven't given any guarantees. I could kill it stone dead right now, with one phone call."

"You won't, Steve," said Tom. "You know you won't. Nor should you. It's in your own best interests to go ahead and do what you've been planning. And you're tough, too, Steve. There's a very hard streak in you, which'll always keep you on top. It'll always make sure you keep one eye very carefully on what's best for you. And there's nothing wrong with that. You've got more than most people to guard against, and it's good that you've also got this tough streak in you to make sure you guard against it. So I know that you'll do what you've planned to do. I just wish somehow you didn't have to do it. Not that you're not going to do it, but that the necessity for it didn't arise. I s'pose I just like security. I like things to carry on the way they are, and I spose I've got used to you. Still," he said, his tone becoming brisk and normal suddenly, "you can't have everything you want in this man's world. I'll get by, I dare say."

But the two boys drifted off, vaguely unsettled by his attitude; and as before, their steps led them to the cricket field. To their disappointment Alfie was nowhere to be found, so they sat on the board floor of the pavilion veranda, and did their agonising alone. They had never missed the old man more. When they had talked their way round and round in circles for two hours or more, they had come to no conclusion except that they could see no alternative to the plan they had already made. They got up, stretched, and started ambling back through the village to the pub.

16

The bar was full that evening, for the rumour had gone round fast that Stephen was planning to make some kind of statement. He made his entry, deliberately coming in through the main door rather than using the entrance from the residential part, spotted Richard, waiting expectantly in their usual corner with their coterie of friends and supporters, waved to him, then advanced into the packed room. The first person he ran into was Gibson. He clapped an arm affectionately round his shoulders. "Well, Pat," he said, rightly surmising that a matey use of his first name would be the thing most calculated to annoy Gibson intensely, "you've won, old man. How d'you like it?" Gibson glared at him, wriggled out from under his long

199

arm, and said nothing.

"Fact, gents," said Stephen, revolving slowly and inspecting the turn-out. "Mr Gibson, your well-known and generous local rugby sponsor, has, as you all know, been saying, noisily, for a long time now — it seems like a long time to me, anyway, but perhaps that was just because of the number of times one seemed to hear the same old drone going on in the background — yes, he's been saying, ever since I inherited this place, that my friend and I were freaks, vermin, perverts, all manner of unspeakable names. He once accused me of being a child-molester, in the full hearing of a dozen people." He glanced about him, and saw a lot of uncomfortable faces. They hadn't expected this kind of rude, crude reference to such matters. A low buzz of resentment sprang up around the room.

"Just lately, he's been blaming Richard and me for the sudden arrival of a lot of new friends from Brighton and places. Well, as a matter of plain fact, that was nothing to do with us, as it happens. But as far as it goes, I was glad enough to have them. Money in my till, no harm done, as far as I could see — or as far as I can see now, for that matter. Still, Mr Gibson and his pals thought it was a bad sign — bringing the tone of the place down, or something of the kind. We've even been blamed for that appalling attack on the little boy recently. It may interest you to know that Richard and I were questioned about it, but only in case we might have recognised anyone from the descriptions. We ourselves were cleared instantly, on the first night of the police's enquiries, because we were nothing like those descriptions. As far as I know the police are no nearer catching the monsters who did that than they were the night it happened. But it may interest you to know also that the gay community has put up thousands of pounds in reward money; I myself contributed a hundred pounds towards it. I wouldn't mention that in ordinary circumstances, but I think it's worth mentioning here. You might compare it with the amount you've offered in the same good cause, for instance.

"But the fact remains, we've been becoming more and more conscious of getting less and less popular. We were blamed when a gang of bikers decided to stop off here for one of their little adventures — though I don't quite know how we were expected to know they were going to stop here, or what we were supposed to do about it when they did. As far as the first's concerned, my second sight's been getting a bit rusty lately; and as far as the second's concerned, well, I noticed a distinct lack of heroism among all parties when it came to chucking our bikie friends out. Even our rugby match — and I confess, Pat, that was all my own idea — even that hasn't helped you to like us much better, despite the fact that practically everybody in the village turned up to watch it, and was demanding a replay afterwards last night.

"I could go on and on, but I'm not going to. I think instead I'll just tell you what I'm going to do.

"I'm told that it's likely that if I stay on here as owner, there will be an objection to my application for renewal of the licence. Well, I thought about that, and I decided that that was getting just a little bit too sneaky. There are limits beyond which I'm not willing to be pushed, and that's beyond them. So, you win. I'm going. I'm leaving the licensing trade, after a short and turbulent spell in it. In other words, I'm selling up."

He looked round, and saw that Gibson's face was clothed in a broad smile of satisfaction. "Mr Gibson, at least, is pleased, gents, as you'll see, if you care to come and look," he went on. "Hmmm. Not one taker, Pat. But beware of rejoicing a little prematurely. 'And makes us rather bear those ills we have/ Than fly to others that we know not of...'"

He left them with the quotation hanging in the air, went to the bar, and got himself a drink from Tom.

"I left you with that quotation," he resumed after quenching his thirst, "to remind you gently of the fact that you have no idea who I've sold out to. Well, he's a very shrewd businessman, wealthy, ready to put a lot of money into any project he likes the look of. He's promised to look after Tom and keep him on, which is one testimony to his very good sense and judgment. But other than what I've told you just now, you know nothing about him. In the circumstances, I'm sure you'll understand my feelings when I tell you that I'm not inclined to tell you any more. No, gents, I think you can wait and see just who I'm selling to. But I hope you'll be very happy. You ought to be, seeing how hard you've been hoping and striving to get rid of Richard and me.

"Just one last thing, gentlemen, and then I shall relieve you of the embarrassment of my presence. There are some here — they know who I mean — who are not included in the things I've been saying. They have consistently made a point of taking our part, sometimes representing us when unkind things were said about us when we weren't here to defend ourselves. To those I say that nothing I've said so far refers to them — though I'm sure they realise that already. To them I say that we shall be very sorry indeed to say goodbye to them, and hope we may perhaps see them again in happier surroundings. To the rest, simply goodbye."

He stopped speaking abruptly, turned smartly about and walked over to Richard. They stood for a few moments, having a word with the Major, Alfie and other supporters, then the two of them disappeared into the residential part of the building, leaving a buzz of conversation going on behind them.

Tom, Major Sealey, Alfie and their group found themselves under heavy pressure from the remainder to tell anything they knew of Stephen's plans. "He's got something up his sleeve, the little shit," said Gibson, almost through gritted teeth. It so happened that Tom was in earshot when he said it; and it happened also that Gibson chanced to glance Tom's way just as he permitted himself a broad grin at Gibson's words.

Gibson immediately homed in on him. "You know more than you're saying, Tom," he snapped. "Now you better let us in on this. You owe it to us."

"Owe it?" queried Tom. "I owe you something? How do you work that one out, Pat?"

"You're one of us, that's how I work it out," snapped Gibson furiously. "You've been here as long as a good many of us, and you've fitted in well here. You're part of this place, part of the set-up here. You were here, and part of things here, long before those two insolent upstart kids came here disrupting things and upsetting everyone. You owe it to us to let us know if he's got anything unpleasant stored up for us. I wouldn't put that past him, the dirty little hound."

"He's not the only one to have played a dirty game, is he?" said Tom drily. Gibson flushed angrily, but subsided into muttered protests.

"I'll tell you as much as he authorised me to tell you," volunteered Tom, amid general surprise. There was an excited buzz of speculation, quickly turning to a hush of expectancy as they waited to see what Tom knew.

"He's sold the hotel, which he owns outright, to an entrepreneur," said Tom. "A very wealthy one, who will do his best to keep the inn, itself, in the traditional way, not tread on anybody's toes. He's also a gay entrepreneur. I gather it took Stephen rather a long time to be put in touch with him, but that we shall never know. But I do understand that the man intends to build on the hotel's land, to convert the place into a full-blown gay amenities and leisure centre — you know the kind of thing: swimming, tennis courts, squash, snooker, table tennis, outings to all manner of places of interest. That's all I know, except that he'll be advertising the place extensively in the gay press. So we're likely to be seeing a lot more new faces round here. Heterosexuals will, he stresses, be very welcome at all times. He hopes that's what you wanted.

"Oh, yes," he added, as if by way of an afterthought. "He knows all about your seedy little scheme to object to his licence, and he's quite used to scotching that kind of back-stabbing effort. You've started a ball rolling here, Master Gibson, that you may live to regret."

He turned away and busied himself with the chores associated with lunch.

When the boys reappeared in the bar, changed and cheerful, they were surrounded by a crowd, all anxious to know if Tom had spoken truthfully. He looked round him at the mass of faces, staring levelly into each pair of eyes. Most of them dropped. Then he strolled easily across the room to where the Major and Alfie Brett were chatting. He gently removed their glasses from their hands and had them refilled at the bar. Then he spoke, again in a profound hush. "I gather Tom's detonated the small firework I left him holding for me," he said mildly. "Is it true?" demanded many voices.

"Yes, it's true," he said. "Cheers," he added, turning to the Major and Alfie.

"Is there any way you might change your mind?" asked someone.

"Who asked that?" asked Stephen interestedly. A man pushed forward. It was Gibson's defecting crony, who had left him at the rugby match. "I said it," he said, flushing a little, but determined to speak. "I was with Pat to start with," he said. "I don't mind admitting that. But I've done a lot of thinking for myself since those days. You may remember I dissociated myself from his ideas when he accused you of... of something in here one night."

"I remember," said Stephen.

"So I count as neutral," went on the man. "And I'd like to say that as far as I'm concerned, I'd rather you stayed on. You'll have no complaints from me if you change your mind."

"Lesser of two evils, as it were?" suggested Stephen.

"No, I didn't mean it like that," protested the man.

"That's how I mean to take it, though," said Stephen. "And it's not good enough. If you people find you've jumped out of the frying pan into the fire, you've only yourselves to blame. Richard and I came down here full of optimism. We brought our home cricket club here on tour, and we both took a very active part in your local club, right from the start. Not an insignificant part, either. I don't intend to stand here blowing my own trumpet, but if you care to look at my batting average in the few matches I played for the club, you'll see that for yourselves. We came here in good faith and in good will. If you find you've brought something you find even less welcome on yourselves, well it serves you right. If you'd been a little more welcoming towards decent chaps like us, you wouldn't now be wondering what was coming. I suggest you might try giving the new chap a bit more of a chance than you gave us. I suspect — I don't know this for certain, mind, but I strongly suspect — that he'll be a very, very much rougher customer to rub up the wrong way than we've been. Still, it's not for me to tell you how to behave. If you need someone my age to tell you that you're beyond good advice anyway."

He turned round once again, and thrust out a hand to Major Sealey. "Goodbye, Major," he said, and all the savage, bitter irony and hostility had vanished from his voice. "It's been a pleasure to have got to know you. And you know where to find us. We'll see you again, and soon, I hope."

The Major shook his hand firmly, his moustache twitching to show the force of his emotion. He murmured his farewells quietly into Stephen's ear, then turned and spoke to Richard, who smiled suddenly, like the sun coming out, and murmured a reply in sudden animation.

"Bye, Alfie," said Stephen, and the old man gave him a brisk handshake and a big wink. "We'll see you again, too, right?" "I dare say," said Alfie. "I dare say you will. Come and see us here, when your pal's installed and settled down. Why not?"

"We'll do that," said Stephen. He moved among the group, saying goodbyes and shaking hands with selected friends and supporters, including a good many of the cricket club. Richard was making his own circuit. Neither of them took very long about it, and they quickly moved to the door. The Major, Alfie and several of the cricketers, including the club captain, came out into the car park to see them off. The Major stuck his head in the side window as Richard started the engine. "You're doing the right thing, my boy," he said to Stephen. "Sorry to see you go, speaking for myself. Dashed sorry. But you're doing the right thing, and you don't want to waste any time worrying over it. But I hope we shall see something of you."

"You will, Major. I promise," said Stephen, and Richard nodded and smiled. "You will," he said.

"Well, that's good, then," said the Major. And he withdrew his white head from the car and straightened up, blowing his nose vigorously to conceal his emotion. Richard eased the BMW over the sleeping policemen and pulled out into the lane. There was a chorus of goodbyes from the small group in the car park. Stephen stuck a hand out of the window and waved, and they were gone.

"Well, that's that over with," said Stephen. "How did I sound?"

"You sounded fine to me," said Richard, and the love in his tone melted something deep in Stephen's insides. He leaned towards Richard and slid an arm round his shoulders. "Back to how we used to be?" he said, very tenderly. Richard turned to glance at him briefly before resuming his concentration on the road. "Yes," he murmured. "Back to normal."

* * *

That night they sat talking to Richard's parents, staying by some tacit understanding on neutral topics, and, quite early, the boys went scampering upstairs to the room, which had become so familiar to Stephen during his tribulations the previous year. They tumbled out of their clothes, into Richard's double bed, and into each other's arms, and it felt for both of them as if a mild nightmare, not horrifying or appalling but generally drab, depressing and seemingly unending, had suddenly been relieved by a grateful, joyous waking-up. "Oh, yes. We're back to normal, all right," said Stephen happily.

* * *

The next morning they sat in the big bow window of Richard's parents' living room, watching heavy rain dashing itself against the glass and discussing, in fairly desultory fashion, what to do next.

"You're absolutely sure you're doing the right thing?" asked

Richard for the fourth time. "I mean, I'd hate to influence you into doing something you didn't really think was right, just because of the way I felt." "Nope," said Stephen flatly. "I've told you, and I'll tell you again, I really, really, really think I'm doing the right thing. I've felt happier last night with you, and this morning, sitting here watching the rain, than I've felt in months. In fact I'll do it now," he said, jumping up impulsively and going to the telephone.

First he called Guilfoyle of the sharp operators, and told him what he was planning. He gave the name and telephone number of his purchaser, and instructed him to handle the matter for him. "I shan't be around," he said, "so I'm leaving it to you to do the deal and get as good an offer as you can from him. The only thing I say is, do sell it. I don't want it, and I want him to have it. Get the top-whack offer out of him, but don't push him so hard that he loses interest. Okay?" There was a short crackle from the other end. "No," said Stephen. "I'm afraid I can't tell you that, because I don't know myself. But you've got Richard's parents' number — that's where I'm speaking from, and it counts as a sort of permanent base camp. And as soon as I know where I am, or where I'm going to be, I'll get in touch and let you know. Okay. Right. Yes, of course. And thanks very much. Sure. Bye."

Then he extracted a card from the back pocket of his jeans and rang another number. After a moment he said "Morning. Can I speak to Mr Hendricks, please? My name's Stephen Hill. It's to do with... oh, you know about that? Good. Right. Thanks." A few moments later the entrepreneur came on the line. "Hallo, Mr Hendricks," Stephen said. "About the Crown. Yes, I've decided definitely to sell — to you, if possible. I liked the sound of the things you had in mind to do there. I'm not going to be involved in the negotiations myself. No, I'm too busy, and in any case I'm not going to be here to take part. I've instructed the firm of law-yers who've been running the place for years to deal with you direct. They've got full authority from me to handle everything. Yes, I've got it here. You need to speak — to start with, at least — to a Mr Guilfoyle, that's G-U-I-L-F-O-Y-L-E, Guilfoyle. The com-pany's name is..." He gave the name, address and Guilfoyle's telephone number, exchanged a few pleasantries, hung up, and went back in a hurry to curl up with Richard once more in the window seat.

"What now?" asked Richard. "Got any of your bright ideas?"

"Like to take you to bed," said Stephen, reaching down and fondling him.

206

"In a little while," said Richard, easing himself into a better position to be fondled. "But what shall we do? In the long term, I mean."

"Well, you know, I did have one idea," said Stephen. "While I was talking to Guilfoyle."

"Yes?"

"Well, it suddenly crossed my mind, all over again — you know, as if I'd almost forgotten it. Odd, really."

"Yes," said Richard patiently. "But what was it?"

"Well, it suddenly crossed my mind that I'm a rich man."

"Well, boy, anyway," said Richard.

"Well said," said Stephen, biting his ear. "Kindly accept this Pat Gibson Award for sensitivity."

"All right," conceded Richard, with his old, familiar gurgle of a laugh. Stephen's heart suddenly ached for a moment, as he reflected how rarely he had heard that laugh in recent weeks. "All right," Richard repeated, "you're a rich man or boy. What about it?"

"Well, guess what I fancy? Apart from you, of course."

"I can't imagine," murmured Richard demurely. "What do you fancy?"

"I fancy a game of cricket," said Stephen, dreamily.

"Eh? There's no cricket now," said Richard.

"There is in Australia," said Stephen. Richard sat curled up in the window, watching the fat raindrops lashing themselves into squirming amoeba-shapes against the window panes, feeling Stephen's strong, supple fingers stroking him gently, and thought about sunshine and the twang of Australian voices, icy drinks in glasses frosted with condensation and white figures flitting to and fro. "Well, love," he said slowly. "You are a rich man..."

Also in the new GMP series:

Ulster Alien *by Stephen Birkett*
A poignant coming-out story set amidst the troubles of Northern Ireland.

Meet Matthew Woodhead - a sensitive child with his beloved best-friend Danny; an awkward teenager struggling to fit in with the gang; a young gay man on the brink of coming out. But in Northern Ireland everything is more complicated. Matthew's journey to adulthood takes place against a background of civil rights protests, terrorist bombings and the Save Ulster From Sodomy campaign. A world where young lives are destroyed by murder, and young minds by sectarian bigotry. Closely modelled on his own experience, Stephen Birkett portrays a world where the bonds of male friendship are strong, but a gay identity is that much harder to attain.
price - £9.95   ISBN : 1 902852 01 X

Foolish Fire *by Guy Willard*
The first in a new trilogy of an all-american teenager's sexual adventures.

Guy willard is your all-American boy, a good-looking, popular teenager with only one hidden secret... a flaming desire for other boys. This first book in a trilogy of his sexual adventures is set at Freedom High School, where he inches his way out of the closet through a series of humerous and poignant episodes. From "Physical Education" to "Technically a Virgin", Guy's personal story is thoroughly true to life: always sexy, but very human.
price - £8.95   ISBN : 1 902852 02 8

Teleny *by Oscar Wilde*

The only complete edition of this erotic tale

First published in 1893, this outrageous novel of homosexual love has been attributed to Oscar Wilde with varying degrees of certainty. This edition, carefully prepared from original sources in the British Library archives, is the only one on sale annotated and unabridged. Ahead of its time in its celebration of uninhibited sensual passion between men.

"It is a bizarre book, alternating porn with florid purple passages, a hymn to sodomy with an angry attack on notions of the 'natural'" New Statesman.
price - £9.95   ISBN : 1 90285200-1

All the Queen's Men *by Nick Elwood*

A revealing account of fourteen years as an openly gay man in the British Army.

"Out for most of my career as a cavalry bandsman, I discovered a gay military world where many squaddies were partial to a bit of cock fun. I indulged in numerous flirtations and affairs. There were no threats and rarely any hostility. Encounters with the Military Police, at first invasive grew into an irrepressible reckless defiance. We banded together, protected by peers and senior ranks alike.

I became engaged to a 16-year-old civilian, lithe and brown eyed Andreas, the summer soulmate of my dreams. Working up through the ranks to Trumpet Major I experienced much during my army career, pride in my sexuality, elation and loss. What a bummer it is to be in love."
price - £9.95 ISBN : 1 902852 03 6

Banged Up *by Jack Dickson*

Detective Jas Anderson, the hero of "Freeform" is imprisoned and fighting for his life in this new adventure.

Detective-Sergeant Jas Anderson, the violent anti-hero of Freeform, ended that story being expelled from the Glasgow police force. Banged Up starts with Jas being framed by his ex-colleagues, and remanded to Barlinnie prison. Soon he is forced to share a cell with Steve McStay, sentenced for Aggravated Assault on two gay men. In this all-male enviroment, inmates don't divide into gay and staight, rather into who fucks and who gets fucked. But resilient as ever, Jas forms an unlikely partnership with Steve in his fight survival.
price - £9.95 ISBN : 1 902852 04 4